NO QUARTER

NO QUARTER

WAR OF THE DAMNED™ BOOK TWO

MICHAEL TODD   MICHAEL ANDERLE
LAURIE STARKEY

DISRUPTIVE IMAGINATION

John Kern
Proprietor
Spurlock's - Henderson NV

Editor
Lynne Stiegler

*To Family, Friends and
Those Who Love
to Read.
May We All Enjoy Grace
to Live the Life We Are
Called.*

— Michael Anderle

The ocean breeze cut through the sultry night air in the city of Los Angeles. It was Friday, the night for parties and, of course, an excuse for demons to come out in search of their seven deadly sins in the city's bars and clubs.

Just a mile or so outside of the center of the city lay the popular nightclub, *Pecher*. As might be expected, the demons could not resist a place with a name that meant "to sin" in French. They were out in full force, threading through the club with their human shells dressed to the hilt, doing whatever it was they did best.

Katie stood in the shadows of the narrow alley beside the club with a group of cops, all of whom were trying to be as inconspicuous as they possibly could. They didn't want to give themselves away, nor did they want to scare off the crowd of infected inside. Katie scanned the building, her senses confirming there were demons spread throughout the club.

"All right, boys, I want you to surround the building.

Try to look as nonchalant out front as possible. Calvin is going to be at the back door. His job is to rack up anyone who may try to escape that way."

"Okay, we got it. Where are you going to be?"

Katie smirked, looking up at the top floors. "I'm going in. I'll scare out the roaches, so save whoever you can first and do whatever with the rest. Once I'm done clearing them out, I'll take out the rats on the upper floors. Don't be surprised if some of them jump out the windows into your very capable hands. They don't like it when I come around."

"How come we don't do this during the day?"

Katie pursed her lips. "The rats only seem to come out of the sewers at night." She shrugged and cracked her knuckles. "Do it right, and we won't have any problems with the dancers. I doubt they'll hear anything over the music, anyway. Still, we don't want to create a panic. If we have people running all over the place we'll miss a bunch of them, and I don't want to have to put on my running shoes tonight, gentlemen."

The cops nodded and headed for their positions. Katie turned to Calvin and stuck out her fist for a bump. "You ready?"

He tapped her fist with his, then lifted a shoulder and pulled his short sword from his back sheath. "I'm always ready. But it still feels weird doing this without the rest of the crew."

Katie nodded and smiled in understanding. "We *are* the crew. Give it some time. We will get in the groove. It's the same every time we lose someone—it takes a bit to get back in the swing of things. But we're still badass demon killers. Nothing has changed there."

"Damned right." Calvin chuckled. "All right, I'm gonna take my position. You and Pandora—you both be safe, okay?"

You too, big guy, Pandora cooed.

"She said, 'you too,'" Katie told him.

Calvin smiled as he headed towards the back of the building.

Katie watched him go until he rounded the corner, then made her way back to the street. She paused to unzip the front of her tight black top just enough to frame her cleavage perfectly. She swung her dark hair over her shoulders and sashayed down the block toward the door.

A couple of the cops stationed by the curb to look for trouble slipped lustful glances at Katie's ass as she passed. They were quick ones, though, since they didn't want to be busted by the female cops in charge of keeping their eyes on her.

Pandora didn't miss it for a second, though. *The Shield seems to like these tight-ass pants.* Pandora chuckled.

Focus. I need to act like a spoiled bitch.

That's a problem?

No, I'll just channel you.

Katie walked straight past all the people in line and stood in front of the doorman. She tilted her head and gave him a pout, affecting pure boredom. He looked her up and down, raising his eyebrow at the dark glasses covering her eyes.

A smirk moved across his lips and he stepped to the side, opening up the VIP rope to let her through. He opened his mouth to speak, but stopped himself when he saw the long demon finger and sharp nail pointing at him.

Katie flashed red eyes at him over the rim of her glasses. "Things were going so perfectly. Don't ruin it by saying something that would make me have to hurt you."

He swallowed hard and looked at the demon digit again, then nodded respectfully and turned back to the line. No one else had seen the exchange, which was good, because she wasn't trying to start a fight just yet.

However, Katie knew from his reaction that he was very aware of the demons upstairs and had assumed she was one of them.

Pandora whistled. *Whoever those bad boys upstairs are, they must have some mighty fine taste in women if he thinks we're part of that crew.*

Or he's just shit-scared of them and doesn't want to give them cause to rip out his spleen and eat it for dinner.

Spleens aren't really the tastiest part, just so you know.

Katie grimaced. *Okay, Pandorabal Lecter. I don't plan on ever finding out what the tastiest part of a human is. In fact, the thought makes me want to give up meat.*

Bullshit.

Yeah, well, I definitely don't want to go chow down on a cow right now, that's for damn sure.

Which is probably a good thing, seeing as we have a party to disrupt.

Katie neared the end of the long dark hall, which opened up into a wide room filled with people and music. Lights shimmered over the crowd, changing from red to blue to green. People dressed in their best occupied the VIP booths, sipping overpriced bottles of champagne and bobbing their heads to the deep bass beat reverberating from the speakers. Katie smiled and peeked over the edge of her glasses. She felt the presence of more than just a few demons in the place.

Looks like our playground tonight has a really good beat to it.

Katie swayed seductively as she crossed the dance floor. Her body writhed in time with the others surrounding her, her progress marked by the rhythm. She put her hands over her head and swished her hips back and forth, smiling at a couple of guys she spotted watching her lecherously.

The taller one stepped forward, his eyes glinting red as he reached out to put his hand on her waist. "Hey, there, sexy."

Katie pulled her glasses down enough for him to see her eyes flash bright red. "Hey, there."

His hand went stiff, and he backed up into the people behind him before taking off toward the door. Katie pushed her glasses back up and laughed.

She turned her attention toward a group of three guys wearing black suits in the middle of the dance floor. She put her eyebrow up and approached them, moving her body slowly to the tempo of the music. The main guy handed one of the others his drink and smirked, then strode over to Katie and made to pull her into him.

Pandora began to chuckle when Katie pulled her glasses down again. *Silly boys! This is too easy.*

When he saw her red eyes he stepped back, dropping the idea quickly. He grabbed his friends and took off, bolting through the crowd toward the back door. As they opened it, Katie could imagine the glow of Calvin's red eyes in the shadow right outside. She smirked when she heard his one-liner.

"You should watch where you're going. You might trip and fall right into the wrong hands."

Calvin stepped out of the shadows with a cop at his shoulder, and the three guys stumbled to a stop in front of him. The cop grabbed one of the guys by his collar while Calvin growled and grabbed the other two. They hauled the infected guys off to the capacious truck they were using to round the infected up.

Calvin opened the back door, revealing several infected already inside.

The apparent leader of the three rolled his eyes and hung his head. "I told you assholes we should have stayed home."

Calvin chuckled. "Shouldn't have let the demon drive, boys."

He picked up both of his at the same time and threw them into the back of the truck, then glanced at the cop, who was obviously trying to figure out how to do the same. Calvin reached over and tossed the last guy in, shutting the doors with a loud bang. He winked at the cop. "Don't sweat it. I was this strong *before* the demon."

"*Riiight.*" The cop watched him step back into the shadows and flexed his bicep, talking to himself as he walked back toward the front of the building. "Maybe that extra ravioli last night was a bad idea."

Katie looked around the dance floor, trying to figure out if she had gotten them all. Pandora sniffed the air for trails.

Looks like you got all the ones down here.

Good.

Katie zipped her blouse back up and stepped off the dance floor. Several of the guys called after her, sad to see the sexy-ass woman leave. She could almost feel the pride Pandora exuded.

You're hot as shit, girl. I'm telling you, men are falling all over themselves.

It was the dancing...and the alcohol.

They're intoxicated all right, by you. You did shake your groove thing, that's for damn sure, and they liked it. We should go dancing to troll men all the time.

Katie walked around the nightclub, scanning for a way to get upstairs. The first thing she noticed when she got to the back of the club was the black-painted door—and the very large guard standing in front of it. He was alert, his shoulders were back, and she spotted an earpiece in his ear. Katie smiled; she'd found exactly where the little bastards were hiding. She sauntered up to the guard and reached for the door.

He blocked her way. "I'm sorry, miss, this area is restricted. Go back into the club."

Katie tilted her glasses down and flashed her red eyes. "You might want to rethink that."

It didn't faze him a bit, which proved beyond a doubt that she was right where she needed to be. "I said go," he repeated, a little less politely this time.

Katie looked around and shrugged. "Oh well, you can't say I didn't give you a chance. I told you to rethink it, so this is on you. You should apologize to yourself after I'm done."

Katie grew a handful of long and super-sharp nails. Before the guard could react she thrust her hand forward and grabbed him by the balls, giving them a thorough squeeze. He crumpled instantly and Katie caught him by the chin, holding him so his ear was next to her lips.

Pandora took her voice over. "If you don't step aside and let me in, I'm going to squeeze just a *touch* tighter. You don't want *that*, do you? Now, open the fucking door."

He drew a labored breath when she twitched her claws, and sweat peppered his forehead. "You don't understand! I'll be killed if I let you up there without at least trying to take you out."

Katie grimaced at the sweat glistening on the top of his big bald head, and after releasing his balls, pulled her arm back and hit him hard under the chin. He whimpered and fell forward onto Katie, who caught his weight with a slight groan.

Katie propped the guard on the seat by the door. "God, you're fucking heavy!" She positioned his elbow on the table and let his head loll. "I wouldn't want you to get killed on my account."

She pulled open the door, letting it shut quietly behind her. She was at the foot of a tall staircase leading up to an archway. Slowly, she began to inch her way up the stairs, working to not make a noise.

Inside the room at the top, two men sat on a black leather sofa, cocaine spread out on small mirrors on the table in front of them. A tall woman in a tight black pencil skirt and a red chiffon blouse stood facing a third man who was looking through a window at the dance floor.

The man took a sip of his whiskey and slammed the tumbler down. "I don't see her anymore," he grumbled.

The woman sighed and rolled her eyes. "Who?"

"The hot-as-fuck bitch I saw on the dance floor. She was wearing this tight black shirt and had tits to die for. Those red pouty lips... I *want* her. I want her up here right *now*. I could bend her right over that desk and make her forget everything she ever thought she knew about how to be handled by a man."

"You're kind of a pig." The woman chuckled and finished her martini.

He ignored her comment. "Maybe I'll get George to go down there and pull her aside. I could really make her walk wrong tomorrow!"

Katie sat just outside the archway with her back pressed against the wall. She was pissed as hell that he was talking about her like her only purpose in life was to gratify him.

Looks like you have an admirer. Pandora snickered.

Yeah, one I've just decided to "make walk really wrong tonight!"

Pandora laughed. *I think we can make that happen.*

What are we looking at here? Three mid-level demons and one getting up there?

I'd say the other three are low-to-mid-level, and that jackass is teetering somewhere in the center. He's pretending he's more powerful than he really is. The others are too stupid to know.

"I'm still waiting for the cops to get off our asses. I saw four of them posted outside earlier," one of the guys complained. "I thought we blackmailed the police chief."

The woman groaned, turning around to glare at him. "That definitely failed, but no worries. I just happen to have a little birdie who's passed along some really nice racy pictures of the good ol' chief with three prostitutes at the Wayward Motel from last Tuesday night. I'm sure his wife and the press would *love* to get ahold of those."

The main guy chuckled and looked at the woman. "Nice job, but let's wait until next week to pull that one out. Make him feel secure."

"But Bailor," she moaned. "I really want to stick it to him."

"And you will get your chance." He smirked. "For now, go get Georgie. I want a piece of that woman's ass if she's still here."

The woman rolled her eyes and set her empty glass down, then walked over to the door and grabbed the handle in a huff.

Katie stepped to the other side and waited for the woman to come through the door. She was looking down at her nails when her eyes hit Katie's shoes and moved up her body to her face, which froze her in place.

Katie smiled and grabbed the woman's throat, silencing her before she could say a word.

She leaned forward and sniffed the woman's skin, catching a strong whiff of the demon inside her. The woman's hands flew up to scratch at Katie's, desperate to get free from her grasp.

Katie lifted her bodily off the ground, her feet dangling just above the floor while Pandora did a thorough assessment. The guys inside had no idea what was going on, but it should have only taken the woman a few seconds to grab the guard from the bottom of the steps.

"What the hell is taking you so long?" one of them yelled toward the door.

The woman's eyes shifted down to the bottom of the stairs, but Katie shook her head. "Georgie's taking a nap," she whispered.

This bitch is toast. The demon has her completely under his control. There's no saving her.

Aw, what a shame.

All emotion left Katie's face. There was just enough time for the woman's eyes to open wide with fear before Katie brought her other hand up and twisted hard and fast. There was a loud crunch, and the woman's body went limp. She hoisted the body into her arms, kicked open the door, and stepped inside. The three men turned around in surprise just as the body turned to dust.

Katie clapped her hands together and dusted herself off. "I swear, you demons can't even fucking *die* normally. You have to cover everything in dust. I have thrown away four pairs of pants because this shit sticks to the fabric like, well...*shit*."

The two men on the couch jumped to their feet and pulled their guns. Katie dodged to the side to avoid the bullets they sprayed into the wall behind her. She pulled her pistol as she rolled across the floor, coming to a halt up on one knee.

She put two rounds in the first guy's skull and he burst into dust, covering the leather sofa with grit. The second guy pulled his trigger, but all it did was click. He dropped the empty gun and ran toward the table in the back where three knives and another gun sat.

Katie shook her head, pulled one of her knives, and threw it. It slammed into the guy's hand, pinning it to the table. She stood up and pulled her separated staff poles from her back sheaths, clicking the buttons as she whipped them down to reveal the sharp blades.

"Got your hand caught in the cookie jar, huh? Let me help you with that."

She raised one pole over her head and swiped down, taking off the guy's arm. Before he could react to the pain, the other pole sang through the air, coming to a stop in the top of his head.

Katie tilted her head and watched his eyes flicker red before his whole body turned to ash. She retrieved the pole from his head and put both back in their sheaths, then grunted as she yanked the knife out of the table.

The one called Bailor looked panicked, stepping back and forth as he tried to figure out where to go. He grabbed the carafe of liquor off the bar and threw it at Katie, then bolted for the back door. Katie ducked to the side and sighed before sticking the knife in her sheath and taking off after him. She groaned in irritation as she pelted down the back stairs and followed him to the door, yelling the whole way.

"Where are you *going*? I thought you wanted to *meet* me? Here I am, and honey, I am *more* than ready to take care of you. More like kicking your fucking nuts so hard, I'll make a hole-in-one on a golf course—*in DC!*"

2

Katie reached the bottom of the stairs and pulled open the door Bailor had just slammed, blinking wildly as the spotlight from the dance floor raked her vision. The music throbbed loudly as she stepped into the crowd.

She narrowed her eyes, looking for the Bailor's clothing in all the movement. She glanced at the VIP tables, but everyone there was a normal, uninfected person—there to laugh, flirt, and have one hell of a night. Just then shouting from the dance floor caught her attention, and she found her target fighting his way through the dancers.

Katie smiled and moved quickly to the edge of the floor, never taking her eyes from her target as he pushed through the crowd. He stopped and looked back, panic on his face when he spotted her closing in.

Katie's chuckles faded when he grabbed one of the dancers and held a knife to her throat. She whimpered and looked at Katie, who was now pissed as hell, with frightened eyes. The guards spotted the knife and began heading over, so Katie bolted toward Bailor. She didn't hesitate when she reached him, just punched him square in the nose. He dropped the knife and pushed the woman to the side, stumbling back before turning toward one of the approaching guards.

He lunged and grabbed a gun from a guard's hip and turned to point it first at Katie, then at one of the dancers. He yelled at Katie. "I know who you are."

She slowed her pace and put her hands in the air, watching him closely. "Then you know that what you're doing is a very bad idea."

The hand holding the gun shook. "Fuck you, Lilith or Katie—whichever one is talking. Do you know who I am?"

"No." Katie shrugged. "And I don't really give a fuck. Put the gun down."

He darted into the crowd and grabbed a small woman in a tight red dress before Katie could stop him. The woman screamed as he dragged her toward him and held her body in front of his. He pressed the gun to her temple, hiding his head behind hers. Whichever direction Katie shifted, he pulled the woman with him. Slowly, he began to back up, dragging her along. The woman was crying at this point, and she stared at Katie.

"Please," she whimpered. "Help me."

"Quiet, you stupid bitch," Bailor growled. "You do what I say, and you might make it out alive."

Pandora sighed. *What a fucking pussy, using a damn human as a shield. I bet he shit his pants, too.*

If he hasn't, I'm gonna make sure he does.

Katie reached behind her and surreptitiously pulled out a knife. She looked the woman in the eyes and tilted her head to the right as she slowly lowered the knife and hid it behind her leg. The woman blinked, understanding what she was trying to say. Katie nodded, and the girl nodded back.

Uh, did you just decide to knock the gun out of his hand with your knife?

What else am I supposed to do? He's desperate. He'll shoot her in a heartbeat.

Do you actually think it will work?

Sure. I just hope he doesn't pull the trigger in the process.

Oh lord, Pandora moaned. *Not that I'm complaining about dead humans, but I* am *complaining about dead humans when it's our ass on the line.*

Relax, I got this...I think.

Katie stared at the woman and gripped the handle of her knife tightly. She mouthed the words, "One, two, three." The woman took a deep breath and threw her head to the left, squeezing her eyes shut. Katie didn't hesitate. She pulled her arm back and let the knife fly. It was like watching a car wreck in slow motion, and even Katie held her breath as she waited for contact. The butt of the knife hit the gun and dislodged it from Bailor's hand, but not before he got a shot off. Luckily, it was already pointing up away from her head and the bullet flew into the lights, raining a shower of sparks over the crowd.

Katie put her arm up to block her face.

Bailor growled loudly, then tossed the woman to the floor and took off for the back door.

Katie stopped near the woman. "You okay?"

"Yeah," she replied breathlessly. "Thanks."

"No problem," Katie told her and took off after Bailor.

By that point, people were starting to realize what was going on and stood back, clearing a path for both of them. Bailor reached the door and disappeared out the back before Katie could get to him. She gritted her teeth and barged out into the alley, where she plowed right into Calvin.

"Whoa, whoa, whoa! Slow down, crazy lady."

She looked left and right. "Where did he go?"

"Who? You mean him?" Calvin pointed to Bailor, who was unconscious on the ground. "I cold-cocked that motherfucker as soon as he came through the door all red-eyed."

Katie glanced down. "Dammit, my foot had a date with his fucking balls."

Calvin's eyebrows rose. "Uh, that sounds serious." He pointed to the body. "If it makes you feel any better, it doesn't look like I hurt him enough. He hasn't turned yet."

Katie and Calvin both looked down at Bailor, and his body burst into dust. Katie sighed and kicked the stuff off the top of her boot, then looked at Calvin and put out her lip.

"Aw, don't worry. There are plenty of demon nuts out there for you to crack."

She stomped her foot and put her head back. "But Calvin, *this* one deserved it the most!"

Calvin chuckled and put his arm around Katie. "How about a donut and some sleep?"

"*So* not the same as the sweet feeling of emasculating assholes."

Yes, it is!

"But I suppose it will do." Katie finished.

"Shut up and sit down. We'll deal with you in a bit," one of the cops yelled into the back of the truck.

Katie let out a low whistle as she looked into the back of the truck. "All of those, just from the club? Wow, that's more than I thought there were."

The cop touched his forehead in respect. "A good day for the city, thanks to you and Calvin."

Katie glanced at him. "That's my job. It was nothing special."

"To *us*, it's pretty amazing. There was no way we were going to get all these guys and the ones upstairs on our own. We really appreciate you helping the precinct." The cop put his hand out and shook Katie's, aware of the strength in her grip.

"Well, we appreciate your appreciation." Calvin smiled and shook his hand as well. "Hopefully, these people can get the help they need, and if nothing else, they are off your streets."

"Exactly. The more we get off the street and the more we treat, the safer the city will be. This war is already hard enough with the demons attacking us every which way. To have the infected let their demons take the driver's seat just forces us to turn our attention away from the more pressing issues. Oh, and the captain said to let you know your consulting fee will be in your bank account within forty-eight hours."

"We appreciate it." Katie smiled, shutting the truck doors and latching the handle. "Do you need us to escort these guys to the holding facility?"

"No," he told her, slapping the back of the truck. "We can take it from here. You guys have done enough."

Katie nodded and turned to Calvin as the cop walked off and the truck pulled into the street. "And I didn't even mess up my clothes! I call that a victory."

Calvin lifted an eyebrow and glanced at the hole in her top, right at the waist. Katie followed his eyes down and ran her finger over it, then lifted up her shirt to find a bullet hole. She sighed and grabbed a towel off the medical cart that was being pulled away.

Were you planning on telling me I had a bullet in me? I don't even feel it.

Excuse me! I only made it so you didn't feel the pain and go down in the middle of the battle. Would you like me to give you the pain back?

No, let me get the thing out of me.

By all means, do it your way.

Don't be like that. I could have bled out and died.

Come on, like I would let that happen? I need your body.

Me, too.

Katie took a deep breath and grew two long demon fingers with pointy nails, then looked down at the wound and shook her head. As she began to dig around for the bullet, she looked up at Calvin. "I wonder how Timothy and Joshua are doing? I hated leaving them behind, but I suppose I'll get used to it."

Calvin grimaced at the sight of her fingers knuckle-deep in the bullet hole. "Uh, yeah, you'll get used to it, but I don't know if I'll ever get used to *that*." He pointed.

"Huh?" She looked down at her fingers and back up at

him. "Oh. Cheaper and faster than the local hospital. Plus, they don't like dealing with demons there."

Calvin grimaced. "Is that even sterile?"

She shrugged. "I mean, I guess? Pandora will take care of the rest once the bullet is out."

Calvin looked up the street while she worked. "Never in my life did I think I would watch a person nonchalantly perform surgery on themselves while standing in the streets of LA outside of a nightclub."

Katie snorted. "You've seen weirder."

He looked back at her and made a face. "Maybe, but this is definitely the most cringe-worthy. My black ass would have been pumping the morphine, telling them to put my ass under."

"If you had Pandora, you would be doing the same thing. Oh! Hold on, there it is."

The demon fingers and nails disappeared as Katie carefully pulled them back out of the wound. She held the blood-covered bullet up to her face and looked at it for a moment before tossing it on the ground. "At least it wasn't one of mine."

Calvin snickered. "Yeah, *that's* the positive we can take from this."

One of the cops poked his head around. "Isn't that evidence?"

Katie looked down at the bullet and back at the officer. "The guy who shot me is dead, so don't think we need to worry about evidence. I mean, maybe if there was a *body*, but all we have is a pile of ash and a few witnesses. I think he's paid for it."

The cop nodded and shrugged. "You the boss, lady."

Katie nodded, looking back at Calvin. "I like that. 'You the boss.' You should learn that phrase."

Calvin grinned. "Dream on, superhero. God, I can't wait until my vacation starts. No bullets, no fighting, no weirdness where my partner digs a slug out of her gut. Just quiet, sun, sand, alcohol, and maybe even a few women."

"And the whole time, you'll be wondering what we're doing over here." Katie chuckled, shaking her head.

"Nope, I'm not like you. I can just float it away in the waves."

"Well, don't float it *too* far away. You're going to need it when you get back here. I am *so* not retraining your ass."

"I think you've forgotten who got here first. I helped train you, you little volleyball player."

Katie laughed. "Details."

The cops were moving out and gave Katie the word that it was about time she and Calvin did the same. She was about to suggest a restaurant for some late-night food when her phone began to buzz in her pocket. She pulled it out and looked at the screen.

Calvin lifted an eyebrow, and she showed him the name with a sigh. He nodded in understanding and went out to the street to give her some privacy. Katie ran her finger over the call button before answering.

Duty never seemed to end.

Katie kept her voice light. "General, it's good to hear from you."

"Good to hear your voice, too, Katie. We haven't spoken

for about six weeks, and I wanted to check in and see how everything's going."

"Of course. Well, we just finished a job, rounded up a bunch of infected and took out three more powerful demons. They had completely taken over their humans, so there was no saving them."

"Too bad, but it's good to hear you're in the game and kicking ass."

"I don't think I could get out of the game if I wanted to." Katie chuckled. "The last six weeks have been a lot of preparation and making deals with the government to help whenever they need it on contract terms. My IT is back at the base streaming intel, and Joshua is busy as always pumping out the ammunition with the company."

"How do you like your new setup?"

"Honestly? I worked with what I had. With Eric in New York, Korbin and Stephanie exorcised, and Damian off on his own adventures with the church, I figured this might be a better option than waiting to get some new teammates. Besides, it gives us a bit more freedom, especially now that the demon issue is more widely known."

The general sighed. "Things used to be so much simpler. Make a call, kill a few demons—that was it. Now there's red tape upon red tape. It's insane."

"No arguments from me!" She chuckled. "I always thought it would be simpler with everyone knowing but that was apparently a fantasy. Things, at least for us, have become much more difficult."

"Oh, for the days of old." He sighed. "Have you met with that stranger again?"

"No, he came, he gave me very little information, and bolted, leaving me with a lot of questions."

"Well, things will become clearer as time passes. They always do. I have to admit, I *do* feel a little better knowing you have some angel blood in there somewhere."

It's bullshit, in my opinion. I would swear Nephilim only had demon blood in them. But noooo—the weirdo guy shows up and all of a sudden you are chillin' with Jesus.

I wouldn't go that *far.*

"How is Pandora taking the news?"

"She has her opinions." Katie snickered. "As she does with most things. How are the battles going?"

"While there sure are a lot of them, none of the big ones are in major cities—at least for the moment. That's why I still need you guys and the teams to be working in the cities to keep the demons out, so they don't create larger infestations within the populace."

"Got that, and it's important to keep the progress we've already made in mind. We're definitely getting to them, though, big chunks at a time. For once, I saw more savable infected than not tonight. It makes me feel like we're doing something right."

"Absolutely, and every bit helps."

"Thank you, General." She looked around while she spoke. "We've definitely come a long way in our relationship."

He grunted. *What time was it where he was?* "That's for damn sure. But now I have to be honest, unfortunately. I did call you for a specific reason."

"Okay, shoot."

Pandora sighed. *Oh boy, here it comes.*

"I know this isn't going to make you happy, but I have to ask you to go to New York."

Are you fucking kidding me? Pandora immediately started bitching. *There's nothing but Dunkin' Donuts in New York City! It is the barren wasteland of donuts. There's not even a good old McDonald's on every corner, much less the evil Chick-fil-A! I'm going to have to eat shitty donuts and even shittier chicken nuggets. I swear to God this man hates me.*

"I can't hear her, but I feel like Pandora isn't happy."

Katie chuckled. "Yeah, well, 'tis life, I suppose."

"We have you booked at the Stewart Hotel. I specifically picked this for Pandora, since it's one block away from Madison Square Garden."

Great. I can take in a show with my shitty donuts.

"And," the general continued, "underneath Madison Square Garden is a Krispy Kreme donut place, which also happens to be right next to one pretty good pizza shop."

I...well... Okay, I can be bought. Let's hit the road, bitch. The Big Apple awaits!

I'm going to stick with the humor of this situation and not worry about how easy it is for your ass to be bribed.

"Sounds good, sir," Katie responded. "Does that mean I'll get to see how Ella's doing while I'm there? It's been a while—Incursion Day, actually—since I've seen her."

"I wish, but unfortunately Ella has gone down to Texas to handle some business. She seems to be kind of in the same boat as you right now, a bounty-hunter-for-hire thing."

"Oh, I didn't know that. I figured she was with the team. What about Eric?"

"He went with her. The two seem to make a pretty good

team, and the truth is, there seems to be more money in the for-hire business right now than with the teams. She still helps them whenever they need her, but the two of them are jet-setting wherever the contracts take them."

"Huh. Well, I hope they're doing well. I'll head to New York soon. I'd like to have a little time in Las Vegas if that's okay."

"Sure, take what you need, so long as it isn't too long. Reboot. Let me know when you're leaving, and we'll get the transportation set up for you."

"Thanks, General."

"No, thank *you*, Katie. And thank you for suffering through the lack of donuts, Pandora."

Whatever, Pandora grumped.

"She said no problem," Katie lied. "We'll talk soon."

She hung up the phone and glanced at Calvin. A little time in the big city never hurt anyone. Well, it did, but Katie knew that if the general had asked, it was definitely important.

3

K atie ducked and opened the front passenger door of the chopper to climb in. They were on their way back to the base in Vegas, having been in Los Angeles for two weeks before the LAPD had asked for their help.

Calvin was already sitting in the cockpit with his head-phones on, running through the pre-flight checklist. He was pretty good at flying the bird, but was never truly comfortable with it. Still, Katie insisted he pilot whenever possible, just in case she had to do a swan dive into some demon situation below.

She buckled her belt and gave him a thumbs-up, then placed the headphones on her head and sat back as the chopper took off from the helipad and they rose to the correct altitude. Katie knew to give Calvin his space while he took off. It was his adjustment time; the period he got comfortable with the bird.

They had enjoyed LA. Not only was it a great place for some relaxation and fun, it was also teeming with demons. They always had something to do out there, some demon to exorcise or demolish, and there was definitely room to make money whether independently or on-call. It was, however, time for them to be getting out of the field again. Get some training done, and just touch base with their people back home.

Once in the air and moving toward home, Calvin leaned back in his seat and let out a deep sigh. "I can't even tell you how ready I am for this vacation. I still say it's not nearly long enough after years of servitude in demon slaying, but I'll take whatever I can get."

Katie smiled. "Sure, sure. We know you just want to get away from us."

Calvin let out a deep laugh. "Sorry, but you mess up my dude mojo. I can't seem to get a date around you."

Pandora cackled inside Katie's head. *God, I'm so bad. Oldest demon trick in the book—a little sleight of hand.*

Katie frowned. *What are you talking about?*

I'm *the one keeping the chicks away from him,* she revealed.

Katie hung her head. *Oh, goodie.* That's *not gonna start a war with me in the middle.*

Hey, if I'm not getting any dick, he's not getting any wet flower.

Calvin glanced at Katie, who was grimacing. "What? Tell me! What's she saying?"

"Ugh." Katie rolled her eyes and leaned her head back. "Apparently, Pandora has somehow been working the women, not allowing you to get any relationship squeeze."

Calvin did a double-take, unsure of whether to laugh or be pissed. Finally, he settled in-between on something even sweeter...*revenge.* "I got you, Pandora. Don't worry. Somehow, some way, I will get you back for that."

Pandora took over Katie's voice for a moment with a deep cackle. "Bring it, Sweet Cheeks. I've been playing practical jokes for millennia."

Katie and Calvin both laughed and relaxed the rest of the way home. When they arrived, Katie couldn't help feeling relieved to be back at the base; to finally be home after the long trip. Everything looked to be on the up and up. Guards scattered as the chopper blades blew around the sand, all the buildings were tightly locked down, and everything else was tucked neatly underground.

They pulled their stuff out of the chopper and moved toward the elevator. After riding down to the main living quarters Katie put her bags down in the hall and climbed back into the elevator, and Calvin gave her a questioning look.

She pushed the unlock button. "I wanna go check on the guys. We've been gone for a while."

"Gotcha." Calvin nodded. "All right, I'm gonna go to my room and get cleaned up and ready for my trip. I'll catch up with you before I leave."

Katie smiled and released the door. "You'd better."

Katie chuckled as Calvin walked off with a spring in his step. She took the elevator down another level and made her way to the IT room. She slowed, hearing Timothy laughing as she approached. As she rounded the corner, Joshua and Timothy both looked up with big smiles on their faces.

"Hey, boss, you've returned!" Joshua stepped over to give Katie a hug.

"It's about time," Timothy teased. "We thought all the fabulousness of LA had reeled you right in. We were waiting to see you on a preview for some big Hollywood movie."

"Yeah, right. Pandora would become the biggest prima donna ever." Katie laughed. "One of those celebrities who demanded there be a bowl of only green M&Ms in her dressing room and four shirtless massage therapists on call at all times." Everyone laughed.

What's the problem with that? I fail to see the humor in such a normal request.

Katie rolled one of the office chairs toward them and sat down. "So, what's going on with you guys?"

Timothy shrugged. "Not too much. Joshua just came down to keep me company. I've been a little lonely without Stephanie around. I actually want to talk to people now, can you imagine that?"

Katie smiled and patted his shoulder. "I was like that at first. I just kept to myself and didn't really embrace my new life too much. That was why I thought you'd come round eventually. I know you're not new to being Damned, but you're new to being part of a family." She smiled proudly at him. "You know, you're doing a great job down here. You've become a valued member of the team, as well as the group. Honestly, our time out in the field fighting demons is probably what's changed your attitude. The bonds we form in war are strong."

Timothy looked at her quizzically.

Katie grinned. "You *missed* us!"

Timothy nodded and chuckled. "Sweetie, you're *so* right. I've spent so long hiding behind my screens that I forgot how it felt to be connected to people. Stephanie changed that. Well, you all did. I have a whole new outlook now."

"There's nothing more life-affirming than facing down the demons inside you, taking them to the ground, and rising victorious."

"*And* living to tell the story," Joshua added. "You should have seen me when I first got here. My Asperger's didn't help, and I was afraid of anything that moved. Now I have friends and a family; a good life and people I enjoy being around. I don't find the need to isolate myself anymore. You all make me feel safe enough to be myself."

Katie nodded at Joshua, proud of how far he'd come. It made her think about Stephanie, who'd had a lot to do with Joshua's blossoming, as she had with Timothy's. Stephanie had always had a way of getting people to come out of their shells without them even noticing it had happened.

She bit her lip and looked at Timothy. "Do you want to head out again? Maybe go see the sights like you did when the rules changed? Promise I won't pull a Korbin on you and send a tail."

Katie chuckled at her recollection of the first time she had gone out on her own. Korbin had sent one of her teammates out to follow her "inconspicuously."

How much more awkward could it get with a new teammate than having to explain why they'd found you in front of a porn shop having an argument with your demon about going inside?

Timothy shook his head. "No, I don't think I want to do that just yet. I'm working on it, though. I love it here, really, and I don't mind staying around. I have my duties, and you guys are all based here. If I have to be somewhere, I'm happy it's this place."

"You don't have to be here anymore. You know that."

"Yeah," he agreed, looking at the computers. "But where would I go? What would I do? Back to my mother's basement? Waste my time hacking into things just to prove to myself that I can do it? After getting a taste of a different life here, that would never fulfill me. Besides, I made a promise to myself: I'm going to start trying to go out and see a few things. Enjoy Las Vegas. God knows things change quickly in this lifestyle. I never know *where* I'll be from one month to the next."

Katie nodded. She saw a look pass between Joshua and Timothy and narrowed her eyes, wondering what the two of them were communicating. Timothy squirmed in his seat, his hands clenched in his lap. She raised an eyebrow. "Spill it."

Timothy took a deep breath. "I was kind of hoping Pandora could maybe have a little talk with my incubus. The last time she put him in his place, I was able to at least have one night out without him forcing women down my throat. I'd be happier about going out if I knew I could be around women without him making it really awkward and uncomfortable. I don't trust him, but I know if he has the fear of Pandora in him he'll behave."

Katie pressed her lips together and shook her head sadly. "As much as I want to say yes, I think you need to come to an agreement with your demon. Maybe figure out some sort of quid pro quo. It is still your body and you make the choices, and your demon has to understand that."

Timothy sighed and pushed out of his chair. "He's *impossible*. It will be ten years before I leave this base again."

Katie could sense his frustration and disappointment. She felt bad for him, but she stuck to her guns. Timothy needed to take control of his life and his demon. She couldn't do that for him.

The IT guy walked toward the door, then turned back. "I'm gonna do a walk-and-talk with this bitch; show him how much of a Queen B I can *really* be."

He shrugged and headed for the door, the faraway look on his face telling Katie that he was already talking to his incubus in his head.

Timothy might play a big game on the outside, but on the inside, it was more of a negotiation. He was trying to figure out a way that they could both get what they wanted.

Okay, I'm listening. What's it gonna take for us to make this livable?

Oh, I don't know... How about some hot, sweaty, nasty sex with a few hot Vegas showgirls?

Yeah, no. Not happening. There has to be a middle ground here. You don't own me, sweetheart. You can delude yourself that you have power over me all you like, but I've resisted your takeover attempts every single time. I rule this dick, not you. I have the power to put it wherever I choose.

And I have the power to make it wet spaghetti any time it goes somewhere I don't want it to.

Okay, but you still don't get what you want, sister.

Ugh, his demon groaned. *We may be able to come to an agreement, but you better bring all your cards to the table because I will not be giving in easily to your flamboyant ass.*

Katie laughed as Timothy disappeared around the corner with a look of indignation on his face. Joshua chuckled. "I told him he had to figure it out too. Hey, do you want to check out the factory? The girls are over there, and I'm sure they'd love to see you."

Katie grinned and got up from her chair. "Yep, that was my next stop after here."

Katie and Joshua took the elevator to the ground floor and covered their faces against the ever-present sand that blew across the empty cement platform. They moved across the grounds to the building across the drive. Katie was hit by a wall of noise when they opened the door. It took her a moment to adjust to the sheer volume of sound coming from the machinery within.

She clamped her hands over her ears. "You should get ear defenders for in here. It's so *loud.*"

Timothy handed her a pair of earplugs and nodded. "Already on top of that, thanks to Rose."

Joshua pointed out the stockpiled ammunition as they walked through the factory; the crates of bullets in the back, as well as the new shipments of military-grade special weapons like grenades, smoke bombs, and new missile prototypes they had been working on. Katie could tell she had left the place in the right hands. Joshua never skipped a beat. The orders were being separated out by the women on his team, who were all rocking their uniform of jeans, boots, and tight black collared shirts. Katie smiled, appreciating how Joshua had taken the initiative to make it a real work environment for them.

"Hi, Katie," the women shouted. A few waved with their clipboards, but they didn't stop working.

Katie beamed and waved back. She had only just realized how much she had actually missed everyone while she was gone, despite her earlier words to Timothy. She'd known the girls a lot longer than she had known him, after all. She'd seen them grow from escorts with no hope of leaving the life of sex-for-money into working women with the power to shape their own lives. Katie felt proud. Stephanie's legacy was helping them achieve that, and she would continue to honor that legacy as long as she drew breath.

They walked back to Joshua's desk, and he opened the order log. "We are at max capacity on orders right now, but General Brushwood has just informed me that more machines will be made available for our use. That means we'll probably be upping the production rate here soon. There's an influx of new soldiers in the military as well, so he'll be able to send over more help."

"Very good." Katie nodded. "You really are doing an amazing job, Joshua. Thank you."

Joshua smiled, letting Katie know without words that he appreciated her too. His life there was actually a *life*. He no longer lived in a van, going from show to show with his tools. He actually had a place to call home.

Katie wished he really knew how important he was to her life and her business, and she hoped that over time she would be able to show him. She smiled and laid a gentle hand on his arm for a moment. "All right, I'm gonna head back to my room and get some rest. You know where to find me if you need me."

"You got it, boss lady."

Katie smiled again and left the armory. She stepped out into the hot desert sun and closed her eyes, taking in the warmth for a moment. The sound of oncoming military vehicles forced her to open them again, and she waved at the half-dozen muscle-bound military boys who were passing her.

They waved back, all checking her out as they went by.

It's about time we got some hotties on the base, Pandora purred. *I wonder how many of them I could seduce at once?*

Let's try zero, k? They work for the general, and we don't need that getting back to him.

You are literally no fun. Zero. None.

Katie laughed and shook her head. She headed back to the elevator and went down to the living quarters, where she grabbed a bottle of water and bag of chips out of the kitchen before collecting her bags and lugging them down to her room.

She was in the master suite now, the one that had been Korbin's. She'd wanted more space and had the run of the base, so she'd figured, why not? She'd paid the girls to paint it and picked out more feminine décor, and settled into her new place.

She tossed most of her bags to the floor and set the main one on the dresser. She pulled out a pair of specially made huge-assed pistols from it, and a slow smile came over her face as she looked them over.

She had gotten them back from the maker in LA a week before, and couldn't wait to give them a try. However, she just wanted to chill right now, so she slid them into her underwear drawer—careful not to put them on Pandora's precious bras—and grabbed her bankbooks from the desk.

It had been a while since she'd updated her finances, so she plopped down on her bed and opened her laptop. She went to her bank account and began transcribing the deposits and withdrawals into her ledger.

She had several accounts at that point for tax purposes, so she liked to keep one big heavy ledger so she knew where her assets really stood. When she was done, she sat back and shook her head.

Damn, I'm rich. Like, stinking, rolling in it like Scrooge McDuck rich.

I don't know who that is, but wealth is a good thing, right?

Katie wrinkled her nose. *Yes and no. Every penny that's in here is watched by the damn government. If I want to do anything or buy anything, they know. It's like they have a magnifying glass on me.*

I don't get it, Pandora replied, confused. *Why does what you want to purchase in your personal life matter to the government at all? Now that things have changed, they take their tax money. I've seen the deposits.*

Because I'm not just some ordinary woman. Katie sighed. *It's just the thought that I can't even buy a pack of gum without the sonsabitches knowing about it. It pisses me off.*

Calm down there, slugger. They also put the money in that account.

I know, but back when I was a nobody—just a lonely student playing volleyball—they didn't care. If I bought a pack of gum, it didn't matter. But now they'll be trying to work out my intentions from my purchases. They want any info they can get. Can you imagine what would happen if I bought a—

Dildo? Anal beads? Oh, oh, a butt plug...or maybe some of those underwear made out of fruit roll-ups? A vibrator with a rabbit on the end. No! A double-sided rubber dildo. No! A spiked cock ring. No, wait, a pair of tickets to one of those sex camps. What's it called? The Bunny Ranch. Even better, a weekend pass to a BDSM event, or shit, maybe a—

Stop! Stop! Katie chuckled. *I should do that just to see what would happen.*

I agree. Do it! Right now! Strike while the iron is hot. Let's buy something to moisten your manhole and confuse the hell out of the government looky-loos while we're at it.

Maybe. Katie laughed as she got up and opened her dresser to pack for New York.

Shit, with your track record, I'm totally satisfied with a maybe.

Good, because a maybe is all you're getting. Right now, though, I need to figure out what to take with me to the Big Apple, and no, a double-sided cock ring did not make the list.

Hey, I'm still reveling in my semi-victory.

"This is Katie. I'd like to speak to the general, please."

"The general is in a meeting right now. This is his assistant. Can I help you with something?"

"Oh, well, I guess I can ask you, and if you don't know, I can call back later. My partner Calvin is about to leave for vacation, and I was calling to make sure he had the" authority to get on an international flight. Figured it was better to call now and ask than wait until he was in line."

"If you could hold for just a moment, I'll get the answer for you."

"Sure."

Katie was slightly annoyed that she had to talk to one of the general's underlings—not because she was too good for it, but because it meant she would probably get the runaround.

The lower-level staff never quite knew how to work with Katie. They were either too nervous to give her a straight answer or too green to understand she wasn't one of the bad guys. Either way, it was almost always a pain in the ass.

The assistant picked the phone up again. "Are you still there?" she asked Katie.

"Yep."

"Oh, good. The general said that Calvin is authorized to get on that flight."

"Excellent."

"However, if you could hold on just a moment, the general will be right on the line. He wants to speak to you himself."

"Oh, uh, yeah, sure."

He never interrupts a meeting unless it's important, Pandora remarked.

I was just thinking that.

Several moments later, the general picked up. "Hey, Katie. Thanks for holding."

"No problem."

"Yes, Calvin can go, but unfortunately, you cannot."

"Okay," she replied slowly. "Why have I been grounded?"

"Think about it. You have the equivalent of a nuclear bomb inside you. It's not an internal order. None of the airlines want to risk their planes. *We* have no problem with you flying, it's a public issue. It's all very new to them."

"I understand." She sighed. "So it's not that I can't leave the country, but rather that I'm limited to my personal resources?"

"Precisely," he replied. "Can I call you a bit later? If that is all, of course. I have a boardroom of testy officers waiting for my return."

"Of course. Thank you, General."

They hung up, and Katie sat back on her bed, slightly deflated. *Well, this pours cold water over my plans for future trips.*

You're just going to have to get your own transport. It's not like you can't afford it.

True, and I guess I could use the company plane in the meantime. I just don't like the feeling that I'm being followed. You know damn well there are more bugs on our plane than in the whole country of Zimbabwe.

Truth. Pandora chuckled.

Just then, Calvin came in from the hall, singing. He stopped in Katie's doorway. "I came to say goodbye, my dear. I'm off to a tropical paradise to bask in the glory of a month-long vacation."

Katie laughed and got up from the bed to wrap her arms around him. "I'm gonna be lost without you."

"Nah, you got P-Dog to keep you company. Besides, how much trouble can you get in while I'm gone?"

Pandora snickered. *Is that a rhetorical question or is he testing me?*

Katie chuckled and nodded. "Go! Enjoy the sun, the sea, and the women, not necessarily in that order. Just don't forget to come back!"

"We shall see." He winked. "I'll see you fools in a month!"

He walked back toward the elevator, singing *Copacabana* at the top of his lungs. Timothy turned the corner from the other direction and stopped right outside Katie's door.

He cupped his hands around his mouth. "That's about a club in New York City, not *South America*, you unwashed heathen!"

Calvin waved back and turned the corner, carrying his luggage, with a towel already over his shoulder. The elevator doors shut, cutting off his singing.

Timothy shook his head and walked away mumbling, "Neanderthal."

Katie shook her head, amused, and walked over to shut her bedroom door. She emptied the dirty clothes out of her suitcases and began to pack for New York. The whole time she was packing she ran through different ideas on just what she was going to do to make some more money.

Money the government couldn't see her spend.

4

K atie sat back on the plane and looked out the window as they took off from the base's newly-renovated runway.

She was taking the corporate jet, since it was easier than taking a military or commercial flight. She wanted some privacy; to escape the stares and the whispers that happened whenever she was in public anywhere.

Besides, with the general's news that her travel was being restricted, she wasn't sure she would even be welcome on *domestic* flights.

Once the plane had reached cruising altitude, she pulled out her laptop and connected to its Wi-Fi. She wondered for a second why she didn't take this jet everywhere, then remembered how much it cost to fuel it and hire the staff.

She was rolling in money, but she wasn't Bill Gates—at least not yet.

Katie pulled up the website for the Stewart Hotel and a map of the surrounding area. She wasn't sure how long she would be there or even what she would be doing, so she figured she might as well check it out ahead of time and get herself familiar with the area in which she would be staying.

Our hotel is catty-corner to Madison Square Garden, so we can take in some concerts while we're there. Also, it's not too far from Times Square, so we can go there easily for food and shopping. It's not really a bad location.

So why did they stick us there? You know those government types. They would put us in a hostel if they could get away with it. Pandora was skeptical.

I believe it has to do with the fact that there's a Krispy Kreme practically right across the street, and they know how picky you are.

They don't know I'm that picky, she scoffed. *According to Google maps, there's a Dunkin' Donuts even closer. It's connected right to the damn hotel.*

Yes, but the Stewart Hotel has little kitchens in the suites. Apparently, we can grab donuts and take them back there. The website says that they have microwave oven drawers.

What the hell is a "microwave oven drawer?"

Katie shrugged. *Apparently, it's a microwave oven where you push a button and the drawer opens. You just lay your food in there, close it, and it microwaves it. Nifty, huh?*

Pandora sighed. *I suppose it will do. Now, what are the options for us getting more money?*

I guess I could go out on more individual raids, rake in the cash for those demons.

You could always sell your body. You already *sold your soul.*

Hey! I still have my soul. You may be wrapped tightly around it right now, but that can be changed.

Pandora chuckled. *With as popular as you've gotten, most*

if not all those men would pay a pretty penny to sleep with you—not to mention the boatloads extra they would pay to sleep with me.

No. *The answer is no. Unequivocally, no. I think I'll just start pulling cash from my account. Of course, I can't pull it all at once, or the government will make waves.*

Wish we had thought of this back in Vegas. We could have just gambled and won.

Only if we wanted to spend time making a lot of small bets. For the larger ones, the government still knows you won.

Ugh, assholes! What happened to a woman's right to shop?

Speaking of shopping...

Katie pulled up a list of the different shops and boutiques near the hotel. She figured if she was going to be in the best shopping place in the country with money in her pocket, she might as well get some new clothes.

There was the small question of what the hell she wanted to buy. She had been draped in black spandex for so long that she wasn't sure she even knew what her style was anymore.

Pandora chuckled. *This is going to be fun!*

Lucero folded his arms over his chest, staring out of the conference room window at New York City. He was thin, almost fragile looking, but those looks were definitely deceiving.

Lucero was the head of the unnamed terrorist organization which was funded by the demons. He led with ruthlessness, and was responsible for some of the most lavish displays of chaos the world had seen since Incursion Day.

Lucero waited impatiently on the thirtieth floor of the office complex for the last of the seven American leaders to enter the room and take a seat.

He knew the humans were nervous around him, especially with his red, beady eyes glaring down at them. Lucero liked the fear in their eyes, but he also knew he needed to keep that at a minimum.

He had a job for them, one that would restart the chaos in the cities.

When the last of the seven were seated, Lucero glanced around the large mahogany table at their nervous faces. "Thank you for coming. Each of you was picked for your bravery, your loyalty to the demon cause, and your resourceful nature. You have been patiently waiting for months for a call, and I'm pleased to let you know *this* is that call."

Several of the leaders shifted nervously in their seats, unsure what to expect. Most of them were there not because they believed in the cause, but because they wanted to reap the personal benefits of helping the organization.

Lucero didn't care what their motivation was. It was almost better that way. Personal greed was one of the most common motivators. The organization really didn't care what their reasoning was as long as they remained loyal and completed their assigned tasks.

"Each of you will be responsible for personally finding sacrificial vessels to use as demon hosts. These individuals must be strong enough to survive possession, but not so strong that they can *reject* the demon. Anyone loyal to the cause is, of course, a preferred option, but in reality, it doesn't really matter. If they aren't a supporter, the demon will quickly change that for them. Once these sacrifices accept their demons, they will then go out into your respective cities and allow the demon to completely take over, causing a catastrophic terrorist event."

"And what about after that event? Will we be able to control those demons afterward?"

Lucero scoffed. "Those who follow the right way will be able to overcome the demons at the end of the day. It is a good way of finding out who is really loyal."

Uneasy looks passed between the leaders, and they began to wonder if they had gotten themselves in over their heads. At that point, though, it really didn't matter.

It was done. The decision had been made, and they were committed to finding the vessels no matter the cost to them or the people of their cities.

Of course, none of them said a word, too entrenched in their personal greed, and too terrified of Lucero to question his authority.

Lucero's impassive face revealed none of his internal snickering. He knew exactly what kind of effect he had on these people. He could feel their fear in his bones, and it satisfied him like a good meal. He was going to get what he was after, and when he did, he would smash pathetic humans like these.

Until then, they were his puppets to command.

Calvin got a glimpse of the beautiful scenery as his plane touched down at the Cabo San Lucas airport.

The plane rolled to a stop on the runway. The staff opened the doors and set up to unload. The passengers had to collect their carry-ons and head down the stairs to catch a bus to the main airport itself. It wasn't ideal, especially since Calvin was ready to relax.

"Talk about old-fashioned. You'd think they would get with the times," he grumbled to himself. He climbed onto the bus and took a seat near the back.

When the bus was loaded it pulled off the runway and onto a small paved road on the side. They were pretty far from the airport, so Calvin leaned back and took in the scenery.

When they reached the airport, he was met by a half-mile line of people that twisted throughout the large room, ending all the way over near the exit doors.

Over a dozen border patrol officers were stationed by the doors, working to get people through the line and into Cabo.

Calvin tensed at the thought of waiting in the long line. *If I end up in Hell when I die, this is exactly what they're going to do to me for eternity.*

He looked around as the line shuffled slowly forward. He heard babies crying, the nervous chatter of parents trying to organize their families, and husbands and wives bickering about passports and luggage.

It was all the things that would usually irritate the hell out of him at an airport, but this time, being on vacation, he sat back and enjoyed the normalcy he had long since forgotten.

He was alive, which was a feat for someone in his profession, he wasn't on a mission or having to kill anyone, and he was looking forward to getting to the resort. It was a change of pace that he quickly let himself acclimate to.

Not even the large group of bros bothered him. Calvin even chuckled at the wrestling match they began from the sheer boredom of waiting.

When Calvin reached the front of the line, he handed over his passport and set down his luggage. The agent looked him up and down and motioned to his sunglasses. "Please remove those. Thank you."

Immediately, Calvin felt the tension rise. His chest tightened as he prepared himself to have an issue. He pulled down his glasses and showed the border guard the flash of red that moved over his pupils.

The guard lifted an eyebrow and opened his passport, reading the information inside. The fold denoted him as being one of the Damned and listed Katie's Killers as his place of employment.

The agent slowly looked up at him with an awestruck expression. "Congratulations, you kick many demon's asses back to hell!"

Calvin was shocked a moment, then smiled and pulled his glasses back up, nodding at the guy in thanks as he took his passport back.

The guy leaned in and whispered, "Is Katie as pretty as on television?"

Calvin pulled his glasses down a little more and winked. "Even *prettier.*"

He left the swooning border guard and went to fetch

his suitcase from the carousel, ready to get his relaxation on.

Before he could even get out to the main doors, he was inundated with people waving their hands in his face and offering him a cab.

He had heard several warnings about the cab drivers out here and really didn't feel like kicking anyone's ass that morning, so he waved them off and headed outside to hail his own transport.

There was a line of them waiting outside, so he picked the one that looked the most reputable and climbed into the back seat, putting his luggage in after him. "The Pueblo Bonito Pacifica in Cabo, please."

"Right away, señor."

As they drove along, Calvin stared out the window. He couldn't miss the vast difference just a few blocks made out there. There was a sharp contrast between the some of the neighborhoods with peeling homes and poorly-maintained dirt roads and the others with their pristine exteriors and manicured lawns.

Children played in both areas, the only difference being that some were barefoot and wearing worn clothes and others looked no different than children back home in the suburbs in the States. It warmed Calvin's heart to see that they all laughed as they played, regardless of their location.

The drive to the Pacifica took about forty-five minutes, so he sat back and relaxed, pulling out his passport to show at the two checkpoints along their route when they entered Pueblo Bonito.

Safety was a huge concern here, just as it was every-where else in the world. When they finally crested the last rolling hill, the vista took his breath away. The ocean twinkled about half a mile below, an azure jewel set in golden sand. The water was the bluest he had ever seen, and even from there he could see the rough, rolling white caps of the waves.

When he arrived at the hotel, he paid the driver and handed his luggage to the attendants. He checked in at the front with a beautiful dark-skinned woman whose nametag read Yvonne. Between the lush yet earthy décor of the adults-only hotel and the beautiful women walking around, he felt like he was already in paradise.

Yvonne eyed Calvin appreciatively. "Welcome. We have you in one of our most luxurious suites. Would you like to purchase our all-you-can-eat option for your stay?"

"That would be fantastic," he replied, ready to chow down.

She held out a plastic band and secured it around his wrist. "You can use this at any of our Pebble Beach hotels, as well as Couples and Lucas."

They're going to lose money on us, his demon piped up.

Calvin had to keep his snicker in check as Yvonne handed over his keys.

Yvonne smiled coyly. "Enjoy your stay…and don't hesitate to let me know if you need anything."

"Thank you." He returned her smile and headed for Suite 1652, the attendant with his luggage following him.

Everything was stone: the walls, the floors, and even the countertops inside his suite. He hadn't stayed in luxury like this in a long time—if ever—and he couldn't have been happier. After the attendant was gone, he picked up the pamphlet for the hotel and sat down on the edge of his very soft bed.

Let's see. What do we have here? Hot tubs on the bottom floor outside. Okay, I can get down with that. Two pools with night service—very nice. I wonder why you would swim in the pool when the ocean is right there, though?

Sharks, his demon replied. *Nasty bastards, sharp teeth.*

Ah, no. It says right here swimming isn't advised due to strong undertows.

At least the view is one of a kind.

I know, right? I haven't seen anything like this in my whole life. It's fucking beautiful.

So, what's the plan? Swim? Party? Buffet? What are we going to do first?

I planned on just chillin' here, maybe getting some room service. Tomorrow, we can go out to Cabo and take in the local scenery.

Calvin flipped off his shoes and yawned, stretching his arms over his head, getting ready to relax. He walked over to the window and stared out at the ocean, his eyes eventually trailing back to the pool below. There were a dozen or more very luscious women around the pool, wearing nothing more than a few strings and small triangles of cloth.

He rubbed his chin. "On second thought, I might go for a swim."

His demon snickered. *It's like I know you...*

5

Matt, Brandon, Dillon, and David were off from school after a long Friday of tests and assignment submissions. They all sat around the picnic table at the local park, where most of the kids hung out when they weren't planning to catch the train into downtown Chicago.

The place was perfectly manicured, just like every lawn and every cookie-cutter house in their nearby neighborhood. They were the kids of middle-upper class families, expectations high, results minimal—just enough for them to still go out on the weekend and party it up with their friends.

Matt drummed his hands on the table, bobbing his head up and down. Brandon reached across and held down his hands, tired of hearing his drumming. Dillon winked at one of the girls across the way. She giggled and shook her head, walking off with her friends.

Matt nodded. "Isn't that the new girl?"

"Yeah." Dillon smirked. "She's in my chem class. Super-smart and super-fucking-hot. Her dad's some kind of surgeon in Chicago, and her mom is a fitness instructor. She seems to be a mix of both—sassy little sexy thing with book smarts."

Brandon laughed, high-fiving Dillon. "Perfect combination, dude. Good girl by day, party girl at night."

David ate his Fritos quietly, just listening to the guys talk. Ever since he had become infected, he felt set apart from the other guys. The four of them had been friends since kindergarten so they still kept him in the group, but he just wasn't feeling the bond anymore.

As far as dating was concerned, he was pretty much looking at a dry life. None of the girls would even give him a second glance when they saw the flash of red in his eyes.

"You guys going to Cynthia's pool party on Saturday?" Brandon asked. "I heard *all* the girls are gonna be there."

"Hell, yeah," Dillon blurted.

"It's on my calendar with like twelve circles around it." Matt laughed. "How about you, David?"

Matt did the most to include David, trying to pull his friend out of his shell a bit. "Nah, her mom said I wasn't allowed to come. Cynthia said that since I got this damn demon in me, she was scared to let me come over there."

"Bummer," Dillon replied.

Matt gave him a sympathetic smile. "Sorry, man. That sucks."

David leaned back, chewing on the straw from his drink, and shrugged. He was pissed; he had been ever since he'd become infected. He didn't understand what all the freaking out was about.

It was a stupid tiny demon he'd gotten messing with

some lame mirror game awhile back. He grabbed his stuff and stood up from the table, nodding at Matt before heading toward his house. He was tired of listening to everyone talk about the things he couldn't do.

His mom was in the kitchen cooking when he got home. He took his shoes off and hung his book bag on the hook by the door, then went into the kitchen and grabbed a cookie off the plate before sitting at the island.

David's mom looked over and smiled as she took a sheet of cookies from the oven. "Hey there, sweetie. How was your day?"

"Stupid," he complained bitterly. "I hate my freakin' life."

His mom put the tray down and came over to wrap her arm around his shoulders. "Hey, hold on! What happened?"

"Nothing happened. It's the same problem as always—the stupid demon inside me."

His mom turned his face to her so she could inspect his eyes. "Is it acting up? Do we need to go back to the clinic?"

"No." He sighed. "It's not that. The demon doesn't even talk. It just sits there. It's everyone else who has the problem. They act like I've got some sort of disease. No one likes me anymore, and my friends' parents' say I can't come to parties or be around them. They act like I'm contagious or something. Everywhere I go, my eyes are a dead giveaway. Everyone treats me like normal until they see that red flash, then all of a sudden I'm a pariah."

"Not everyone will treat you that way, sweetie," his mom told him gently.

David snorted. "I offered to help some old lady across the street with her groceries the other day. She was thankful until my sunglasses slipped off and she saw my eyes, then she pretty much just snatched the bags from me and hobbled off like I was going to eat her or something. The world is going to hell, and I'm stuck right in the middle of it. The worst thing of all is, I have no one there with me—it's just me and my damn demon."

The barracks were loud and rowdy, full of soldiers freshly returned from PT. Brock looked at the floor as he always did when he passed through the barracks, not wanting to give his succubus the pleasure of viewing sweaty, half-naked men.

He grabbed a towel from the locker and wiped his face, letting the other guys pile into the showers ahead of him. He was out of boot camp now, so he had a little more control over when and with whom he took a shower these days.

When his succubus was behaving herself, he showered alone. Otherwise, he would shower at the same time as Phillips—a guy on his squad she absolutely loathed—and the sight of him naked pushed her deep down inside. That day she had been quiet, which he was thankful for.

The Rapid Reactionary Force was interesting.

They were barely even friends yet; just a bunch of guys who had no choice except to band together as brothers at the drop of a hat. When the siren blared they got their shit together, teamed up, and were out the door within twenty minutes.

There were no load-ins, and there was no long-winded

explanation of the task. They boarded the planes with whatever weapons they could carry, got a minor briefing on the flight or drive over, and dropped in.

That was it.

The whole point of his sector of the military was that they were able to buy the military time to load their shit in and get there. That, or help the cops when the incursion wasn't big enough to call out all the forces. They were like the mercenary teams for the United States government, the main differences being that they were not trained nearly as well as the others, and their freedom was not their own.

By the time Brock had gotten in and out of the shower, everyone else was dressed and taking advantage of the downtime. The men talked, played cards, wrote letters or emails—whatever they wanted to do.

Brock never wrote letters or emails, he didn't take naps, and he wasn't overly friendly with the others yet. Music just made him miss home. He always hated it when the guys would blare his CD when he came into the barracks although he always smiled and laughed, not wanting to give in to the homesick feeling in the bottom of his gut.

"Brock," one of his brothers called. "Come hang out with us."

Brock hung up his towel and went over to take a seat in one of the chairs they had pulled up around the end bunk. The guy slapped his leg and leaned back, putting his arms behind his head. "Rutger here is telling us about his imaginary girlfriend back home in Boise."

Everyone laughed except Rutger. "She's *not* imaginary. We've been together since middle school, and one day, when this demon shit is gone and we're both back to normal, I'm gonna marry her."

"Let's just hope whatever demon's inside of her isn't too wild." Another soldier chuckled, thrusting his hips forward with one hand out in front of him.

Rutger rolled his eyes and looked away, shutting his notebook. He glanced at Brock, realizing that he had no idea what kind of demon was inside him. He was a quiet guy, and no one really knew much about him except that he'd been the lead singer of a successful rock band.

"How about you, Brock? How did you get your demon?"

Brock shook his head and leaned back with a groan. "I was fucking around with that mirror game, playing it with some chicks I met on tour."

"Aw, man." Several of the guys chuckled. "That sucks."

"I've heard groupies do that," another chimed in, making a lewd gesture as he spoke.

The first soldier leaned forward and nodded at him. "You must have been pulling in some mad fucking sweetness as a rock star. And shit, now, with that demon... Is that where you go when we get liberty? To fuck all the chicks? Seriously, I don't know why you left being a rock star. You could be doing whatever you want out there on the road, and never get fucking tired. Five, six, seven chicks a day."

"Yeah, man," another joined in. "Tell us stories from the road, bro! You didn't come here the moment you were infected. You had to have a taste of the wild life."

Brock put up his hand and shook his head. "I haven't

slept with a single woman since I became infected, not once I left tour—which was the next morning."

The first soldier snorted his disbelief. "*What?*"

"Yeah, right, dude. Give us the details. Don't hold back," another urged with a laugh. "He's fuckin' with us. He's gotta be."

Brock shook his head in resignation. "Nope, dead serious. Not a single one." He sighed. "The thing is, well...my demon isn't the normal garden variety. She's a succubus."

The soldiers loved that.

"Whoa!"

"That's fucking sweet. I bet she's like talking kinky shit in your head all the time."

"I've heard stories about what they can do to men if they infect them. We're talking like sensations whenever you want it."

Brock rolled his eyes. "That's definitely not the case with my succubus. She's a bit of a bitch."

I can hear *you, asswipe.*

"It sounds awesome, but the reality of it isn't as fun as you think. She's strictly-dickly, loves herself some sausage. She *only* drives stick."

The guys got quiet for a minute, looking around at each other while that sank in. Once it did, their faces turned and they all expressed sympathy for Brock, really feeling for him. A couple of them stifled snickers, but the rest of them were Sorry Central for poor Brock.

Brock let out a half-laugh before his face became serious. "Look, we are going into some bullshit together, and I've got your backs. But if any of you offer my succubus dick, I'll shoot you myself."

The guys broke out into laughter, patting him on the shoulder. "Thanks for taking one for the team, bro."

Just then the alarm went off overhead and the green light that signaled support for a small incursion came on. Brock was on that sub-team, and so were the guys around him.

They suited up and headed out, ready to kick demon ass.

Katie pulled up in front of the Stewart Hotel in the blacked-out SUV and looked up at the hotel logo written elegantly in black and white on the front of the awning of the tall stone building.

Two doormen came over, and one opened her door and held out a hand to help her out of the car. The other went to take her bags, but she stopped him with a shake of her head and loaded the luggage rack herself. The doorman raised an eyebrow when metal clinked in one of them as she set it down.

She gave them a bright smile and walked straight inside to the front desk. There was no one at the desk, so she waited a moment, taking in the light, airy feel of the hotel. It was beautiful; the décor sumptuous but understated, not overdone like so many of the hotels she had stayed in before.

After a few minutes, she tapped the bell on the counter and sighed. *Are they getting it on back there, or what?*

Pandora sniffed the air. *They want to, but no. Sadly, they are not doing it right now.*

A young woman came out from the back, her cheeks flushed pink. She rushed over to take care of Katie, slightly flustered as she spoke. "Sorry about your wait, ma'am."

Katie ignored her discomfort, putting on a polite face and giving the woman her information. The woman began to type quickly into the computer just as a tall young man with bright blue eyes emerged from the back.

His eyes were on the young woman's ass as he came out, but as soon as he saw Katie, he straightened up and hurried off to his duties. Katie stifled a comment, looking down at the brochures on the counter instead.

The young woman was still flushed as she handed Katie the key cards. "Here you are, ma'am, Room 1928. The bellhop will help you with your bags. You are on the nineteenth floor. It's a beautiful view from up there."

"Wonderful." Katie smiled. "Thank you, but I'll take my own bags."

The bellboy looked crestfallen. "Are you sure, ma'am?"

"I am, thank you." She took her key cards and pushed the luggage rack over to the elevator. Service was nice and all, but the last thing she needed was for the bellboy to drop one of her bags and cause an accidental gunshot or explosion in the elevator. She would never live *that* one down.

As she entered her room, she thought back to it and cringed at the word "ma'am." Had she already aged so much?

Maybe if you got some sleep, like I keep telling you.

Like you keep telling me? Do you mean like you 'kept telling me' while we were on vacation? Can it, Pandora. Let's just get settled in.

Touchy. Pandora scoffed. *Maybe you need to get laid more than I thought.*

Katie ignored her and looked down the small hallway straight ahead. There was a closet on the right that could accommodate her entire wardrobe from back home in it.

To the left was a door that led into an expansive bedroom with its own bathroom. The colors were light and earth-toned, and the bed looked like it was made out of clouds. Katie leaned against the doorway and gazed longingly at the bed, imagining the deep sleep she would get in it, cocooned in the mountain of blankets and pillows.

It was a dream come true.

The bathroom was small but all marble, a sleek and shimmery design that screamed luxury and pampering. The government didn't usually spring for a place like this, but then they didn't have another hunter who could do what she could. In a way, she was a specialty weapon, and the funding to fight the greatest threat to mankind was relatively endless these days.

Katie made her way out of the bathroom and down the hall, where the suite opened up into a plush living room. Floor-to-ceiling windows gave the impression that the room was much more spacious than it actually was. Toward the front was a small desk, where several menus for local eateries and room service sat by the phone. The room was simple but stylish, with a large comfortable couch and a large flat-screen television with a small bar next to it.

Katie ran her hand over the amber throw on the back of the couch. *Oh, that's soft.*

This is great and all, but I need to see this microwave.

Katie chuckled and walked around the half-wall into the kitchen, where she made straight for the fridge and looked inside.

Yes, I can work with that, Pandora hissed. *I can fit a fair number of donuts in there.*

And here's the microwave.

Katie pulled out the drawer and looked at the dials. Things for heating, things for toasting, and then there was the full-power cooking capability. She opened out the lid and mentally noted how many donuts would fit.

Eight, Pandora answered before she could finish her calculations. *Krispy Kreme? Excellent! We can reheat those babies without leaving the room. I was worried I would have to ask the front clerk to run over there a few times a day. Come on, put your shoes back on. Let's go out and get donuts right now!*

Katie laughed at Pandora until she realized that she was dead serious. *All right, all right, but you'll have to wait just a few. I want to unpack my suitcase first. I don't need to roll back up in here covered with sugar and get it over everything I brought.*

You are really testing me today, you know that?

Katie smiled and went into the hall to fetch her luggage. She was half-tempted to take her time, but Pandora's constant sighs were already getting on her nerves. She folded her clothes and put them in the dresser, then shoved that suitcase into the closet. The rest were her weapons. In the hotel, she didn't really want to just set them out for anyone to see, so she placed them in the closet and shut the door, dusting off her hands. She put the 'No Disturb' sign on the door and left.

All right, madam. Donuts await us.

6

Katie stood at the Krispy Kreme counter gazing in wonder at all the options. The 'hot' sign was on, and the smell of glazed deliciousness was making Katie's stomach growl expectantly. They watched each donut roll down the conveyer belt and come to a gentle stop in a shimmering pool of them at the end.

Pandora gasped. *Hot and Ready, just how I like my donuts —and my men, for that matter.*

The woman behind the counter gave Katie a bright smile. "Welcome to Krispy Kreme, how can I help you?"

"Hi." Katie smiled. "So many options. Let's start with one dozen of your glazed, and I'll let you know from there."

"Sounds good. Having a get-together?"

Katie chuckled. "No, but you'll be seeing me quite a lot while I'm here. I guess you could say I have a sort of donut fetish. We're staying at the Stewart. There's a Dunkin' there, but they just don't give the fix Krispy Kreme does."

Pandora snickered. *That's putting it nicely. Dunkin' blows goats compared to Krispy Kreme. In fact, there is no comparison. Krispy is supreme.*

The woman winked at Katie. "Of course, they don't. Even before I worked here, I would go out of my way *not* to go to Dunkin' Donuts. I do understand those who do, though. You have to come a ways to find us."

"We made sure we knew exactly where you were when we were on our way here."

A short guy with a manager tag poked his head around the corner. "I like it. True Krispy fans—we don't find that too often around here. There are too many options for food. You go out for a donut, you go home with spaghetti and a taco from somewhere you saw along the way."

Katie laughed, nodding. "There were definitely some tempting spots on the walk here, but I had my eyes on the prize."

The woman set the box of hot glazed donuts down in front of her and handed her one with a napkin wrapped around it. "On the house."

"Thanks." Katie smiled. "I'll also take a variety dozen. Just put whatever in there, as long as it's not apple. I don't like apple stuff."

"You got it," the woman chirped, grabbing another box.

Don't just hold that donut. Let me have a bite.

All right, all right, don't get your panties in a twist.

Not wearing any. Pandora snickered.

I don't even want to discuss how that makes me feel, since you're squatting inside my body.

She took a bite of the donut to shut Pandora up before she had a chance to make another comment. Pandora groaned as Katie chewed and swallowed, and Katie had to stop Pandora from vocalizing her ecstasy.

Pandora sighed happily. *At least the general understands the basic necessities of life.*

"All right, here you go." The woman put both boxes into a large Krispy Kreme plastic bag and rang Katie up. When she was done, Katie grabbed a few extra napkins and waved at the workers.

"Thanks, guys. See you in a day or two."

More like an hour or two.

Let's try to pace ourselves this time, please.

The manager waved cheerfully. "We'll be here."

Katie headed back to the hotel, Pandora trying to convince her that waiting wasn't an option the whole way back.

The cab stopped at a corner in downtown Cabo San Lucas. The driver looked at his meter and then back at Calvin. *"Trescientos diez pesos, por favor."*

Calvin nodded, pulling out some cash. "Not bad, just fifteen bucks US. I'm used to much more expensive cab rides."

The man held his hand out and smiled like a man who had no idea what Calvin was saying. Calvin chuckled and handed him the cash, giving him a little extra for a tip. He climbed out of the cab and stood on the corner, moving out of the way of the tourist foot traffic roving down the street. He'd gotten some sleep the night before, and now he wanted to explore the town.

Cabo was a beautiful mixture of the past and the modern. Vibrant colors peppered the buildings, and brightly-dressed people thronged the streets. It reminded him of a West Coast city—a beach town—and exactly what he imagined a Mexican street market would look like, all at once.

Canopies shaded almost every doorway. Some were brightly colored, and others were woven from dried palm leaves. Behind Calvin was the inlet, where the people docked their sailboats to party the days and nights away. Farther down the block was a street market where vendors had tents set up all over the place to sell fresh foods, homewares, and arts and crafts. Some even had typical touristy stuff like Cabo T-shirts and oversized beach towels. He took a deep breath of the salty ocean air, which was mixed with the coconut of suntan lotion and hints of local culinary delights.

This is definitely going to be a good vacation.

I concur, Calvin replied. *All these years, and you've never been to Cabo?*

His demon sniffed the air. *I was always too busy doing, you know, demon shit.*

Well, welcome to paradise, my demon.

Calvin took a step and nearly fell ass over elbow on the uneven sidewalk. *Dang, that's a pothole from hell.*

Not really. There's no lava.

Calvin rolled his eyes under his dark glasses, wishing his demon wasn't always so very literal. He glanced along the street to map out his path between the tourists and the crumbled walkways. The street itself looked as if it had been redone recently, but the sidewalks were a maze of holes and missing chunks. Someone could break an ankle real fast stumbling out drunk from one of the bars.

Man, back at home this would be a lawyer's dream. They could make a living just off the number of people suing after falling into one of these holes.

Americans are weak. Other countries expect you to actually use your brains and figure out how to walk around *the holes, not into them.*

Calvin wandered around the streets, mingling with the locals. He talked with them about the different goods under their tents and purchased a few things to take back with him. All along the roads were taco stands, and the aroma wafting around him was heavenly. It didn't take long for him to hit up the first one, opting for a pulled pork taco and a regular shredded beef one. As soon as he took a bite he was in love, and so was his demon.

Hot damn, this thing is delicious. Seriously, the best taco I've ever had!

When he finished those, he stopped at the next stand and looked up at the menu. There were all types of dishes; from the typical beef and bean burrito to the California—which he wanted, but figured packing potatoes in on top of all the tacos he had planned on eating was probably not a good idea.

Get the fish taco, the demon pleaded. *I spent some time in California—San Diego to be exact—and they had the best fish tacos. I can only imagine the real deal would be even better. Get it fried.*

"I'll have *uno* fish taco and *uno* ground beef taco. *Gracias.*"

The man took Calvin's money and handed over two steaming hot tacos wrapped in aluminum foil.

Calvin sat down and went for the fish taco first. Dribbles of the creamy sauce dripped down his chin as he ate. He wiped his mouth and groaned. The thing was heavenly. He ate the beef one, then sat back and rested his hands on top of his stomach. He glanced at his wristband.

I still don't know why I'm buying all this when I can have all the free food I can eat back at the resort.

Because it's local cuisine, and I have decided that tacos are my new favorite food.

Calvin lifted an eyebrow as he walked through the thoroughfare, not sure that picking tacos as a favorite food was going to work out that well in the end. He had never been a fan of anything too spicy, and some of the tacos were lighting him on fire. He had gone through four bottles of water already. They weren't cheap, but drinking the water here was a major no-no, demon or no demon.

Calvin continued to wander around the streets, browsing the shops. He stopped and leaned against a railing to watch for a while as the sun lowered itself toward the water. The air cooled as the sun sank, and a gentle breeze caressed the city. When the sun finally disappeared below the horizon, the people began to flood the streets in their hottest nightclub wear. Calvin straightened his black shirt and checked his shoes. It was time for him to get out there and start partying. He had been looking forward to it since he'd decided to take a vacation.

He scoped the venues laid out before him like a banquet. He knew *exactly* where he wanted to start his night of dancing and drinking. He was in Cabo, so there was no *way* he could not go to Cabo Wabo, even if it was just for a couple of drinks. The place was already beginning to fill up, so he found himself a seat at the bar and ordered a whiskey and Coke. The band was doing their sound check, and the people on the floor were ready to dance. Cabo Wabo had been started by Sammy Hagar and his Van Halen bandmates and drew a huge tourist crowd.

People of all ages mingled. Their conversation created a buzz throughout as they chatted about the pictures on the walls or ordered some of the cantina's noted fried foods. Some bobbed their heads to the Van Halen pumping through the speakers. It wasn't really Calvin's scene—or at least, it didn't feel like it. He hadn't been out like this in a very long time, so he was kind of rediscovering himself.

He sipped his drink as two scantily clad women came through the front, which was open from wall to wall. They snuck a look at him and giggled as they leaned against the bar, then flirted with the bartender while they ordered their drinks. Calvin glanced at the one closest to him, checking out her ass. She turned and gave him a coy smile.

Calvin leaned back and took a sip of his drink, watching them strut off to find a seat. He chuckled to himself; he still had it. About twenty minutes later some touring cover band who had gotten lucky enough to book themselves at Cabo Wabo got up on stage. They had the typical band look: mid-twenties, long hair, rolled jeans, and Van Halen ripped sleeve t-shirts. It was exactly what he expected.

This is an interesting place. His demon chuckled. *But I doubt you'll get the action you're looking for here.*

Oh, you underestimate me, my dear demon. I'm gonna get up there and show em' what I got.

Calvin put his empty glass down and headed to the dance floor. He sauntered over to the woman whose ass he'd scoped and held out his hand with a smoldering look. She batted her eyelashes and allowed him to pull her in, shaking her body with his groove. He looked around, a lone black man in a sea of white, and couldn't help but laugh. He would be one of the best dancers out there, especially since there were more middle-agers than young people.

He let go of his preconceived notions and got into the music, losing himself in the feel of the woman pressed against him. When the song was over, everyone clapped and cheered loudly. The place was so full at that point, it was standing room only. The woman's friend came over and whispered into her ear. She leaned up to kiss Calvin on the cheek and spoke into his ear. "Bye, handsome."

"You leaving?" he yelled over the music.

"Gonna test out another club. We're headed to the Blue Marlin Ibiza. Check it out—it's pretty hot right now."

Calvin smiled and bit his lip, shaking his head as she was pulled away by her friend. He chuckled and looked around him, feeling the death of the scene for him. He paid his tab and headed to the next place on his list. He would definitely check out the Ibiza. He had heard it was a pool-side club, and anywhere there were hot, bikini-clad women he was down, but first, he was off to the Rooftop Lounge at the Cape.

Calvin had seen flyers touting that night pasted everywhere, and he'd been pleased to see they had DJ Tiesto gracing the decks. Calvin had seen them filming the video for his song *Red Light*, which was all about Vegas. He found he really liked that rhythm and could get into it in a heartbeat. He headed over to the club and went through the line rather quickly. As soon as he emerged on the roof, the deep beats and low drops of Tiesto filled his ears.

Calvin didn't even grab a drink, just went right out into the crowd and began to move. Song after song the melodious tunes soothed him, creating a steady flow of energy that he hadn't felt since before he was Damned. Sweat poured down his body, and he pulled off his wet shirt. His muscles glistened under the blue lights around the club, and women began to flock toward him, dancing all around him as he wound to the rhythm.

He was still wearing his dark shades, but the crisscrossing stage lights kept the light just right for him. He didn't want to raise a panic if his eyes flashed red. He was too enthralled with the women on the dance floor to fuck that up with too much demon. He was surprised to find there weren't too many red eyes in the crowd, but at the same time, he had promised himself that unless there was trouble, he would forget all about that while he was there.

The DJ took a set break, and house music pumped through the speakers. Calvin went to the bar and picked up a napkin to wipe the sweat from his face, then ordered a bottle of water and a whiskey and Coke and walked over to the edge of the rooftop terrace. All across the city, he could see the magic of the night scene. Some people danced through the streets on their way to the next club, others hailed cabs, and the lights on the party boats strobed wildly as people enjoyed their cocktails on the water.

Before I leave, I definitely want to hit up one of those party boats. I've heard once that they pull away from shore, some really wild shit happens.

Hey, I'm totally down, his demon replied.

The people at the rooftop club were still dancing, and although he was having a blast, he was thinking it was about time to jam over to the Ibiza and find himself a woman for the evening. He flapped his shirt in the wind and headed out of the club, tossing a smile and a wink at several women who were watching him leave.

When he got to the street, he saw a vendor still selling on the nearby corner. He picked up a pair of blue and gray boardshorts in his size.

"Those would fit you well, *señor.*"

"I think they would." He smiled and handed over the cash. "Can you tell me how to get to the Ibiza?"

The vendor grinned and pointed. "Oh, nice choice. *Muy caliente.* Just go down two blocks, and you'll see the blue lights, okay?"

Calvin nodded. "Thanks."

He ducked into one of the local taco shops he had visited twice that day and went into the bathroom to change into the shorts. If he was going to a poolside club, he was going to be ready for a dip.

When he reached the place he bobbed his head and smiled, hearing the melodic beats pumping from the sound system. Once inside, he couldn't believe his eyes. The place was filled with nearly-naked women dancing and laughing and having fun up and down the walkways around the lighted pool.

After a few songs on the dance floor, where he got close

to more than one hot chick, he headed to the bar to grab a drink. The bartender handed him the house special, a twist on the margarita, and he sat back on the stool to watch the crowd. A woman he had danced with on the floor walked over to the bar and sat down on the stool next to him, crossing her long, tanned legs. She was wearing a blue string bikini, the triangles barely large enough to cover her nipples. She leaned forward and put one hand on Calvin's thigh.

"I was just curious" she purred into his ear. "Just how big *are* black men, really?"

Calvin raised an eyebrow and looked at her closely. "Pandora?"

She smiled. "No, I'm Patricia. But you got so close! How did you know that?"

He chuckled, looking at her sexy curved hips before tapping his drink to hers. "Just checking. One can never be too sure, with the friends that I have."

"Mmm, you sound like someone who takes risks. I like that about a man…as long as he knows how to take control too."

Calvin looked at her and took a big gulp of his drink. It had been a long time since he'd had a woman hit on him like this, thanks to Pandora and her tricks. He caught the bartender's attention and indicated Patricia. The bartender brought her a martini, and she touched the glass to Calvin's. "Thank you. Cheers, handsome."

She took his free hand in hers and tugged gently. "Come on, let's sit in the shallow pool with our drinks."

Calvin couldn't help but appreciate the little bounce Patricia's breasts made when she skipped, which she did on purpose every time his eyes rested on her. He held her martini while she sat down in a quiet corner of the shallow pool, then got in beside her. The music beat loudly, creating a shimmer across the pool as the vibrations passed through the water.

"So, are you here on vacation?" Calvin asked.

"I guess you could say that." She giggled. "I came here on vacation a year ago and just couldn't get myself to leave. It's too beautiful, and the people here are so hot. How about you?"

"Yeah, I'm on vacation. I came from Vegas."

"Oh, I love Vegas," she babbled. "The shows, the people... Just the *wildness* of it all, you know? I couldn't imagine living there, though."

"I live...outside the city. But yeah, it's definitely a wild town. I've grown accustomed to it. Needed to get away from the lights, though, and get something tropical into my life."

"Well, all of us long-timers are *definitely* a good dose of tropical." She winked and giggled, going pink. "How long have you been here?"

"I just got here yesterday. Figured, why waste any time? I just hopped right in."

"That's the best way to experience this place—just dive right into it. Have you been to the beach?"

"Not yet. I spent the day walking around Cabo, taking in the sights, and then went to Cabo Wabo, the Rooftop Bar, and then here."

"A man with a plan...that's sexy. You even remembered a bathing suit."

"Ha, actually I bought this from a vendor on the way

over. Figured if there was a pool, I should probably be prepared."

"You could have just come in with your boxers. We wouldn't have minded." She smiled and took a sip. "In fact, if you hang out long enough and enough drinks are served, bathing suits become optional around this place. It's my favorite part of the night. So many hot bodies under the stars getting crazy. No inhibitions—just the way I like it."

"That sounds like...the perfect way to live." He chuckled, putting his arm around her. "That's kind of my motto for vacation."

"Just vacation? That's a bore! Trust me, by the time you're done here, you'll go back to your life a changed man."

"Hopefully, not too changed." He laughed. "My job kind of requires me to be on my game. That's why I came out here for a few weeks—to recharge after a long strenuous stretch."

"Aw." She walked her fingers up his chest. "Poor baby, work has kicked your butt. Don't worry, though. I won't make you work too hard. Just relax and take it all in."

"That's the plan." He smiled. "The relaxation part, at least. I don't get that at home hardly ever. It's either training or work calls or personal issues to handle. It's a lot."

"What do you do?"

Calvin bit the inside of his lip, unsure whether he should tell her. What he did wasn't really a secret anymore, not with the media coverage of what was going on, but he had never actually come out and told anyone. After a few moments of deliberation he shrugged, figuring why not?

He was on vacation, and would most likely not see this woman again after it was over.

"I'm one of the fighters in the war against the demons."

She leaned forward and looked at him with excitement. "Really? Are you like military, or what?"

"No, I'm ex-military actually, but that was long before the current task forces were created. I'm a mercenary, working on one of the teams in the States."

"Wow," she marveled. "I'm impressed. That's amazing. What are the demons like? I mean, the ones that aren't that dangerous."

"They're humans with a propensity for trouble." He chuckled. "People like you, who were in the wrong place at the wrong time and struggle to battle that demon."

"Huh, doesn't sound much different than regular people. We all constantly battle our demons. But wait…if you are a mercenary, then don't mercenaries have to be Damned?'

"They don't have to be. We had a guy who wasn't, and he was kick-ass at the job."

"But you are?"

She didn't seem scared in the least, which was new for Calvin. Almost all uninfected were terrified of anyone who might even be close to demon status. Instead, she had a mixture of excitement and curiosity dancing across her face. He chuckled and looked around before turning toward her and tipping down his glasses. His pupils flashed red, and she threw her hand to her chest and gasped.

"That is really sexy, like the ultimate bad-boy status. You know what I think?"

"What's that?"

She ran her finger down his chest. "You and I should get out of here and find somewhere a bit more...private."

Calvin cleared his throat and set his glass down on the edge of the pool. "You don't have to ask *me* twice."

He stood up and straightened his suit, then offered his hand to help Patricia out of the pool. They headed over to her things, and she pulled on a sheer cover-up and put her bag over her shoulder. Next thing Calvin knew, the two of them were laughing as they tumbled out of the club and onto the street. Calvin put his hand to hail a cab like he did on the streets of Vegas.

The car pulled up, and the driver rolled down the window. "Where you headed?"

"The Pacifica," Calvin told him.

Patricia was even more impressed. "Ohhh, that's fancy. Very hot." She leaned against his body as she whispered into his ear. It was obvious that his clout was scoring him some major points.

The cabbie nodded, and Calvin opened the back door. "Ladies first."

Patricia gave him a dazzling smile. "A gentleman, too. Looks like my lucky night."

Calvin chuckled, sticking out his chest in pride as they climbed into the back seat of the cab. He double-checked that he had everything and nodded to the driver. Patricia leaned over and began to nibble her way along his neck, and he knew this night was going to be a good one.

7

K atie got up from the couch in her hotel room and paced, looking at the box of donuts each time she passed it. All the sugar she had eaten had filled her with nervous energy, and she knew it was time she either did something to take her mind off it or eat more donuts. Considering she had already eaten a few, she figured doing something would be much more reasonable. Of course, Pandora had a different view on things, but Katie ignored her, knowing that more sugar would only lead to more anxiety.

Katie pulled out a pair of stretch pants, a tight black top, and a sweatshirt in case it was chilly, then left her room and headed out for a night walk to get some of the sugar out of her system. There were a lot of people out on the streets, dining, and enjoying the evening. The air was thick with noises and smells—so many things to keep her senses occupied. She couldn't go ten or fifteen steps without hearing a siren somewhere in the distance. It was a stark contrast to the quiet of the desert, but she didn't really mind. It was New York, and she couldn't expect anything less from the city that never sleeps.

Katie shoved her hands into her pockets, watching everything that was going on around her as she strolled down the block.

Pandora fed her a steady stream of information as they went. *The girl in the tight blue dress is a demon, though not a very strong one. The guy with her is not, but I can tell he knows. The old guy reading the paper on the corner definitely has a demon in him. It feels like he's had that demon a long time. Old mob-family head.*

They still have those out here?

Oh, yeah, throughout history, and almost all of them are infected.

Katie chuckled. *Doesn't surprise me at all.*

Katie rubbed her chest and grimaced slightly when a particularly strong burning sensation bubbled. She swallowed hard, thinking at first that it was indigestion from all the donuts she had eaten, but after a few moments, she recognized the feeling. There was an infected person relatively close by.

Someone with a strong demon.

Uh-oh, your Spidey senses are going off.

Katie didn't say a word, just turned down the next block and headed in the direction the feeling was flowing from like someone had turned on an inner demon GPS system for her. She walked down two blocks, weaving in and out of the pedestrians until she came to a nice clothing store that was open late. The mannequins in the window were decked out in high couture, none of it really Katie's style, but she wasn't there for fashion. She pulled open the door and walked inside.

The woman at the counter looked up and smiled before going back to her tasks. She was used to all types of people coming in and out of the shop, but few of them spent very much money. Katie glanced around the mostly-empty store. There was nobody at the racks of clothes lining the walls, so she went into the center of the store. Everything was organized according to color, and the rainbow of the colors cascaded around the open space. She was looking for the source of the feeling; she knew it was coming from in there somewhere.

"Oh my *god*," a voice rang out from the back of the store. "This would be *too* hot for the party next week. The boys would swarm me."

A gaggle of giggling girls emerged from the changing area. In the center of them was a young girl somewhere around eighteen with several layers of clothes hung over her arm. They were trying on the more expensive pieces in the place, and Katie wasn't sure whether they could actually afford the clothes or if they were on a shopping spree with Mommy and Daddy's credit card. Either way, she had found her demon.

The girl was tall and slender, with long naturally-red hair and bright green eyes. However, from the constant red glow of her pupils, Katie could tell the demon had gotten its clutches deep into the girl. She could sense that the girl had almost lost control of the situation; the demon was right below the surface, just waiting to take the reins.

This needs to be taken care of, Katie stated.

Pandora fully agreed. *Whatever we do, it can't wait much*

longer, or she'll be completely gone. It needs to happen right here and now.

You work your magic, and I'll work mine, Katie told her, heading toward the girls.

The five girls glanced at Katie curiously as she approached. She flashed her red eyes at them and they parted like the Red Sea before her, leaving a pathway to the infected girl. Katie gave the girl a comforting smile to put her at ease, but from the look on her face, the demon inside her already knew who she was.

All right, you fucking dick, let go of this girl, Pandora commanded.

The demon sneered. *Fuck you, she's mine.*

Pandora cackled. *Do you know who I am? Do you know who the fuck you're messing with?*

The demon started to laugh, then cut out suddenly when Pandora revealed herself for a brief second. *Lilith! Shit, I mean, yes, Your Darkness. I'm leaving.*

The demon trembled inside of the girl and released his tight grip on her soul. Katie could see the transition occurring; the girl relaxed a little, and the red in her eyes faded just a touch. Katie reached out, using her newly-discovered angelic powers. Her palm glowed white as she reached inside the girl and gently pulled the demon out. The other girls' eyes grew wide when they saw her holding the demon by its throat. Light surrounded her until the demon's throat was crushed.

The after-image of the demon faded like dust in the wind. The girl swayed, and her friends grabbed her arms to support her. The red was gone from her eyes, leaving just the beautiful green hue.

Katie put her hand on the girl's shoulder and looked her in the eyes. "Are you all right?"

"Yeah." The girl shook her head. "I just felt this intense fear, then a calm like I never knew before. It's gone. My demon is *gone*."

"You're Katie," one of the girls breathed in awe. "That mercenary—the leader of Katie's Killers."

"Oh my God," one of the other girls gasped excitedly. "Can we have your autograph?"

"Sure." Katie chuckled.

The girl ran over to the desk, where the saleswoman was recording the whole thing with her phone. She walked back with the girl and handed Katie the footage.

"Can I release this?"

It was obvious the woman was afraid to do anything without Katie's permission. She wasn't infected, and from the look in her eyes, she was terrified of demons. Katie pressed Play and watched the whole thing transpire, surprised at the white glow surrounding her in the playback.

That's new.

Pandora scoffed. *Yeah, an effect of all that angel bullshit.*

Katie handed the phone back to the saleswoman. "You can release it as long as you hide the girls' faces. All you can see of me is my back."

"Thank you." The woman smiled, taking the phone back.

Katie signed the autographs, talking some with the girls about being out at night on their own. They were shopping for a party coming up before they all headed to college, and had been out looking for clothes since that morning. Just like any teenagers that age, they didn't think twice about the dangers out there.

"It's not just demons," Katie told them, handing the last autograph back. "There are plenty of regular weirdos out there too. Anyway, be safe."

The girls closed in, talking excitedly to the redhead. Katie smiled as she walked out the door, glad she could help and that it hadn't been any worse. Too many lives had been lost to demons, and an eighteen-year-old girl was the last person she wanted to see taken down by the forces that fought against the demons. She could hear the girls and the woman from the counter asking the redhead how she was feeling.

"I'm okay, thankfully. Until the demon was gone, I had no idea just how far gone I truly was. I can't believe that Katie from Katie's Killers saved my life—her *and* her demon."

Katie smiled as she left, amused by the babbling teen's rush of words.

You're a fucking rockstar, Pandora told her. *You have fangirls!*

You too, Katie reminded her. *She was just as happy that you were there.*

She headed back to her hotel. That had been more than enough action to get rid of the sugar jitters. Moments like tonight reminded Katie why she did what she did. It was good for the soul.

So dramatic. Pandora snickered.

Katie's stomach growled as she rounded the last corner before the hotel. She was hungry for something more than dough and sugar, but when she glanced at the moon shining in the sky, she realized it was later than she'd thought. She passed two different Chinese restaurants and a Thai place, but all of them were closed. As she approached the hotel, she made peace with the fact that she wasn't going to find anything decent to eat, even in New York City.

You could find one of those nice greasy diners.

Yeah, but it'll give me a stomach ache, and they'll all be packed with the after-hours bar crowd at this time. You know that if there are demons I won't be able to help myself, and I'm tired.

Suit yourself. There're always more donuts.

Katie groaned. *I know.*

She walked into the lobby of the hotel and stopped by the concierge desk. "When does room service open for breakfast?"

He looked at his watch. "In two hours," he told her.

"Okay, thanks."

Katie headed back up to her room. When she got inside she paced for a moment, trying to force herself not to give in to the donut cravings. However, her stomach growled low and deep, and she was left with no choice. She opened the box and heated up three of them. She figured it would at least hold her until she could chow down on some bacon and eggs for breakfast.

As the donuts heated in the microwave, she opened the fridge and looked inside, finding nothing but the leftover donuts. "Damn, forgot the milk."

I knew we forgot something!

No matter. Katie sighed. *When I get up in the morning, I'm sure we'll need more donuts. I'll pick up milk while I'm out, as well. For now, I will enjoy my sugary late-night dinner with a Diet Coke from the bar.*

There's a reason the first three letters of diet are D, I, and E. Anyway, you're about to chow down on all those donuts, so why would you drink diet *soda?*

I have to make some *attempt at eating healthy. Besides, I like it, and it doesn't have any calories.*

Yeah, but there isn't any flavor in it either. It's just brown water, and you're already eating donuts. You may as well just go for full-sugar yumminess.

Very true. Katie chuckled and switched the silver can for a red one. *I feel like I should have an angel on the other side of you telling me to stick with the diet.*

Pandora snorted. *That's a good human. Don't worry, I'll take care of the calories for you.*

You're a real pal. Katie laughed. She took her plate of donuts over to the bed and leaned back against the headboard to eat.

At least they taste good together. I don't understand the people who buy that strawberry milk shit. It tastes nothing like strawberries. I tried it on my last trip to Earth and nearly barfed.

Hey, I'm just glad you don't have a broccoli fetish. That might have broken me.

Pandora snickered. *Duly noted.*

The chopper hovered high above the large patch of grass

where the other helicopters were landing. Brock looked through his window at the line of soldiers surrounding the property, all guns blazing. The other guys were finishing strapping on their protective gear and loading their weapons. The chopper landed and his team disembarked, ducking as they raced over to the commanding officer on the scene.

"Welcome to a new kind of hell, boys," the CO shouted, laughing loudly as a medic attempted to patch a bleeding tear in his shoulder. "For those of you don't know me, I'm General Triphorn, and I'll be your tour guide through this funhouse. Welcome to Georgetown, Mississippi, just a shit-click away from Jackson, where the demons rage and the help arrives just in time to watch you kiss your ass goodbye. Once upon a time we scoffed at countries who allowed war to touch their homelands, but now we are *all* facing the enemy on our home turf." He ducked his head, much to the medic's consternation. "Guess we'll just have to show them what happens to anyone who brings that shit onto American soil, eh, boys? Gather 'round."

The boys chuckled as they surrounded the general to receive the word. The medic continued to struggle with bandaging his arm, the main issue being that the general wasn't one of those men who would sit quietly for proper medical treatment. He finally got the tape in place to hold the bandage down and hurried off, shaking his head and muttering under his breath about PITA patients who wouldn't hold still.

Triphorn bounced on his feet as he paced back and forth. "Here's the deal, boys... The demons have taken over that ranch behind us, but they were caught before they could chow down and move on. They'd been eating the cows in the main barn—the one over there in the center with all the bullet holes. We've penned them in there, and are attacking in waves. These little bastards are not very strong, but they are fast and shifty."

"Who made the call?" Brock asked, looking around.

"The farmer who runs the property. She walked in on them and then took off across the field. She was able to get a 911 call off before the bastards tore her to pieces and hung her torso from the weathervane on top of the barn for show. They seem to have a taste for drama, so I figured we'll surround the bastards and show them some serious theatrics. That's where you boys come in, with your quick action. I want those sonsabitches lit up like the Fourth of July. I want to see their demon balls flying through the air before they unceremoniously turn to dust. Do you understand?"

"*Yes, sir,*" they answered in unison.

"Good," he replied. "Now, try not to get yourselves killed. They have sharp claws, as you saw from the gash I took from one as it ran from my bullets. There are men in the field, but they've been instructed to stay back. They're only there if we need some backup."

The soldiers nodded their understanding.

Brock put his helmet on and fastened the strap under his chin, then checked his rifle one last time and followed the guys toward the perimeter. Beside the barn was the large portal the demons had used to come to Earth. The military had surrounded the barn, and had been able to position their men around the portal as well. Bullets flew everywhere as they killed the last few demons coming out.

It didn't look like any more would emerge from the portal, but they couldn't know for sure.

Grim determination painted the faces of the soldiers surrounding the barn. Brock's brothers were the relief team, there to swap out with the primary team so the others could back off for a rest. They had been at it for hours at that point, and most of them needed a reload, a bite to eat, and a drink of water at the very least.

Brock lined up with his boys and waited for the nod from their team leader. When the doors of the barn creaked apart they opened fire, spraying the doors with bullets. The leader raised his arm and pointed forward, and the team advanced one synchronized step at a time toward the barn, continuing to fire as they approached.

Suddenly, the doors flew open and a demon headed straight toward Brock. Brock dropped his weapon and threw his arms out as the demon landed, pushing the hell spawn to the ground. More demons were charging out of the barn, so the team had to focus on stopping them while trying to keep one eye on the wrestling match beside them.

Brock growled as he rolled across the grass, scrambling frantically to keep the demon's claws as far from his face as possible. He was able to free one hand and he punched the demon hard in the face, stunning it for a second. In that small open window, he grabbed his knife and thrust it upward into the demon's throat. The beast snarled and growled, but then its eyes rolled back and it burst into dust.

One of Brock's teammates clapped as he walked over, then helped Brock to his feet. Brock chuckled, picked up his gun, and slid his knife back into its sheath. When he looked up at the guy, there was a demon running straight for his teammate's back. Brock raised his gun and aimed over the guy's shoulder. "Watch out!"

His teammate spun and opened fire on the demon. Chunks of the demon's body flew as the bullets blasted it and the demon turned to dust mid-stride, and the guy wiped his forehead. He nodded his thanks to Brock before turning back toward the field.

The last demon ran in zigzags to evade the bullets, its only objective to get back to the portal. The boys raked him with bullets, and he screamed in pain and turned to dust. There were no signs of any more demons close by. Brock held a hand over his mouth and nose when the portal slammed shut and blew the usual cloud of foul-smelling wind over the field.

Everything went quiet. The only sound Brock could hear was the lowing of the surviving cows.

8

Katie lay motionless in the cocoon of blankets and pillows. The soft mattress almost swallowed her, and the layers of blankets she had wrapped herself in rendered her invisible to the naked eye. She was dreaming of donuts and pizza—something obviously conjured up by Pandora—when a loud siren sounded from the street far below, startling her awake.

She grumbled, keeping her eyes clenched shut in an attempt to go back to sleep. She didn't want to get up yet. It had been a long night, and she hadn't even fully fallen asleep until the sun was starting to peek over the buildings.

"So much noise," she griped. "Can't a girl ever fucking sleep *in?*"

Don't get shitty with me, princess of the angels. I am not the one creeping into the room being an unexpected pain in the ass.

What are you babbling about now? Katie snapped. *I promise you that you will get your damn donuts as soon as I can function. Just let me sleep!*

Look, woman! This isn't about donuts.

Then why are you throwing a fit?

Didn't you hear what I just said? There's a stranger lurking in the shadows of your room.

Katie contemplated the words for a moment, still a bit groggy. When she finally realized what Pandora was bitching about, she sat straight up in the bed and pulled her gun out from under the pillow. She stared hard at the shadowy spot behind the bedroom door. Standing there was a figure she couldn't quite make out.

"Who's there? Show yourself!"

The angel who had come to her before, Gabriel, stepped into the light, his silver hair shining softly in the morning sun. Katie narrowed her eyes and dropped the gun, feeling irritation bloom in her chest.

"Look, I know you're like a messenger from God, or whatever, but that doesn't preclude you from having manners. You can't just come barging into a woman's room while she's asleep. Creep factor aside, it's rude. Besides, you could get an eyeful of something that would shock you."

Gabriel chuckled. "I have been all over the world and to other worlds, and I can promise you there is nothing in this room that could shock me. Besides, I could sense you were dressed and alone, so I waited here for you to wake."

"Waited there? How long have you been staring at me?"

"Long enough," he told her. He walked over to the window. "Although, I was worried you were going to sleep the whole day away."

"Great." Katie sighed. "Another being who thinks eight

in the morning is sleeping too late. I guess I need to come to terms with never getting a good night's sleep again."

"From the looks of the donut sugar all over your mouth, you weren't expecting any company."

Katie narrowed her eyes and brushed a hand over her mouth, finding the grains of sugar. Visions of the feast Pandora had put her through ran through her mind. She had fixed three donuts, but that hadn't been enough for Pandora. They had eaten *all* of the donuts left in the boxes. Katie felt nauseous just thinking about it.

You bitch. I said three *donuts, and you made me eat like a dozen after I gave in and drank the full-sugar Coke!*

Hey, you picked them up and put them in your mouth. I wasn't controlling your movements.

You think you're so smooth, and now look! There's an angel in our room, I'm a mess, and you have no donuts. Guess who the only person who can rectify your donut deficit is?

Oh, come off it. It's not like you'll make me miserable. You know I can do the same right back to you, so just suck it up. I told you I'd take care of the calories. You just get this white-glowy silver-haired freak out of our room. He's starting to get creepy with his constant patient smile.

Katie returned her focus to Gabriel; she'd almost forgotten for a moment that he was there. "Since you're here, there were a couple of things I wanted to ask you. Like, how do I work on my abilities? What kind of powers do I have, beyond taking demons from people? And what the hell is up with the white glow? It makes no sense."

Gabriel gazed impassively out the window with his hands clasped firmly behind his back. Katie guessed that he was going to pull the same mysterious act he had the last time he had visited her, which irritated the hell out of her. She wanted to know more about what she was and why she had angels popping up in her hotel room and watching her while she slept. However, she could tell that anger and intimidation would do nothing for her case.

Gabriel remained facing the window when he finally spoke. "I am here to tell you one thing."

"What's that?" Katie asked, crossing her arms and pouting.

That he dyes his hair and goes to raves. Pandora snorted.

Gabriel turned around and smiled at Katie as if he could hear what Pandora was saying. He gave her a look that made Katie sure he was reading her very soul, which made her slightly uncomfortable. Katie lifted an eyebrow and looked around to avoid his intense eye contact.

"Okay, the secretiveness is killing me. What do you have to tell me?"

"There are entities in New York City who are planning to use demons as terrorist devices."

Katie's eyes grew bigger. "In the city?"

Gabriel nodded solemnly.

"And where are they? What are they planning?"

"Find them," Gabriel told her softly, his body becoming transparent.

"No, no, no." Katie moaned, climbing quickly out of bed.

By the time she got to where he'd been standing, Gabriel was gone. "Wait, wait! What do they look like? Who's funding them? Come on! You can't be just the evil-puzzle-giver."

She sighed, finding herself alone again in the room. So, there were terrorist demons, who were obviously planning something, somewhere in a city with millions of people, none of whom Katie really knew. She was supposed to find the demons and—she assumed—dispose of them.

Great.

Pandora snarked, *Just like an angel, giving you a sixteenth of the puzzle and then buggering off. I told you angels were assholes.*

Oh, kind of like demons who con their humans into eating a dozen donuts and then bitch and moan about those who want to help us?

You enjoyed scarfing down all that creamy white filling, don't lie.

Katie did her best to sound innocent. *I'm saying nothing.*

You don't have to say anything, sister. Your shirt says it all, loud and clear.

Katie looked down at her shirt. Sure enough, she was covered in small white flakes of sugar, the remains of the small pebbles that had been stuck to her face. Apparently, she couldn't even eat like a civilized human being. She brushed at the remnants, leaving the tips of her fingers sticky. Katie walked into the bathroom and leaned over to brush the sugar off the front of her shirt. She sighed and pulled the shirt over her head, banging her elbow against the tiled wall. She tossed her shirt on the floor and washed her hands, staring at the sparkling flecks of icing in her hair with something like shame as she dried her hands.

She turned, banging her knee against the cabinet. "Dammit! This bathroom is so small I need to step out of it to change my mind."

Did we read that somewhere recently? What's got you so wound up? Maybe I shouldn't have made you eat that last donut.

Katie leaned her head back against the bathroom doorway and closed her eyes. She was pissed, for so many reasons. Between the lack of sleep and the creepy-ass angel with his half-assed clues, a demon-induced sleep feast wasn't that big a deal—especially since said demon was going to take care of the consequences of all her actions. She sighed and banged her hand on the doorframe. *How are they going to use demons in terror attacks, and how am I supposed to stop it when I don't even know where to start?*

Tell the cops.

Oh, sure... I'll just march right up to the captain's office and let him know that after falling into a diabetic coma, I woke up to an angel in the corner of my hotel room. He told me demons are using other demons as terrorist devices, but that's the only information I have.

What's the worst that could happen?

They might lock me up in a mental institution, regardless of my being Damned. It's not like the soaps where I can claim insanity and get out if I've committed a crime. They'll chain us to the bed—and not in the fun way you're thinking.

Oh, I'm sure it's not that bad. Humans like to help. They wouldn't leave you there long.

You obviously haven't heard of electroshock therapy.

No, but it sounds sexy.

Katie rolled her eyes and headed toward the living room, hesitant to see what kind of major damage Pandora had done while Katie was asleep. The donut boxes were strewn about, and there was sugar all over the counter and crumbs on the floor. Katie growled and stacked the boxes angrily.

Seriously, you had me sit there and eat that many donuts but not pick up the trash afterward It's so fucking embarrassing I can't even have housekeeping clean this up. Not to mention that with all the sugar on the floor, we're going to wake up to roaches and ants in the damn room.

Really? Can ants and roaches go up to the nineteenth floor to find food? How do they get there? Do they tip the doorman and ride the teeny-tiny elevator, or do they take the Mission Impossible route and use tiny little suction cups to climb up the building? And how do they get in? Tiny little glass cutters to open up a hole to the inside? Personally, if an ant or roach goes through that kind of trouble, I'm going to say they deserve all the sugar they find.

Katie grabbed a roll of paper towels from the kitchenette and rummaged around under the sink, knowing that housekeepers always kept spare cleaning supplies in the rooms. She went for the toppling pile of donut boxes with her hand as she stood, and watched the top box land, open and upside down, on the floor.

Seriously, if you were outside of my body, I would give you such a fucking ass-kicking right now. I'm supposed to be here to slay demons! I'm not here to wipe mounds of sugar off the floors and table like some kind of maid for you, Pandora. You need to learn how to eat with a little more grace. For fuck's sake, get a napkin or a plate or something. It looks like I danced around and threw the sugar like confetti.

Pandora just listened, finding Katie's temper tantrum amusing.

Katie flung the paper towels into the trash. *What about*

Gabriel? He shows up out of nowhere with no warning and then gives me only a tidbit of information to go on. Obviously, it's important. Otherwise, he wouldn't have shown up, so it's something I need to focus on.

Katie stalked back to the bathroom and turned on the shower. She undressed, tossing her clothes into a pile as she thought about what Gabriel had told her, which was a big bunch of fuck-all. She climbed in and let the hot water rush over her. It stilled her mind, but only for a moment. She opened her eyes and pushed her hair back from her face, then grabbed the bottle of shampoo and squirted a bit into her hand. She knew she probably shouldn't be so frustrated with the angel, but hell, he was being mysterious, and it wasn't cool. In fact, it was downright *frustrating.*

How in the hell am I supposed to find a group of terrorist demons in a city this size?

The waves crashed against the shore on the beach a short way from Calvin's room. The waves were wild but the weather was perfect, with bright sunshine and blue skies as far as the eye could see. Birds flew overhead, swooping down over the waves every now and then, and those not hungover from the night before began to creep out of their beds and head for the sandy stretches and beautiful views.

Calvin, on the other hand, lay face down in his bed wearing nothing but the sheet draped over his ass. He took his time waking up, not moving a muscle as he lay there and listened to the ocean. It was one of his favorite sounds, and he'd been longing for it during his time in the sands of

Vegas. To him, the desert was nothing more than a tease. It had all the things he disliked about the beach—the sand, the boiling-hot sun, the weird insects—but nothing of what made the whole day at a beach worthwhile. It was just grainy grit that liked to get lodged in every crevice of his body.

Eventually, he opened his eyes and peered out the low window opposite his bed. The whitecaps of the crystal-clear waters lapped against the shore. Calvin saw a woman in a polka dot bikini trailing through the edge of the surf, and he recalled that he had not gone to bed alone the night before. He reached behind himself, finding an empty spot in the bed. Patricia was no longer there, but on the pillow was a folded piece of paper.

He opened it and smiled as he read her short note.

Calvin, didn't want to wake you since you looked so comfortable. I had a fabulous night, something I love so much about this place. I very much enjoyed myself, and I wanted to assure you that I'm damned glad I ran into you. Enjoy your time in Cabo,

P.

xoxo

He chuckled and lay back, staring at the ceiling. He wasn't sure how he felt about being a one-night stand. He had grown up in a household with a momma who had explicitly ground into his head that women were to be treated like the queens they were. Even here in Cabo her words stuck with him, and not just because he feared her wrath. The woman last night had made *him* into a one-night stand, not the other way around. He decided it wasn't such a bad thing.

He rolled over and pushed his face into the other

pillow, which still held the floral scent of her perfume. He took a deep breath and turned his head to the side, his mouth quirking at the memories she'd gifted him with. He pulled the covers up and shut his eyes, thinking about all the tourists who flocked to Vegas to get away from reality. That was what he was doing—getting away from reality—and it had started out really well.

"Well, when in Cabo, do as those who come to Cabo do."

Katie bit her bottom lip as she stared at all the donuts. The woman from the night before was still there, or had come in again for a new shift. Either way, she knew exactly who Katie was. The other two stood by, waiting for her to finish her order of three dozen donuts.

"Two chocolate crème filled—"

The woman smiled as she placed two of them in the box. "Please tell me you have a bunch of friends eating these?"

Katie shrugged. "I wish. These hips don't lie."

The two other women looked her up and down. One put her hands on their hips and raised her eyebrow at Katie. "I just want to point out that your hips are to die for. There is nothing about your body that screams three dozen donuts, *especially* not your hips."

Yessss, Pandora hissed. *I am sculpting you into the ultimate female specimen! Men want to do you, and women want to be you. I told you—you're fucking hot, not just when you don the spandex suit but all the time. Even the other night in your broken-down hoodie, men were stopping and staring as you walked by. You're a h-o-double-t-i-e, and you are welcome for that.*

Calm down, Gillian Anderson. It's not like I was morbidly obese to begin with.

No, more like pathetically weak; all skinny and ironing board-like. You could have been knocked over by a strong breeze. Now you have ballast. Again, you're welcome.

Katie sighed and tried not to roll her eyes. She spotted the refrigerated case next to the counter and let out a squeak of happiness when she saw the milk there. She grabbed four of them before she forgot to buy any again. The girls bagged up her three dozen donuts and milk and handed them to Katie. She dropped a twenty in their tip jar and waved as she walked toward the door.

"I will probably see you again soon!"

They made their way back to the hotel and up to the nineteenth floor. She took out a shelf to make room in the small fridge and stacked the donut boxes in there, putting the milk on the shelves in the doors. She pulled a chocolate-sprinkle donut from the top box and kicked the door shut with her heel.

I'm eating one. *Just* one. *Do you understand that?*

No hablo Ingles.

I am not messing around here. Besides, I gotta get out of here before the day is gone. We can eat more later. I'm telling you now, Pandora, I expect those donuts to last us a couple of days at the minimum. I'm thinking like three to five.

Riight. Pandora cackled. *I love how you dream big. It's cute.*

Katie rolled her eyes and wiped her hands, then grabbed her jacket and headed out of the room. There was no way she was going to binge, especially not in the middle of the day.

9

Katie put on her sunglasses as she stepped up to the curb and checked out the NYPD office a little farther down the street on the opposite side. She walked down to the pedestrian crossing and waited. She nodded to the runner bouncing to the sound of the music blaring through his headphones beside her. When the light changed, he took off at a run and Katie crossed carefully, checking both ways to make sure no one had decided a hit and run was in order for the leader of Katie's Killers.

You're getting paranoid.

Better safe than sorry, my friend.

She walked into the precinct and smiled at the large-ish middle-aged sergeant behind the front desk. He was on the phone telling a woman who she needed to call to get a cat off the roof of her apartment complex. He was obviously annoyed but kept his tone even and reassuring. When he finally hung up the phone, he sighed and shook his head.

Katie chuckled. "One of those days?"

"Every day is one of those days in New York. How can I

help you? And please don't say your cat is stuck on the roof."

"No." Katie chuckled. "I'm here to see Lieutenant Alvarez. He's expecting me. My name's Katie Maddison."

The sergeant did a double-take, showing he recognized the name, and picked up the phone, pressing three numbers in quick succession. "Lieutenant, she's here."

He hung up the phone and nodded. "Take a seat, ma'am. He'll be right out to meet you."

"Thanks," Katie told him.

Before she had a chance to sit in one of the chairs, a short brown-skinned officer came through the door and extended his hand toward her. "Katie, I'm glad to see you."

"Lieutenant. I'm sorry I didn't check in earlier, but I had important nutritional tasks to accomplish first."

"Not a problem." He chuckled. "We know about the Krispy Kreme obsession."

Katie groaned. "Of course you do."

"Come on. We'll go have a seat at my desk."

Katie followed him through the precinct, taking note when they passed a couple of red-eyed criminals hand-cuffed to a bench. She was tempted to take their demons, but didn't want to step on any toes. She knew how protective the city cops were of their catches. They walked up to a desk at the back of the pit, and the lieutenant nodded at the chair.

"This is Detective Crowder. He's gonna take your contact information and introduce you to the detectives who work directly with the incursion calls. You can also exchange info with them, so they know who to call while you're in town."

"Sounds good." Katie smiled. "Thanks for your help."

"No, thank *you*, Katie. If you need anything while you're here, just let me know."

The detective took down her cell phone number and where she was staying on a handwritten form. As she stood there, she could feel eyes on her from across the room. One of the detectives put his things down and came over to give her a high five.

"We all saw that video from the store last night. That was some excellent fuckin' work."

The detective inputting her info into the system looked up and smiled. "It *is* you. I thought it might be, but I didn't want to make assumptions. That was a really good thing you did."

"Just doing my duty." Katie chuckled uncomfortably.

"I'd say you did more than that," another guy argued. He walked over to shake her hand. "You saved a life, and that's a big deal."

"Well, I hope she uses her second chance wisely."

"We all hope that," the detective behind the desk agreed with a smile.

They all congratulated her on a job well done, and Katie wasn't sure how to deal with it. Until Incursion Day she'd just handled what was put in front of her, no more or less, and nobody had made a big deal about it because they had been busy doing the same. It was her duty as a Damned to use the advantages she'd been given to take care of inno- cents and protect them from demons on Earth. She didn't expect praise for it.

Pandora, however, was ignoring the whole thing completely. Instead, she graded every man who walked through the precinct. *That guy in front of us is a seven: nice arms, strong chest, but a flat fucking ass. No, I want something I can grab. The guy across the room, though, he's a ten and a half. Ho-ly shit! Look at the way he moves that body. And his package...whooo! I can tell he's got girth just by looking at the bulge in his pants. My tongue could do some serious damage to that boy. Just need to get him out of that monkey suit and into...well, his birthday suit.*

Aren't we vulgar today?

Hey, men do it to women all the time. No shame in giving it back. Oh, oh, look at this big boy coming at us. Yeah, boy. I have to give him a six for swagger. I mean, normally I'm not into the chubby ones, but he's got some attitude behind those hips. He is not taking shit from anyone.

Katie tried to keep a straight face and answer the questions she was being asked, but it was an effort to keep it together under Pandora's sexist banter. However, she had to admit that Pandora had a point. There were some pretty sexy men in that precinct, and most of them had an eye on Katie.

Look at Macho Man over there. The guy with the perfect jawline, arms as big as your head, and thighs that could hold you up in the air for hours. I wonder what kind of package he has hidden under that uniform. Pandora sniffed when the cop turned to the side, giving them his profile. *Oh. Well, that's disappointing but not the smallest I've ever seen. With that tight-ass body, I could definitely work with that. He looks like a take-control kind of guy, but underneath, I bet he secretly wants to be told what to do. A little ribbon, a metal headboard, and some lube and we could have ourselves a real good time.*

Three of the detectives came over to give Katie their

contact information. She suppressed a smirk as each one of them wrote their personal numbers on the backs of their cards. She knew there was no need for that, since they could be contacted through their work phones. It was obvious they were all hitting on her.

When she was done with the last one, she gave them all a bright smile. "Thanks, guys. I'll reach out if I need you. And please feel free to call on me for help with any of your cases."

"I will." The cop returned her smile with a hopeful one of his own.

Meh, he's a five and a half, tops.

Katie stood up from the desk, straightened her shirt, and headed for the door. She could feel the awkward heat of everyone's stare as she walked out, but decided not to flash her eyes. She might actually need their help in coming days, and she didn't want them all to be terrified of her. Katie had come to learn that there was actually some correlation between men's affection and getting things done fast and efficiently. She knew if she called any of the guys who'd given her their numbers they would move in a heartbeat for her.

Well, that was a fucking bust, Pandora grumped. *I would say the hottest cop who asked for your number was a six, and that is being gracious. Not one of the tens asked for your number. Maybe I need to do a little more work.*

Maybe they have significant others, or I'm not their type.

Pandora rolled with laughter. *They are* men, *honey. They don't have monogamy on the plate. And you are* everyone's *type —I made damn sure of that. I'd like to meet the man who is genuinely not attracted to you. Those tits, those hips, and our signature snarky personality...it's a ten all around. Just gotta get one of the tens to notice it.*

I do have to admit, there were a couple of guys in there who looked good enough to eat.

Whaaaat? Kajesus, you actually said something I can agree wholeheartedly with—about a man!

They both started to giggle as Katie left the precinct. Katie thought about it once they were back out into the street. *Hey, it's been a while, and I think I'm finally over the whole, "the last guy I slept with was killed a few days later" thing. I might just be interested in seeing that package you speak of on one of the tens. But if they die, I'm going full nun until I'm no longer infected.*

I'm going to place a protective shield against the next guy. You do pick men that live a dangerous lifestyle. You can't blame yourself for their death.

I can't live with myself if it turns out I have the vagina of death.

They both burst out into laughter.

Katie and Pandora wandered the streets of New York, checking out the scenery as they continued their discussion on men. There were many people there from all walks of life, and one thing Katie liked about Pandora was that she gave no shits where the guy came from. Her ratings were strictly based on appearance, from the mid-thirties guy begging on the corner to the record store clerk and up to the CEO walking from his building to the limo parked out front. No one got a break from her scrutiny.

Personally, I find that the boys with the money aren't very open or they're freaks. Like, super-freaky freaks.

I figured you would like that.

Yeah, most of the time, but honey, there's some shit you humans do that even I would walk away from. You guys can definitely be weirdos.

Katie stopped in her tracks. She was getting the feeling that something just wasn't right again, emanating from her chest and seeping into her bones. She was drawn to a building farther down the block.

What's going on? she asked Pandora.

I was just about to ask you the same thing.

You're not doing this?

Nope, don't even feel what you're feeling.

After a few moments Katie took off across the street, stopping to let a car pass before she stepped off the curb. Pandora cleared her throat nervously.

Are you jaywalking? Because I'm not leading you down the road to perdition, at least not for jaywalking. That would be the lamest thing ever.

Katie ignored her and hurried over to the source of her feeling. She reached the building just as a guy put his key in the door of the tenement on the corner and walked inside. She grabbed the handle right before it closed and slipped into the atrium to wait for the guy to disappear into his apartment. She looked down the empty hallways, listening to everything around her. She could hear a television down the hall, playing some game show. On the other side, a baby was crying.

Katie climbed the staircase, allowing the feeling to draw her to its source. She paused on the landing of the second floor to make sure it wasn't coming from there. When she reached the third floor the feeling pulsed in her chest, almost taking her breath away with its intensity. She stood at the end of the long hallway, waiting for any clue that would tell her where the feeling was coming from. It was so strong she could feel the individual emotions inside it. There was fear, sadness, anger, and even a bit of relief.

I'm all about this adventure thing, Pandora remarked, happy to be going along for the ride, *but I sure as hell wish I knew what you were up to.*

Suddenly, there was a loud clatter, followed by yelling and the crash of breaking glass. Katie rushed to the third door on the left and pounded on it, her anger starting to fill her. She heard a man yelling at someone, and his voice grew louder as he approached the door. He yanked the door open and sneered at Katie through his messy beard. "Whaddaya want?" he yelled, attempting to intimidate Katie.

Katie looked him up and down, singularly unimpressed despite his easy six-and-a-half feet. She held her ground, trying to figure out exactly what was going on. Her face showed no fear, since she really couldn't care less about his size. He was small compared to some of the demons she and Pandora had taken down in the recent past. He would be a warm-up in an incursion, but right now he was the main event.

She looked behind him to where a young light-brown-skinned woman huddled on the floor against the hallway wall with her face in her hands. Her shoulders shook with silent tears, too afraid of the prick in front of her to even make a noise. Katie's jaw clenched when she spied the bruises peppering the woman's beautiful skin, marring her hands and arms and neck. There was a burn mark on her right arm that looked like it couldn't be any older than a couple of days, the skin puckered angrily around the wound.

Katie ground her teeth and balled up her fists, beyond pissed.

Pandora barked. *Oh fuck, no, motherfucker! You're never going to put your hands on a woman ever again. Time to school this scuzzball, Katie. This motherfucker has got to learn his lesson.*

I couldn't agree with you more. We got time for this piece of trash?

I don't give a damn if the complex burns down around us. We will *make* time.

The man followed Katie's gaze to the woman behind him. He didn't give a crap that Katie had seen her. He chuckled to himself, finding the situation more than amusing. It wasn't the first time someone had tried to stop him from what he saw as his right, but it was the first time the person was a fine piece of ass like Katie. He rubbed his hands together, ready to have some fun with her.

Katie curled her lip and cracked her knuckles. This malfunctioning asshole had no clue that she was Damned —or that if he were still breathing at the end of this it would be due to Katie's benevolence, rather than because he deserved it.

He turned back to Katie, his eyes lingering on her breasts as he spoke. "Would you like a little roughhousing too? Does that turn you on? I have plenty of room inside here, and plenty of energy to expend on a feisty little bitch like you."

Katie raised her boot with a snarl and kicked him back into his apartment. She removed her glasses, and the glow of her eyes bathed the hall in red. The guy scrabbled backward like a crab to get away as she stepped over the threshold and slammed the apartment door behind her with a cold smile.

"I thought you'd never ask."

Calvin sat underneath the round dome inside the main restaurant of the Pacifica, anticipating his main course. He had already plowed through his appetizer, perfectly-grilled *ojillo* octopus served with an avocado puree, jalapenos, and smoked chili butter. His Miraflores salad was sitting prettily in front of him like a work of art, and his main course was being prepared as he admired the salad.

He looked out of the window, enjoying the scenery. The blue water and rolling waves were so peaceful, and the ladies around the pool areas were definitely a welcome addition. There were, of course, a few "white whales," as they called them back home.

What in the hell is a 'white whale?'

Calvin chuckled, taking a bite of his salad. *White people who come from the North. They tend to be a little overweight and have absolutely no tan. In fact, they usually have the opposite of a tan. They'll be the ones barely able to sit down on the plane ride back. Lobster red.*

That is not very appetizing.

Meh, let them be free.

I'm starving, his demon complained.

And I'm nervous. I can't believe I let you talk me into having the chef make us specialty tacos. I did not come to Cabo to try the hottest sauces on the menu.

Oh, live a little.

I am, but my intestines may not after this. You'd better make sure I don't have flames coming out of my ass later.

The demon chuckled. *I got your back...literally.*

Calvin's brow furrowed when a thought hit him. *I hate to ask this after so long, but what is your name?*

Martaliustonkofielline, his demon replied.

Martali—shit. That's right. I could never figure out what the hell you were saying the first time, so I just kept calling you "demon."

Didn't think you cared, he responded. *I assumed that a human stronger than his demon would have more pressing things to worry about than said demon's name.*

I've never been good with names. Don't get me wrong—if you try to call yourself David Hasselhoff I'll give you a different name, but if it's something I can pronounce, then sure. I don't see why it matters.

Well, give me a nickname then. I'm not down with the human shit. Something easy that your tiny brain can remember.

The waitress came over to the table and set down the tacos and another glass of soda for Calvin with a sly smile. She already knew he was going to have one hell of a fire in his mouth. Calvin returned her smile and waited until she walked away before sniffing the tacos. His eyes watered and his nose began to run just from that, so he pushed the plate away for a moment and thought about his demon's name.

I'll call you ... Fireballs.

Um...no. How about "Marty?"

Like Marty McFly? Calvin wrinkled his nose.

Don't know who that is, and Marty is a bit emasculating for a demon in my opinion, but I think you can wrap your human brain around it.

Calvin shrugged and bit into his taco. *All right, "Marty" it is. I'll probably shorten it to like Marts or Mars or whatever happens to come out.*

Please don't.

10

Katie straddled the big dude and pounded his face. He groaned and tried to block the punches, but Katie pushed his arms to the floor and pinned them with her legs. She got a couple more shots in before he bucked and the weight of his huge body flipped her off him, but before he could get up, she was back on her feet.

She crouched, ready to attack. "Strong? Maybe. Huge and slow? Abso-fucking-lutely. Come on, big man. You're so strong and tough you have to beat up on women to get your kicks. Well, I'm a woman. Here I am. Come and get me, bitch."

He tried to grab her, but she evaded him easily, slipping around him. He twisted, but she was already in front of him.

She darted in and out, each movement punctuated by a ringing slap made harder by a little boost from Pandora, who was determined to get her licks in on this bully. Each time it looked like he was going to fall, she slapped him open-handed again. "It's not so fun when you're the one getting roughhoused, is it?" She was getting really good at controlling her battles. She managed to throw a glance in the direction of the woman, who was no longer crying but was instead staring at Katie with a mixture of awe and hope.

Katie's eyes blazed red as she glared at the scumbag. "You see?" she told the woman. "You don't have to put up with weak shit like this from assholes like him."

The scumbag squeaked and backed up a few steps. "You're one of those fucking demon things, the kind that likes to take over bodies and do all kinds of screwed-up shit."

Pandora laughed, taking over Katie's voice. "You don't know the half of it. Men like you are perfect for hell. They torture pricks like you first. They'll string you up above the lava pits and flay you slice by slice while your flesh is scalded by the steam rising from below you. Then, when you think you can't take anymore, they'll heal you and start all over again. You won't be able to die, because you'll already be dead. Even demons don't like woman-beaters."

He grimaced and tripped backward, narrowing his eyes at Katie. "What was that?"

She growled. "What?"

"In your eyes, there was this flash of sparkling blue-green. I've never seen anything like *that* before."

Katie was momentarily taken aback. She had no idea what he was talking about, and she could only assume it had something to do with the angel side of her.

He took advantage of her momentary distraction to throw

a punch at her, but Pandora, sensing her distraction, took control of Katie's arms and popped it away like it was nothing. She let Katie's hand fly and bitch-slapped the shit out of him.

"Who the hell do you think has her back?" Pandora railed from Katie's throat as he flew into the wall and landed on his back with a thud. "Motherfucker…just *try* to hurt my human!"

Katie looked down at the groaning man on the floor. She walked forward, her bootsteps loud on the old wood floors. She bent over him and hissed, "If you try to hurt *any* human I will be back, and if you hurt this woman again I'll drag you down to hell personally." She flashed the red in her eyes when the guy tried to get up and laid her best right hook on his jaw, and he crumpled to the floor, unconscious.

Katie's phone began to buzz loudly in her pocket. She fished it out as she stood up, and accepted the call. "This is Katie," she answered chirpily.

"It's Detective Travers. My partner Schultz and I want to know if you could meet us at the Starbucks on Pennsylvania Avenue, right near Madison Square Garden. We want to talk to you about a few things and get some clarification on the demons. We were hoping you could help us. We don't often get someone with the experience and knowledge you have, so we'd like to take advantage of it— if you don't mind, that is."

"Not at all," Katie replied. "I'll be there in about twenty minutes, if you can hang on?"

"Perfect. See you then."

Katie hung up and turned her attention back to the

woman. She was scared, staring at the big lug on the floor next to her.

Katie held out a hand and helped her to her feet. "I know this is a lot for you to take in, especially after you've already been through so much, but I need you to focus for me for a second, okay?"

The woman nodded and wrapped her arms around herself.

"Do you want to live here, or somewhere else?"

The woman grimaced, favoring her injured leg. "I don't have the money to go anywhere else. He hasn't let me work or have any money."

Katie shook her head and reached over, swiftly picking her up in her arms. She had to get out of there and over to the Starbucks, and didn't have time to wait for her to limp around.

"You can come with me."

The woman looked around frantically and then down at the guy on the ground. Katie really hoped this wasn't a bad case of Stockholm Syndrome, where she wouldn't leave her attacker. Either way, Katie couldn't leave her there to be hurt.

"What's wrong? What do you need?"

"My clothes, maybe a few other things."

"Is there anything that can't be replaced?"

The woman sighed and shook her head. "No, all of it can be replaced. He took everything that was precious a long time ago."

"He won't be taking anything else from you. Please trust me. I'll make sure you get everything you need. For now, let's get out of here. This asshole can take care of himself from now on."

Pandora growled, *He's lucky I didn't brand his ass.*

Katie set the woman down when they were back on the street and supported her as she hobbled along. They stopped at the local CVS and Katie left her on the bench out front while she ran in to get some first aid supplies. She sat down beside her on the bench when she came back out and lifted up her sleeve to apply ointment to the burn before covering it with a square patch of gauze and some tape.

"Bring your injured ankle up here."

The woman lifted her foot onto the bench, her head held low as people passed by. Katie looked at it for a moment, deciding it was probably sprained but not broken. She wrapped gauze tightly around it and then pulled on an ankle brace. The woman put her shoe back on and set her foot down on the ground.

"Try to stand up."

Katie put her hand out, the woman wobbled a little but was able to stand. She smiled weakly and nodded. Katie threw the trash away and held out her arm.

"Come on, I want to take you somewhere."

They headed to the store where Katie had taken the demon out of the eighteen-year-old girl. As soon as she opened the door, the woman behind the counter recognized Katie. She hurried over and shook Katie's hand.

"It's so good to see you! I tell you what. You made me a

superstar that night. Business has been amazing! And people all over the world have messaged me to say how thankful they were to have people like you out there helping. They loved your angel glow."

Katie chuckled awkwardly, unsure of what to say. She smiled and glanced at the girl.

The woman sensed her discomfort and put her hands together, resuming her professional demeanor. "What can I do for you today?"

"I would like you to pick out or help her pick out four sets of nice clothes for this lady, and seven sets of day-to-day wear. You can put it all on one bill for me. She will need everything from head to toe."

"Oh, how fun."

"Yeah." Katie chuckled and handed the woman her credit card. "Here, this is my card. If I'm not back by the time you're done, you can charge it. I have to go and talk to my police colleagues a few blocks over at the Starbucks on Pennsylvania Avenue. If you need anything, you can find me there. I'll try to be back as fast as I can."

Katie turned to the woman. "What's your name?"

The woman smiled. "Angie. And thank you so much for saving me from him. I don't know what I would have done without you. You've really done enough. This is all so expensive."

Katie patted her on the shoulder with a kind smile. "I have a lot of money, and not a lot of reasons to spend it. *You* are one of my reasons. Now, try to enjoy yourself. I'll be back really soon."

The detectives stood to greet Katie when she arrived.

"Thank you so much for coming. I'm John Travers, and this is Detective Martin Schultz."

Schultz held out a hand for her to shake. "How d'ya do?"

"Nice to meet you, guys. I remember you from the station, but I think we missed introductions."

"Yeah." Travers chuckled. "You were being bombarded and we didn't want to add to it, so we got your information from the system."

"I see." Katie smiled. "What can I do for you?"

The three of them took a seat at a table in the corner. Both of the cops had a coffee, but Katie chose to pass, not being a big fan of their brew. Travers looked at Schultz and back to Katie nervously.

"Schultz and I, we've been with the NYPD for almost twenty years now, so you can imagine all this demon stuff is a lot to catch up on. We were used to normal everyday robbers, murderers, drug busts...that kind of thing. This is a complete game-changer."

"I can understand that." Katie smiled, recalling when she had first found out about demons.

Travers shifted in his seat. "We're responsible for finding the evil infected, not those who are infected but still okay."

"We find the ones causing the problems," Schultz interjected.

Travers nodded. "Right. We are wondering if there are ways to do that without causing a scene? I know it seems like a stupid question, but when lives are on the line, the last thing we need is mass panic."

"No, I totally get it." Katie nodded. "Actually, I just came off a job with the LAPDF, where we had to get rid of some of the demons that were running clubs. As you can imagine, in a club setting it's vital not to cause mass panic. I don't have any specific tactics to share, and no tricks of the trade, either. But what I *can* do while I'm in New York is work with you to find out exactly what's going on."

Travers sighed. "That would be great."

"Now, these things get a little wild sometimes," Schultz confided. "Will you be okay in a firefight? Have you done anything like that before?"

Katie struggled to keep a straight face. Pandora busted into laughter, giggling so hard she couldn't even get any words out. Katie's stomach was tight from Pandora's outburst. She cleared her throat and nodded at the detectives.

"I've been involved in a few scuffles."

The detectives looked relieved. She could have told them about the all-out battles she had been in, but she didn't want to make them feel stupid. From all the media coverage they should have been aware of who she was, and they definitely should have researched her before they'd reached out to her for help. It seemed she had a bit more education to take on with the two of them.

"If we were facing a club scene like that, what would you suggest?" Travers asked.

"Get about ten officers to surround the club and send me in on my own. I go through and flush out the demons who are all scared of me because they are weak."

Schultz furrowed his brow. "How will we know which ones are humans and which ones are these demons?"

Katie blinked at them for a long moment before answering. "The demons will be the ones running as though they've just seen God himself, of course."

Schultz raised an eyebrow at his partner.

Katie held back a chuckle, thinking that maybe this could be a little more fun than she thought. She pushed back her chair and stood up. "I have something to attend to right now, but why don't we meet at the station around eight thirty tonight?"

"Sounds good." Schultz nodded but had a worried look on his face.

These boys are in for a treat. Pandora giggled.

Katie rushed back over to the store to find Angie all done and packed up. There were lots of bags of clothes on the counter in front of her, and she appeared to be much more relaxed than when Katie had left.

Katie smiled, running her hands over the fabric. "Boxed it all up. We'll take a business card and call you to tell you where to ship it in a little while...and I like that outfit. Very nice."

Angie did a little twirl to show Katie her button-up shirt and wide-leg black pants and blushed at the compliment.

They left the store. Angie followed Katie, clearly nervous about asking any questions.

Katie smiled at her. "What's up, Angie?"

"Where are we going now?"

"Well, I get the feeling I might need my own place here. However, I'm not always going to live here, so I'll have to find something large enough that you can use one of the rooms."

Angie looked around the area, realizing how close they were to Madison Square Gardens. "It can get expensive in this area of the city."

Katie shrugged. "I need something to spend my money on."

11

A ngie's back was straight, her long, dark hair meticulously pulled back into a ponytail, her clothes pressed and perfectly fitted, and a hint of makeup brightened her eyes. She held her head a little higher than before. She and Katie had toured several different buildings in their search for a condo near Central Park. Early on, Katie had spotted a real estate office and steered Angie toward it.

She hoped to find a list of the condos for sale, but that wasn't how it worked. The girls were instantly accosted by Iris Grey, a middle-aged woman with the kind of enthusiasm that you couldn't help but get caught up in.

"Come on in and sit down. Welcome to my office. I tell you, I'm so glad you walked in today. I had the most horrific day coming in. Two appointments canceled, and I thought, 'Iris, just trust in the Universe. It will send you a sign.' And what do you know? You two lovely ladies just popped into my life. Tell me your names."

Katie chuckled. "I'm Katie, and this is my friend Angie."

"Katie and Angie, perfect names. I love it. Now, tell me

what you're looking for so I can show you exactly what matches your taste. There are tons of places to live in this city, but we only represent the best of the best. Award-winning designs, affluent and prized architecture, and amenities you don't get even at the Waldorf."

"I'm looking to be close to Central Park, three bedrooms minimum."

"Excellent. And are you looking for anything specific regarding finishes, amenities, things like that?"

"A modicum of security in the building would be nice. A gym, and maybe a pool? And a view would be lovely."

Iris tittered. "Oh, honey, I won't show you *anything* without a view."

Angie put her head down, stifling a laugh, and Katie did her best to keep the giggles at bay.

Pandora dissolved into stitches. *Oh, I love her,* she gushed. *I didn't know humans could be this funny!*

The woman was very interesting, but Katie had come to expect that from the people in her life. She always seemed to attract those with alternative personalities. Iris wasn't infected, which might mean she wouldn't help her to find a place. Then again, it might not make a difference if she were scared enough of Pandora.

Iris got up and grabbed her purse. "We have a big day ahead of us. I hope you ate your breakfast, ladies. Almost all of them are within walking distance, so let's go."

As Iris guided them deftly through the streets, Katie and Angie almost had to jog to keep up with her brisk pace. Angie looked at Katie as they slowed down at a crosswalk. "Three bedrooms? That's a big space for just you."

"I want a room for me, obviously. But I also want a

room for you, and one for anyone else who may come to stay with us. I have quite a few friends in the business. I'll probably get a pullout couch as well. Hell, I'm sure there are plenty of hotels near here for the overflow."

"That there are," Iris chimed in over her shoulder. "There's the Plaza, the Mandarin, the Lowell, the Dream Hotel. The list goes on and on, and you'd have your pick. I love it when I have clients who have friends. They're *so* much fun to work with."

Katie chuckled. *If only she knew who my friends were.*

All I know is that there'd better be some donut shops near whatever we pick. I'm not playing this game. Pandora was indignant, not really understanding the need to buy a condo in New York.

"What about donut shops?" Katie yelled ahead to Iris.

"Donuts? Oh, if you like donuts, this city has everything. Tons of little patisseries pop up constantly all over the city, and then there are, of course, Dunkin' Donuts on just about every corner."

Of course, there is.

"We're not really Dunkin' fans."

"There are at least three family-owned bakeries within walking distance, and there's a twenty-four-hour shop over in Chelsea, which is just a quick cab ride away—or you can have the complex call you a car. Most of the buildings we'll be looking at have concierge service, so you can send someone out to get whatever you need."

Pandora brightened. *I love Iris! She knows exactly what a woman needs.*

They walked down East Eighty-eighth Street, where Iris paused in front of a stately renovated brick building. It was very chic and clean-lined, yet it looked to have been in New York for decades. The complex had a doorman who nodded at each person as they came and went. He was a middle-aged man with the perfect gentlemanly smile and dark hair flecked with silver. As soon as he saw Iris, his eyes lit up.

"Ms. Iris, so good to see you."

"You too, Robert." Iris turned to Katie, her cheeks a little flushed. "Now, this is 12 East Eighty-eighth, one of my premier listings. This complex has been in existence since the 1920s, when everyone began to move to the Upper East Side. It was the last of the buildings to be created by the renowned Twenties architect Rosaria Candela. The building was not completed until the Thirties due to his service in the military, but he is the architect behind some of the most luxurious living spaces in New York, including the family home of Miss Jacqueline Bouvier."

"I like it. It's got spirit." Katie smiled.

Iris ushered them through the front door, Robert smiling and nodding at each of them. Iris stopped in the center of the large marble atrium and spun around, arms wide. Katie pressed her lips together and chuckled quietly, finding Iris to be *more* than spirited. She was in love with the building.

"So, here at East Eighty-eighth, you will need for nothing. The building has twenty-four-hour door and concierge services, a private courtyard, a residents' lounge with television, onsite storage, a bicycle room if you ride one of those, a fitness center, and of course, you are just steps away from the beautiful Central Park. Now, let's head up and take a look at the condo that's available."

They took the elevator up and followed Iris down the hall. Their eyes darted around, taking note of all the prewar finishes that had been preserved in the hallway. They arrived at apartment 3A and Iris took them inside, smiling as she welcomed them into the broad open space.

"This is a three-bedroom. They do have four and five bedrooms available as well, just so you are aware. Now, to your left through this doorway is your dining room, which opens up into your spacious kitchen. To your right is the very large living room with beautiful views out the front windows. Down the hall you'll find the three bedrooms, including a master suite, and there's a total of two and a half baths in this apartment."

"It's very nice." Katie walked through the dining room and went into the kitchen to inspect the fixtures.

"The floors are white oak, all cabinets have under-cabinet lighting, and the countertops are Covelano Oro marble. The faucets are none other than Dornbracht polished chrome, and there are a wide variety of Wolf and Sub-Zero appliances to choose from."

Katie returned to the hall and made her way into the master suite. It was smaller than she had hoped, but she was in a New York City condo. Most apartments in the city could fit inside this bedroom. Iris came in behind her and flipped on the switch in the master bath. Katie walked in, blinded by the white and gray opulence.

"This is the master bath. The ceilings, counters, walls, and floors are all Dolomiti white marble, and the fixtures are polished chrome Dornbracht. The cabinets are glass fronted, and the oversized tub is cast iron."

Katie's heart skipped a beat when she saw the tub. "I could *swim* in that thing."

They walked through the rest of the place, listening to Iris namedrop designers, architects, and companies that had been part of the design, none of which Katie had ever heard of before. It was obvious from Angie's face that she hadn't either, but both of them acted impressed or shocked, depending on how Iris presented the information.

When they were done touring the apartment, Iris brought them back to the foyer. "What do you think?" she asked Katie.

"I love it. It's beautiful, but I would like to see other options."

Iris did a little skip of happiness. "Of course! Come on, we'll head over to The Astor. It's on my top five list of the most beautiful places to live in Manhattan."

Katie and Angie followed Iris as they made their way back to the busy New York streets. As they walked along enjoying the air, Angie looked at Katie.

"These are all so swanky," she marveled. "I've never met someone who could afford something like that."

"I haven't always been able to, either," Katie told her. "It's pretty new to me. I guess I got lucky, in a way. I have to work hard to keep the luck, but I've been letting the money pile up instead of spending it. I think it's time I let my hair down a bit."

"Gosh." Angie chuckled in shock. "I've never known what it was like to have too much money. Even before I was with that guy I was lucky to keep my account in the black most of the time."

Katie smiled. "I have a business out in Nevada that throws off a lot of money. The product is invaluable to very important people. It kind of runs itself now, and I have a great staff constantly striving to reach that next level in productivity. I do, however, plan on adding additional businesses that aren't related to it, and I'm thinking New York would be a good place to start. What do you do?"

Angie reddened. "I haven't had much experience at anything, but I've had one year of college. I made some bad life decisions. Never believed I could make anything of myself."

"I can only offer the opportunity." Katie shrugged. "If you don't step up I'll make sure you're okay, but you'll miss out on further opportunities."

Angie pressed her lips together as she processed everything that had happened in the last twenty-four hours. She had gotten out of a situation she'd been dead sure she would only leave in a body bag. She'd been given a safe place to stay and clothes, and now here was an opportunity to leave all that behind and move on to the kind of life she'd never even dared to dream of. It was like her fairy godmother had waved a magic wand, and everything had changed in a heartbeat. A song from Hamilton played softly in Angie's mind. *I'm not going to miss my shot.*

At that moment, she made her decision. She was going to make it happen one way or another, and she wouldn't let her doubts overtake her like they usually did. She had always battled with the concept that she might be capable of anything outside the normal day-to-day struggle to survive, and now she would no longer be ground down by life. She was being offered a once-in-a-lifetime opportunity, and she was determined not to screw it up.

She didn't want to live the old way anymore.

"Angie, you coming?" Katie called. She waved to her as Iris entered the next complex.

"Oh, sure!" Angie giggled, realizing she'd stopped and had been staring into the distance. "Yes, sorry."

They walked into the lobby of the Astor, instantly wowed by the marble ceilings and floors. Like the other place, there was both a doorman stationed at the front and a concierge at the desk inside.

Iris led the way up to the fourth floor and down the hall to apartment 801, giving them the rundown as she walked. "This building has been lovingly restored with the utmost respect for the original features. Each condo includes a library and separate office, vaulted ceilings, and the finishes have been completed to the highest standards. This particular condo is close to two thousand square feet, with custom moldings, three-paneled doors, double-paned bay windows, and original hardwood flooring throughout. The foyer leads down the hall. On the right, you'll see three doors. These are the two bedrooms with the adjoining full bath between. There's also a half-bath across the hall for guests. At the end of the hall is the open living and dining area, and the kitchen is beyond, which you'll see is very spacious and bright. The left turn at the end of the hall takes you down another shorter hall to the master bedroom and master bath, as well as two large closets."

"This is beautiful, though not as open as the other,"

Katie pointed out. "It's more like a home than an apartment."

The kitchen was beautiful, with a table built into the stone-topped island, shining hardwood floors, and spotless white cabinetry. Katie could definitely see herself learning how to cook for herself, Angie, and Pandora in the space. Even if she didn't, there was plenty of counter space to order in. She could see them heating up leftovers and chowing down around the chunky wooden table in the middle of the night. Iris guided them through the large bedroom and into the master bath, which included a beautiful clawfoot tub.

"Now, this is my absolute favorite thing," Iris gushed, pushing them back down the hall to the living room. "All the fireplaces have been restored to full working order, so you can relax in front of a crackling fire on cold New York nights."

"That *is* nice." Katie smiled. "Reminds me of home. I always loved a fire."

Pandora snickered. *Reminds me of home too.*

Iris clapped her hands gleefully. "You're very close to the park, shopping, donuts, and transport links."

Katie nodded as she considered the information. "How much is this one compared to the other?"

"Let's see," Iris replied. She scrolled through her phone. "Eighty-eighth Street is 4.95 million, and this one is 5.7 million, so you would make an offer to the owners in that ballpark."

Angie's eyes grew wide, but Katie wasn't sold. She had more than enough to buy either one, but she hadn't seen enough to make a decision just yet. She liked the Astor better, of the two so far. It had that old warm charm, with sleek touches of modern design. She wasn't even sure how much she would be staying there, but she had come to learn that her home base was very important, so she had to get it just right. Doing the kind of work she did, the comfort of home was the only thing that really kept her grounded, and there was no way she wanted to get stuck with the New York equivalent of sand in her mouth.

I like this one, Pandora pointed out.

I do too, but I think I want to see one more before I make a choice.

It was as though Iris had read her mind. "I do have one more property I'd like to show you. It backs up to Central Park."

Katie smiled. "Perfect."

They headed out of the Astor and down about twenty more blocks to the Circa, which was a more modern take on the condo. They went inside and took the elevator up to the eighth floor.

Iris led them to the door of 8A. "Now, this condo boasts magnificent views of both the park and the city from terraces around every apartment, and a modern architectural style that you won't find too much of in this area. They tend to stay more traditional up here."

They followed her into the condo. The bedrooms were to their left, and the master was in the back corner with its own private bath. There were two bedrooms with a connecting bath, and a half-bath in the hallway. To the right was the expansive living room and kitchen, both of which had tri-fold doors in place of the walls leading out onto the terrace. The kitchen was a little smaller than the one at the Astor, but not by much, and it had all the same amenities.

Katie ran her hands over the blue marble countertops and admired the grayish-white finish on the wood flooring. It was open and airy, and the wall of windows made it even more so with the light cascading through the floor-to-ceiling glass of the terrace doors. It was just what she'd had in mind—a space that didn't feel claustrophobic like so many of the places in New York did. It had a level of luxury she could afford and the space to entertain if she wanted to, or just take in the park from the terrace in her downtime.

"This one is on the market for 4.995 million," Iris mentioned as she pointed out the Bosch appliances and the large pantry.

Angie and Iris began to chat about the area, giving Katie a moment to slip away and look around on her own. She stood at the terrace doors and drank in the view of Central Park, which was lively with lunchtime joggers and walkers. She also had a beautiful view of the city. She was just high up enough to see over the buildings across the street and off into the distance. She had never thought of herself as the type to live in the middle of a big city. Frankly, she had never been bold enough to consider it.

As she'd grown into her role as a Damned, she'd found many things in life that should frighten her. Living in a city as vibrant as New York and building her future *her* way wasn't one of them, though.

12

Just outside of town, nestled on the beaches of Cabo was The Office, the perfect place to get your grub on with the warm sand between your toes. Brightly-covered tables inhabited by happy patrons dotted the beach just feet from the lapping water.

Calvin had gone back to town that morning to buy some things he had seen at the market. While looking at different items at one of the local craftsmen's booths, he had run into someone he only knew by face and the way he put pen to paper.

Calvin approached a little nervously. "I'm sorry to disturb you. Are you Russell Blake? The author of the *Jet* series?"

The guy looked up, shifting his baseball cap to shield his eyes from the sun. He smiled, the creases at the edge of his eyes giving Calvin an impression of thoughtfulness. He put down the knickknack he was looking at and rubbed his goatee before nodding, then offered his hand to Calvin, who introduced himself. "Good to meet you, Calvin. I'm very surprised that you recognized me."

"Your books kept me going through a tough tour. I recognized your face from the picture online and on the back of your books. It's actually pretty strange running into you here."

"I'm on vacation, and I figured I would take a look-see at what was in the market today."

Calvin nodded. "I'm in the same boat. On vacation, just came out for a late lunch and some shopping."

"Where you headed for lunch?"

"I was thinking The Office."

"Funny you should say that. So was I. It's the perfect place. Would you like to join me?"

Calvin nodded. "That would be awesome."

The two men made their way to The Office, getting a bright green table off to one side. They sat on the same side, so they were both facing the ocean. Calvin ordered the cheese dip for an appetizer and three shrimp tacos with cheese, while Russell, ordered the crab.

"It's always so nice to meet a fan of my writing."

"I'm a *huge* fan of your *Jet* series. I'm one of the mercenary fighters, but before that, I was in the military. I read the entire series."

"Wow, that's impressive."

"I read some of the *Day After Never* series, but I preferred *Jet*. It was good, don't get me wrong, but I think it just hit a little too close to my work efforts at times. I find myself getting lost in your books, transporting myself to another life and time. You know, the way books are supposed to do. With *Day After Never*, I was going from real life to a daydream that was exactly the same as the world I was trying to escape."

"I can understand that one." Russell chuckled. "I'm just glad my books went to someone who could really use them at the time. It always feels good as an author when I hear stories about people going through hard times and turning to my books to take them to another world. It's a privilege to be there for those who are there for me, even if I don't always know it—so thank you, Calvin."

"Feels strange having *you* thank *me*." He laughed. "But you're welcome."

"So, are you enjoying your trip?"

"So far, so good. I've gone to a few clubs, relaxed, met some people, gotten to know a few beautiful women."

"Is this your first time in Cabo?"

"Yeah." He sighed happily. "I couldn't have imagined it any better. I'm glad I chose to come here instead of touring Europe like I initially thought about doing."

"You have time for that. This beach life is mesmerizing. I swear every time I turn around I find myself here again."

"It definitely seems like it can be addictive." Calvin smiled at the waitress as she set his dip down in front of him.

"How many margaritas have you had since you got here?"

"Surprisingly, only one, and I love tequila."

"Me too." Russell chuckled.

"What's your favorite kind of tequila?"

"Depends on what it's for. In margaritas it's hard to go wrong with 1800, but for sipping? I'd have to say either Atelier del Maestro or *Herradura Seleccion Suprema*, both of which are amazing in different ways. The *Seleccion Suprema* is like a fine single malt scotch, perfectly balanced, whereas the Atelier has more barrel flavors and is lusher in the mouth. For margaritas, 1800 *Anejo*, and the *Servando* is disappointing."

Calvin nodded his head through the whole spiel, realizing Russell was a touch more passionate about tequila than he had anticipated. From the corner of his eye, he idly watched the women playing in the surf in their tiny bikinis. The unreality of the moment brought a dry chuckle to his lips. He was in one of the most beautiful places in the world, surrounded by beautiful women, eating an incredible meal with a man he'd admired for a long time. He felt like he was in another world. It was definitely fantastic enough to have come from the pages of a book.

Two *very* attractive women caught Calvin and Russell's attention. One wore a bronze one-piece that was mostly straps and had a short sheer sarong tied around her waist. Diamonds glittered at her wrists and neck, her tanned skin shimmered with oil, and her brown hair cascaded over her shoulders. The woman next to her wore a white bikini that made her skin appear to glow. She was wearing a long sheer cover-up over her bottom half with the same diamond bracelet on her wrist. Sparkling out from under her long dirty-blond hair were four-inch-long sparkling diamond earrings.

Calvin couldn't help but stare. They were like the poster women for a "Come to Cabo" commercial.

Russell sat back in his chair with a wistful sigh as the waitress delivered their entrées.

Calvin looked at Russell and took another glance at the

women before shaking his head and chuckling. "They make the women out here like supermodels."

"I wouldn't be surprised if those two were, or at least they were for the men who footed the bill for all of those diamonds."

"You don't think they bought them for themselves?" Calvin asked.

"No." He scoffed, turning back around. "You see those two men about ten yards away from them? The ones walking along the beach all suited and booted?"

"Yeah." Calvin noticed that their suit jackets bulged in all the wrong places; they were packing in the center of a crowded beach. "Shit, they're armed." Calvin narrowed his eyes, looking closely at the guys in black suits and sunglasses on a sunny beach. They followed the women down the strand, their eyes constantly roving the surrounding area.

Russell chuckled. "They're bodyguards for the girls. The drug lords hire guys like them as protection for their harems or whatever. See the matching bracelets? Those two are one man's buffet."

"Huh, I never thought that was actually a thing."

"Oh, yeah. In fact, many of the murders reported out here are drug-related crime killings. Not all of them, of course, but it's mostly rival drug cartels taking each other out for a bigger slice of the profits. They're constantly trying to claw territory from each other. There have been small wars over who controls the streets."

"Are there demons involved?" Calvin asked, wishing he hadn't.

"Probably." Russell shrugged and cracked open his crab.

"Mexico isn't at quite the same level as many of the larger countries, including the US, when it comes to trapping and taking care of demons, but then they don't seem to be as prevalent here either."

Calvin grimaced. "They want the US, since it's considered the most powerful country in the world. They think if they can take America, they can take everything. Mexico is small fry to them; they aren't worried about it at all."

"Good. It'll keep some peace here for now." Russell chuckled. "But I wouldn't be shocked if it came out that some of these drug lords were demon-infested. Of course, at the same time, people aren't as innocent as we'd like to make them out to be. Some don't need demons to do horrific things."

"That is *very* true." Calvin let his gaze wander back to the two women by the water. They looked like they didn't have a care in the world, but Calvin thought that if you needed bodyguards to ensure you survived a walk on the beach, you might need to reevaluate your life. Still, they were perfectly-sculpted and absolutely gorgeous women. He looked at Russell, who was smiling and shaking his head.

"The view is free, right?"

Katie left Iris at her office and collected Angie, who was hanging around outside, her mind obviously somewhere else. They made their way through the city, deciding a long walk was better than taking a cab through the traffic.

When they reached the Stewart Hotel, Katie went straight to the front desk.

The concierge looked up from her computer with a friendly smile. "How may I help you?"

"I'm currently staying on the nineteenth floor, and I want to rent another room on the same floor as close to my room as possible," Katie told him.

The concierge nodded. "Yes, of course. Let me just see what I have available. Will there be a specific length of stay?"

"I was hoping it would be open-ended, like the one I'm staying in."

"Of course, madam." He typed for a few more moments, then pulled out a key and handed it to Katie.

"You are all taken care of, madam."

"Thank you."

"Room 1926, just a couple of doors down from your own."

"Perfect." Katie handed the key to Angie. "We will be having a few deliveries to that room over the course of the day, and Angie has my permission to charge whatever she wants from room service to my account."

The concierge smiled as he finished typing. "Very good, madam."

Katie steered Angie to the elevator, relieved that she was finally settled in and everything was taken care of for her new friend. Katie didn't know why she had felt the need to take Angie under her wing, but in her mind, there was nothing else she could do. She needed to make sure she was okay after what she had been through.

"I want you to call the store and have your clothes

brought up to you in the room. If you're hungry, go ahead and order food from room service." Katie handed her a hundred dollars. "Use this to tip with. I usually do ten to twenty, depending on the trouble they went through. Use your judgment. I suggest that until we know that bastard is going to leave you alone for good, you just stay here and relax."

Angie cursed herself for flinching when Katie patted her shoulder. There was a tiny part of her that feared Katie, no matter what she had done for her. She was *almost* sure she could trust her, but there was still the question of the demon in her. She hadn't forgotten how easily Katie had delivered the violence that had freed her. She didn't want to ask, but she couldn't hold back any longer.

"Katie, do you really work with the cops?"

Katie looked at Angie quizzically. She didn't understand why Angie would question that. Angie's eyes flicked to hers and quickly away again, and she realized what had spurred the question.

Katie was infected.

Don't take it personally, Pandora told her. *She hasn't met my fabulousness yet. She'll come around once we get to know each other.*

You're right. She must be scared.

Well, of course.

Katie gave Angie a reassuring smile. "Yes, I'm working with the cops at the moment. I'm helping them take care of the demon situation in the city. I know that's probably hard to believe seeing that I am infected, but it's true, I swear. The only demon I've met today was the creep of a guy you were living with, though."

Katie sighed and looked down at her hands. She understood why Angie was skeptical. Katie had come out of nowhere, kicked her boyfriend's ass, and turned her life upside down in the space of a day without a word of explanation.

"You know what you should do?"

Angie shook her head. "No, what?"

"You should drop your things in your room and head back down to the first floor. There is a bank of Mac computers there for guest use. I want you to research Katie's Killers. You'll find a full explanation of who I am, and what my team and I do. I think once you know a bit more about me, it will alleviate some of those fears you have. I understand that in order for you to work for me, to start fresh, you first have to understand what the hell you're getting into. I apologize for not explaining earlier. It's been a crazy day."

Angie chuckled. "It's all right. You were busy saving my life."

Katie smiled and reached a little hesitantly for Angie's shoulder. This time Angie didn't flinch. "I'm going to go meet with the cops, and I probably won't be home until two or three in the morning. If I'm still asleep at ten tomorrow morning, knock hard, and keep knocking until I get up. I might be grumpy, but I'll get over it as soon as we get breakfast. I have a lot to do tomorrow, so I can't just lie around in bed all day. It's unfortunate, but it's the truth. We usually get food in the morning too, so we can head out for breakfast. Room service gets old after a while."

"All right." Angie clutched her purse in front of her. "I

really *do* appreciate everything you're doing. I don't want you to think I don't."

"It's okay." Katie nodded. "It's understandable, really."

You know what I don't find understandable?

What's that, Pandora? Katie asked.

I don't understand how you think I'll wait until ten in the morning for you to go get my donuts. And yes, I fully expect donuts. Sure, we can have a nice little breakfast with your new project, but I will be getting donuts.

I am fully aware. Relax. I can't help this girl by feeding her dozens of donuts. She obviously hasn't had nutritious food in a very long time. She's skin and bones.

Maybe she needs a demon to help her.

What? No!

Pandora snickered. *Hey, it worked for you.*

Did it? Katie growled. *Because right now, I want to strangle you and send you back where you came from.*

I don't think even your angel fingers are that strong.

You are impossible.

Katie had another thought. "Something else you can look up while you're on the computers is high-end furniture shops. We're going to have to furnish the new condo, and I don't want to put too much thought into it. Find someplace where they'll assist us with all of that. If we need an appointment, make a note so I can carve out some time for it. For now, I've got to get going and make some money if I'm going to pay for all of this stuff."

"All right." Angie nodded. "Be safe."

Katie grinned. "Thanks, and you enjoy that room, okay?"

She saw Angie onto the elevator and turned toward the

front door. There was a reason she had found Angie, a reason she felt the need to take care of her, and a reason that all of it had fallen into place so easily. She just hoped that reason came to light soon.

Katie changed direction and walked to the front desk instead. She smiled at the concierge when he looked up at her.

"Yes, ma'am?"

"I'm going to be gone until late, but I was hoping you could keep an eye on my friend Angie, the woman in my extra room. Not babysitting her or anything, just make sure she's comfortable and has everything she needs. She came from a bad situation, and she's pretty scared."

The concierge gave her a look of admiration. "Of course, madam. I'll make a couple of calls to her throughout the evening and take up some dessert after her dinner on the house. I believe we also have some hampers with oils and bath salts. I can send one up to help her relax."

"That would be wonderful," Katie looked at the manager's tag, "Mr. Pine. I appreciate the accommodation."

"Of course, and have fun while you're out and about. The night concierge will be here when you return."

Katie nodded her thanks and left the hotel. It felt really good to take care of someone like that. It was a stark change from her usual kill-first-ask-questions-later mindset.

atie walked into the Midtown South Precinct, the same one she had been to a couple of days before, and the cop behind the desk recognized Katie from her first visit. He pressed a button, then a buzzer sounded and the door to the back clicked open. She made her way to the pit, finding it just the same as the last time she had been there. Cops milled around, and business was booming. There were suspects handcuffed to benches and others sat sulkily at desks being questioned by the detectives. This time there weren't any with red eyes, but that was going to change very soon.

Schultz stood up from his cubicle and waved to Katie. She smiled and skirted the desks, making her way over to the detective. He shook her hand and indicated the office on the right.

"Thanks for coming. We're going to meet in Travers' fancy-ass office." He chuckled. "It's a little more private, and away from all these knuckleheads."

"Sounds good. Lead the way."

Katie followed Martin over to Travers' office, closing the door behind her. Travers was on the phone, and he waved for them to take a seat without moving it from his ear. Katie sat down in one of the leather-backed seats in front of his desk and glanced at the awards and photos on his walls. He was obviously very proud of his service to the NYPD, and the number of commendations he had displayed spoke volumes about his commitment to the force.

"Katie, good to see you. Sorry about that, and thank you for waiting. Just a final mop-up on the last murder investigation we had. Messy deal. We thought we might be working with a serial killer, but it turned out to be some kid who had watched too many episodes of the new Hannibal show and decided to try a human art sculpture for himself."

"That sounds horrible." Katie grimaced. "Demon?"

"He wishes he could use that defense, but no, he was completely clean. Just your friendly neighborhood psychopath."

"Well, they're definitely out there. So, what are we doing tonight?"

"Right." Travers took the blueprint from Schultz and spread it over his desk. "This is Lavo Nightclub on East Fifty-eighth Street. It's a swanky combined restaurant and club that's a notorious hangout for our more affluent Italian...businessmen, shall we say. Anyway, there's been a serious influx of red eyes in the joint, and the owner actually reached out to us and asked us to help. He's losing business because they're the first ones in and the last ones out. He knows it's only a matter of time until someone takes it too far."

"Okay, and who do we have on this?"

"The Nineteenth Precinct," Schultz answered. "Technically, it's their patch, so we'll be working directly with them."

"Exactly." Travers nodded. "We respect the precinct boundaries whenever we can. Anyway, we took your advice and came up with a plan. We'll have the Nineteenth surrounding the building, stomping on the cockroaches as they come out."

Katie smiled. "I love it when a plan comes together. I would suggest you use stun guns, since the demons won't be strong enough to help their human hosts. Then you can cuff 'em and stuff 'em.'"

"Perfect," Travers replied, writing it down.

"Once you've caught the demons who are actively trying to run and hide—they're the ones who have a strong grip on their human hosts—you can send them off and get help for the humans who still have a chance. We want to save as many lives as we can, and more often than not these low-level demons are more like hitchhikers than tenants. They can be removed."

"Absolutely." Schultz nodded. "If we kill everyone who's infected we're doing the demons' job for them, so we want to save as many humans as we can—not just rock up and start shooting."

Katie was beginning to love this consulting business. She grinned at the detectives. "That's the plan."

Travers returned her grin as he shut the file and stood up. "All right, then. Let's get out there."

Katie followed the detectives to their car. All of the cop cars were backed onto the sidewalk at an angle so they were able to fit on the street. It wasn't legal for civilians, but in a place where cops had to move at the drop of a dime, creating their own parking solution like that was both brilliant and necessary.

Katie sat in the back of the unmarked detective car, looking out the window as they passed through town. As they moved through the traffic, Katie felt a hot band tighten her chest, along with an unwavering need to change direction. She had no idea why or how, but she was being drawn to something, just like when she'd found Angie.

She cleared her throat and rubbed her chest as they came to a stop at a red light. She looked to her right, and the sensation intensified. She couldn't see anything special, just a row of dingy houses with bars on the windows. There were very few people outside. A splash of yellow against the faded brick caught her attention, a piece of crime-scene tape fluttering from the front of a house halfway down the street which was cordoned off.

"What's down there?"

Schultz turned to see where she was looking. "It's a gang-infested area. There's at least one murder a month down that way. It used to be a really nice area, but once the gangs moved in, the poverty level began to rise and the place went downhill. There was a big project a few years ago to clean the place up, but the dealers are harder to stamp out than roaches. They waited until the attention died down, and it just went straight back to what it was before. It's a shame, really."

Katie nodded as the light changed and they lurched forward. She made a mental note to come back when she was on her own time. She could feel the surge of evil coming from there, and after all those donuts last night she could definitely do with a workout.

They pulled up to the curb about a block away from the club. Katie climbed out of the back and took her hair out of its ponytail, then shook her head, letting the locks cascade over her shoulders. She glanced down at her cleavage and adjusted her top for maximum impact.

Maybe just a little lower?

Katie rolled her eyes. *Any lower and they get to see the whole show.*

Suit yourself. You look just fine. Finer than fine, actually. I'm a true artist.

Both detectives shuffled awkwardly on the sidewalk, trying not to stare.

Katie scoped out her surroundings and spotted nine plainclothes cops spread out all around the club. There was a large truck parked in the alley. It was just like LA, only she didn't have Calvin there to back her up this time.

A guy in jeans and a button-up shirt came over, with an older guy smoking a cigar close behind him.

Schultz got the introductions over with. "This is Lieutenant Brown, who's in charge of the Nineteenth crew, and this is Detective Lowery, also from their precinct."

Katie shook their hands and nodded. "Nice to meet you."

"Any words of advice?" Brown asked.

"Just be ready. Some of these bastards are strong."

They all nodded and moved off to their positions.

Katie headed down the block and walked straight up to the front of the line outside the club. She winked at the doorman, who winked back at her and lifted the rope for her to slide right past. Once in the club, Katie walked to the side and took note of her surroundings. The interior was a series of open rooms, with tables down one side for people to have dinner and a wide dancefloor as the centerpiece of the room. Lights flashed around the stage at the back where the DJ pumped out electronica and house music.

Nothing too big in here, Pandora commented. *Easy-peasy.*

Good, because I don't know if those boys are up for anything too hardcore just yet.

Katie got out onto the dancefloor and began to shake it. She twined her way through the press of bodies, looking for demons.

Where are they?

All around us. Just wind those perfect fucking hips of yours, sister. I'll do the rest.

Katie threw herself into the music, and people were immediately drawn to the motion of her hips swaying to the beat. There were several demons on the floor around her, and even the female infected began to circle Katie.

She waited until almost all of them were close by.

Power pulsated warmly in her chest. She gathered the energy and wound it tighter, until it was a writhing knot inside her.

Now, Pandora whispered.

She released the energy. It rippled out, a translucent shockwave visible only to the demonic eye. Katie snickered when the infected bolted as one for the exits, the demons inside them panicked to the core.

None of them were stupid enough to fuck with Lilith.

The detectives had watched Katie disappear into the club, the three of them gathering farther down the street. The night was warm and there were tons of people around, but none of them had realized what was going on. They sat nervously glancing at the doors, looking down at their watches sporadically as they waited for something to happen.

"What is taking so long?" Lowery bitched through a cloud of cigar smoke.

"She's working her magic," Schultz replied.

"Hopefully in this millennium," Lowery huffed.

Without warning, the doors to the club flew wide open and eight red-eyed people came bolting out into the street. The cops jumped into action, using their stun guns to take them down. In the chaos, two of them managed to slip through the net. The ones they caught were thrown into the back of the truck and sent off to their local holding facility.

"Goddammit, we missed two of them," Brown growled, walking up to the detectives. "The sneaky bastards. They crept right past while we were dealing with the others."

"You got six, though, and that's a record," Schultz pointed out.

Brown sighed. "Yeah, but we do things to perfection in the Nineteenth. That should have been a cakewalk. She might as well have gift-wrapped them for us."

A few moments later the door to the club opened again

and Katie walked out, pulling her hair back into a ponytail. She nodded at Schultz and walked up to the group. "How did it go? It wasn't too bad in there tonight."

"They got six out of the eight," Lowery replied.

"Where did the other two run?"

Brown pointed down the block, and Katie sighed.

Don't do it. It's not your freaking job.

I know. Katie sighed. *I need to let the other two go. If I don't, they'll assume I'll always be there to fix all of their mistakes. It's fucking annoying, though. I served them up on a platter for them, and they should have had them in the bag. I know I've got to teach them what to do. That's why I'm here.*

Precisely. Besides, those two will get caught eventually. They ran, which means their demons aren't going to stay hidden for long.

"We'll wrap things up here," Lowery told her. "Thanks for your help. We don't work with the Damned often, but this was good. We'll round up the other two, and next time we'll get 'em all."

Katie nodded and followed Travers and Schulz to the car. They headed back to the station across from the Stewart and dealt with all the paperwork. Katie had to sign a couple of things, but mostly she was just there to make sure everyone got updated. When they were done, Schultz handed her an envelope. "Here's your consulting fee. Thanks again for helping."

"No problem." Katie smiled as she stuffed the envelope into her back pocket. "I'm sure we'll be working together a lot in the future."

Katie left the precinct and crossed to the Stewart Hotel, thankful she was done much earlier than she'd thought.

The night manager had come on duty, and he waved Katie over to the desk.

Katie hoped nothing was wrong. Whatever it was that had drawn her to Angie, she still had no idea who the woman was or what she was capable of.

"The young lady staying in the room upstairs—"

"Yes. Angie. Is everything all right?"

"Oh, yes. I wanted to let you know that she has been taken care of while you were away, per your request. She's a very nice lady. She was only in her room long enough to put her things away. I personally delivered the shipment from the clothing company to her room. She's been on the first floor in the computer room since then. We delivered her dinner and dessert there to make sure she'd eaten. She's still there."

"Great. Thank you so much for doing that."

"Not a problem. Is there anything I can get for you?"

"No." Katie smiled. "I'm going to check in on her, and then I have a date with that glorious bed."

The manager smiled. "Very good, madam. Have a good evening."

"You too."

Katie took the escalator to the first floor and headed to the room where the guest computers were situated. Angie was the only one there. She was typing away and taking notes on a pad to her side. Katie smiled, hoping she'd found what she was looking for, both regarding Katie and furnishing the new house. Katie went over and sat down in the chair next to her.

Angie dragged her gaze from the screen and blinked at Katie owlishly. "You're back early."

Katie chuckled. "Not *that* early."

Angie rubbed her eyes. "I got caught up here, I guess. I lost track of time."

"Did you find what you came to look for?"

Angie pulled Katie into a surprise hug. "I'm so sorry I treated you the way I did. I feel terrible for doubting you! I know now that you're one of the good guys. I researched you and your team like you told me to, and you're all heroes, demons or no demons."

"No need to apologize. I can understand your apprehension. It's smart of you to be cautious around people you don't know, especially after everything you've been through." Katie quickly changed the subject before the moment got emotional. "So, what did you find in the way of furniture?"

"Well!" Angie flipped through her notes excitedly. "There are a *ton* of upscale furniture places in the city. That's not a concern, but I thought maybe you would want to go a different way."

"What way would that be?"

"You're a very busy woman. With the mercenaries and your businesses, you're always on the go. Even though there are multitudes of nice furniture stores out there, I was thinking that it would be easier for you to hire someone who does this for a living. I mean, there's sourcing, shipping, and being here for deliveries and installation. Unless you know how to do all that?"

Katie laughed. "No."

"Me either." Angie smiled. "But there are some really excellent interior designers in this city who *do*, and they'll help you with the personal touches that will put your stamp on the place. I mean, you can go the furniture way, but all you're doing is placing furniture in a house with no real meaning behind it. You want to make your house a home, right?"

"Oh, absolutely. That's very important to me."

Angie raised an eyebrow. "Besides, why have a multi-million-dollar condo with an amazing view of the park and not have any fashion sense to go with it?"

"I think you might be right." Katie smiled. "Tomorrow, will you start looking for someone to help us? Someone who is traditional, but versatile at the same time."

"I've already started that list, and I left off anyone who didn't have traditional styles in their portfolio. I had a feeling you were going to want more of a mixture of styles than anything specific."

Katie chuckled. "Look at that—you're already on the ball. I like it, so keep that up. Now, it's late, I'm exhausted, and you need to get some sleep. You've been through a lot today. There's the most comfortable bed ever in your room, just waiting for you to pass out in it."

"I know." Angie groaned happily. "I sat down on it when I dropped off my things. I have to admit, it's the nicest bed I've ever sat on. I didn't want to get up. I just wanted to curl up right then and there and pass out."

"But you didn't, and that showed initiative. Good work."

Angie flushed with pride. Katie recognized that something had changed in her, and she hoped with all her heart that the change stuck.

Angie gathered her things and the two headed for the nineteenth floor. They didn't say much in the elevator on the way up since they were both exhausted. It didn't hit Angie until she was in the elevator, and Katie only held it back until she stepped out into the hall with her room key in her hand.

Katie stopped at her door and smiled at Angie. "Everything is gonna work itself out. We just gotta keep pushing through, right?"

"Yep." Angie smiled. "Sleep well. I'll knock at ten if you're not up."

"Thanks." Katie smiled as she opened her door. She was more than ready for a good night's sleep.

14

Calvin leaned his head back and spread his arms wide as he wound his hips to the music. Bikini-clad women danced all around him, which confirmed to him that his decision to return to the Ibiza that night was sound.

He was spoiled for choice. Everywhere he looked there was a woman who wanted to take a walk on the Calvin side. He hadn't hooked up with anyone specific so far that night, but he definitely had a lot of options. This time he'd made sure to wear swimming trunks and bring a towel so that he could take a swim or cozy up with some beautiful ladies in the hot tubs—maybe even stick around for the after-hours party, which he'd been told had an even looser dress code.

As one song ended and the other began the crowd put their hands in the air, jumping up and down. Calvin jumped with everyone else, feeling the connection to the music and the people around him. He wondered how he had managed to get lucky enough to be where he was and doing exactly what he was doing at this moment.

He was starting to understand why Russell kept coming back to Cabo. The place and the women were hypnotizing.

Calvin grooved to the sound. He spied a group of stunning women dancing together off to the side, nodded to the one who met his gaze, and danced his way toward them. However, as he inched closer he saw the security guards hovering behind the women. Their eyes roved the area surrounding the women, and their hands moved closer to the butts of their guns whenever a man dared to approach.

It suddenly became clear to Calvin why the women were dancing away from the others. They were not allowed to dance with other men, and the guards weren't just protection but chaperones as well.

Three of the four women laughed and giggled, dancing and drinking together. The fourth appeared distant, her mind far from the fun her companions were having. At first glance, she looked just like the others. Her hair was perfect, her makeup flawless. She was draped in diamonds and wearing immaculate couture.

Then Calvin spotted the black and blue marks on her legs when she shifted on the barstool.

It pissed him off, and he felt the anger rising in his chest. A glance at the human bodyguards—who'd noticed him staring—reminded him that it was none of his business. There were no demons involved that he knew of. He was here on vacation, and taking on drug lords was definitely not on his list of things to do.

She looked at him again with those sad, dark eyes.

Dammit, guess my vacation is over for the night. However, this wasn't the place to make a scene. He made a show of shrugging and danced his way back to the center of the dance floor, where the women were waiting for him.

He passed the night dancing with a plethora of women, but beneath the party-guy exterior, Calvin's mind writhed as he tried to figure out a way to get a moment alone with the woman so he could offer her his help. Every now and then he stole a glance at the corner to make sure he didn't miss them leaving, and as the bartender handed him his bill, he saw the guards and the four women walking toward the door.

He threw a few bills onto the bar, enough to cover the tab and leave a generous tip, and headed out behind them. Calvin hung back while the guards escorted the women to the curb, where they waited at the valet point for their car to be brought around.

Before Calvin had a chance to act, a black SUV pulled up on the opposite curb, and half a dozen men dressed in black jumped out and began shooting at the guards.

The women screamed and scattered when the two guards went down in a hail of bullets. One of them lay on the ground in a rapidly spreading puddle of blood, but he still returned fire as three of the men grabbed the fourth woman from the bar.

She screamed and kicked in an attempt to get away from them, but they were too strong for her.

Calvin took off toward them. He couldn't help but act, but as he picked up the pace, he started to remember that he wasn't at home here. For all he knew, her abductors might actually be her family come to her rescue or something.

He rejected that thought almost instantly. From the rough way the kidnappers were handling her, Calvin seriously doubted she knew any of them. They weren't careful with her at all, and Calvin's gut told him that if she were pulled into that car, she wouldn't be alive much longer.

He ran over to the two dead guards in the street and snatched up their weapons. He also swiped the extra clips from their belts. He didn't have time to stop and see if he could help them. He had to save the woman. The men had been taking too much fire in the beginning, so they'd sent the SUV around the block to pick them up in a safer location.

Calvin shoved the spare clips in his pocket and raised the gun in front of him as he cut behind the building, keeping his eyes peeled for the three guys and the woman. He found them a minute later, and stayed in the shadows at the edge of the building while he figured out the scene in front of him.

One of the guys had his hand over the woman's mouth, trying to muffle her screams as he dragged her toward the SUV. She screamed anyway and thrashed wildly against her captor's grip. She threw her head back against him, and Calvin heard the guy's nose crunch.

Calvin smirked. She was a fighter, that was for sure. Down the street, headlights flashed to hurry the kidnappers up, and he knew he had to help her right then and there, because once she was inside, there would be little he could do.

It would be his only chance

You got this, Marty whispered. *You've taken on way bigger assholes in the past, and they're not even demons.*

Thanks for the moral support, but shhh... I'm trying to think here.

Fine, fine, whatever. Humans—pieces of damn work every time.

Calvin ignored Marty's comments and began shooting as he ran to the rescue. The guard in the front went down with a shot to the head and the second turned with the woman, using her as a shield. She was still struggling to get free. Calvin didn't flinch. He maintained his pace, tossed the gun into his other hand, and punched the guard as hard as he could. The man let go of the woman and dropped to the ground like a brick.

Broken Nose came straight at him and Calvin shot him point-blank, then held his hand out to the woman and pulled her into the alley. They ran as fast as they could until they were across the next street and hiding behind a dumpster.

"*Esos sucios hijos de puta. Me iban a secuestrar. Necesitamos salir aquí. No hay ningún lugar seguro para estar aquí. Sabía que esta mierda iba a suceder. Solo lo sabía.*"

Calvin shook his head. He was trying to understand her, but he didn't speak Spanish. She wrung her hands in frustration, standing up and pacing back and forth. Calvin grabbed her arm and pulled her back down just as the SUV passed by, the men inside looking up and down the streets. She shook her head, not looking at Calvin.

"*¿A dónde voy? Que esta pasando? Sabía que esto era algo malo desde el principio. Nunca debería haberse conectado con él. Me ha metido en un mundo de problemas y ahora estoy aquí,*

165

con un hombre extraño y necesito calmarme, pensar. Vamos, piensa."

"Hey, slow down, I can't understand you." Calvin pointed to himself. "American, Calvin."

The woman gave him a snarky look and pointed to herself. "Bilingual, Sofia."

Calvin nodded and looked around the corner and back at her. "Do you need some help?"

She tilted her head at him. "How many bullets do you have?"

Calvin shrugged. "Probably not enough, but there are plenty of weapons one block over if we need them. Look, Sofia, I will help you if you want. It's what I do. But if my assistance isn't welcome please tell me, because I'm happy to go back to the Pacifica and sleep the night away. I'm supposed to be on vacation."

Sofia bit her lip while she considered Calvin's offer. She knew she could disappear into the city and probably be okay, but she wasn't sure she could make it all that way without being spotted and dragged back. On the other hand, she could go with this guy and try to figure out what to do next. It was a crapshoot either way, but she had no idea if she would be safe with him. He had saved her, killed two guys and knocked the other one out, so either he was some freak who wanted her all to himself or was actually the guy he seemed to be.

Finally, she looked up at him with a serious face. "Can you really help me? I mean *really*? Not just some crazy American gunslinger fantasy, but actually help me be safe?"

Calvin met her eyes, allowing his to flare bright red.

She let out a little gasp and took an involuntary step back. "You have a demon!"

He smiled gently to soften the effect for her benefit. "For some of us, the demons are our bitches." He half-expected Marty to complain about being called his bitch, but his demon didn't even scoff.

Calvin didn't wait for her answer; he didn't have time for that. The SUV would be back any minute, since it was clear that they wanted her and they weren't going to let go that easily. Whoever had ordered her kidnapping was bold enough to make it happen in the middle of the street in front of a busy club.

They returned to the end of the alley, and Calvin picked up all the dropped ammo and weapons. He filled his bathing suit shorts with the clips, and stuck the handguns in the waistband of his board shorts.

He made sure his shirt covered the weapons. Sofia jerked when the squealing of tires cut the night.

Calvin instantly went on full alert. He grabbed Sofia's wrist and they pelted to the next street over and hid in the shadows, but the car that went by was filled with loud, drunken tourists. They both sighed with relief, and Calvin pulled out his phone and dialed the number to the cab service the hotel had suggested. Sofia waited in the shadows while Calvin watched the street for the cab.

When the cab pulled up, Calvin glanced around to make sure it was safe before nodding to her. She ran over and jumped into the back of the cab, and Calvin got in after her. He slammed the door shut and nodded to the driver.

"The Pacifica, please."

As the cab set off down the street, Calvin indicated to Sofia that she should get out of sight. He bent over her as they passed by the SUV, and the cabbie raised an eyebrow and took the next right turn.

Sofia slowly sat up, pulling her hair to the nape of her neck. She shook her head, rubbed her bruised cheek, and peered out the window. Calvin put the gun down next to him on the seat and leaned his head against the window.

"*Gra—* Thank you...for stepping in like that," Sofia told him.

Calvin shook his head. "I couldn't just leave you to get kidnapped. Sofia, that's a pretty name."

"Thanks," she grumped. "Pretty names don't keep you out of ugly situations, unfortunately."

"No, but the person behind it can, at least most of the time."

She scoffed and crossed her arms over her chest, looking out the window and muttering to herself in Spanish. "*Gilipollas ignorante Él no me conoce. ¿Cómo se atreven a juzgarme? Lo que sea.*"

Calvin chuckled to himself and resumed his window-watching as the cab sped through the night toward the Pacifica. He cracked his window, and though he couldn't see the ocean in the dark, he could smell the salt and hear the waves hitting the sand. Sofia was a complication to his vacation, but he could not have turned his back on someone who needed help. He just wasn't built that way.

After they went through two checkpoints, the cab pulled up in front of the resort. The doorman opened the door, and Calvin paid the cabbie before he ushered Sofia to the entrance. He saw the fear Sofia was trying to hide.

"I want you to get another cab and wait for me. I have to grab my stuff, then we can get out of here."

She grabbed his arm. "No, I will go with you. I cannot take the chance of being seen."

Calvin scanned for threats as they hurried through the lobby of the resort to the elevators. Once they reached his room, he showed her inside and started to pack his bags. He hoped he would be back, but with the way things had spiraled out of control so quickly he was going to make sure he had all of his things.

Sofia stood in the living room, looking around with her hands clutched in front of her. "This is nice."

"Thanks." Calvin came out of the bedroom with a bag in each hand. "It was supposed to be a nice *long* stay."

"I know. I'm sorry. I—"

He dumped the bags and waved her off. "Not now. No time, and really, no need."

He smiled kindly at her as he picked up the phone and dialed the front desk. "I'd like to request a VIP transport as soon as possible, please. Yes, tinted windows would be preferable. You can charge it to the card on file for my room. Excellent, thank you."

He hung up the phone and looked at Sofia. "They'll ring twice when the vehicle is out front."

She nodded but didn't say anything. Calvin put his duffel bag on the stool at the breakfast counter and began to check through his newly-acquired loadout. He glanced at Sofia as she rubbed her arms. She was still wearing just a bathing suit and a sheer wrap. He didn't have anything that would fit her, but he figured a knee-length button-up was better than nothing until they could find somewhere to grab her some clothes.

"I still don't know how I got into this," she murmured, looking out the window. "I'm a foreign exchange student from the University of San Diego. If I had my passport, we could get out of town."

"Where is it?"

"My house about a mile away from here, but they'll probably be looking for me there."

"The people who tried to kidnap you?"

She shook her head. "No, the other ones."

Calvin was about to ask who the other people were when the phone rang twice, signaling that their ride had arrived. He sighed and placed one of the guns into the back of the jeans he'd changed into. He zipped up the bag and slung it over his shoulder, then grabbed the other one and nodded to Sofia.

"You ready?"

She returned his nod and followed him to the door. Calvin remained on high alert as he opened the door. He was pretty sure no one had followed them, but he wanted to be safe. The last thing he needed was a gun battle at the Pacifica.

They headed back downstairs, and the doorman was holding the door open for them. She jumped into the car, and Calvin surveyed the street to make sure no one was watching as he threw his bags into the trunk. He stopped for just a moment, watching the palm trees swaying. He couldn't escape his life. Trouble found him wherever he went, even in a beautiful place like this. He chuckled.

"Looks like my vacation is over until further notice."

Sofia might not be infected, and maybe none of the others were either, but he was in the middle of something now and there was no way out of it other than to fight. Protecting Sofia was the objective here. He shut the trunk, climbed into the car, and looked longingly at the Pacifica one last time.

It will still be there mañana, Marty told him. *Besides, there's nothing more relaxing than a good fight.*

15

Katie sat next to Angie in one of the hotel's boardrooms. Across from them was Debbie, the first of three interior designers they were planning on seeing that day. Katie had told Angie to pick the candidates as a test of her judgment. Debbie had a resumé that would make most mouths drop wide open. She had designed for some of the biggest names in New York and beyond, including some of the Kennedys, Meryl Streep, and one of the Bush twins. She was very professional but was a little nervous around Katie.

"So, I contacted your real estate agent and toured the home. It's very beautiful, and will be easy to work with."

"Thank you," Katie answered politely.

"Tell me what you're looking for. When you close your eyes and picture your home, what do you see?"

"I love light, but only in the living spaces, not the sleeping spaces. In my line of work, I often have to catch zees in the middle of the day, or whenever I can. I want something soft, without a bunch of hard edges, but the bathroom and kitchen must be modern. For my bedroom, I want to feel like I'm in a Victorian boudoir, and I need custom closet fittings for my lingerie collection."

"That sounds lovely. How about the main living area and the other bedrooms?"

"The living area is all about comfort. Soothing colors, a place to kick back and relax after a long hard day. As far as the other bedrooms, I would like to incorporate an office into the spare if possible, but it also needs to be a welcoming place for a guest to sleep. I was thinking white and fluffy like the hotels in New York."

Katie looked at Angie. "Angie, how do you want your room?"

Angie blinked. "Oh, well, I didn't really give it much thought. Comforting, secure, safe. I suppose that's not what you're asking..."

"No, that's enough to go on." Debbie smiled. "I can have this back to you tomorrow."

"Perfect." Katie smiled. "I would love a quote with it as well, though it can be an estimate. I understand things can change as we go."

"Will do." Debbie smiled back, standing up and shaking both women's hands.

"Now, if you'll excuse us, we have another appointment a couple of blocks away."

"No problem. I will speak with you tomorrow." Debbie closed her books and watched as Angie and Katie rushed out of the boardroom and out of the hotel.

As they hurried down the street, Katie looked at her watch and picked up the pace. They were going to be right on time to speak to Teresa, the second designer on the list.

She didn't have as much experience as Debbie, but Angie had loved her portfolio and the way she worked with light and created flowing designs.

The meeting with Teresa went a little faster since they were covering the exact same ideas for the space and discussing timeframe. Katie liked Teresa. She was spunky with a little bit of sarcasm in her, and not at all afraid of Katie. They ended their meeting with her and rushed back to the hotel restaurant, ready for their last meeting of the day. Sarah, the last designer, was already waiting for them, having gotten a table and ordered everyone salads as appetizers. Katie liked the take-charge attitude, but Pandora was less than pleased with a bowl of lettuce.

She's gonna lose, hands down, Pandora grumped as Katie went through the spiel for the third and final time. *There better be enough room in that kitchen for the donuts. Just saying.*

At the end of lunch, before Katie and Angie got up, the third designer excused herself, telling them she was eager to get to work since the deadline for quotes was so tight.

Katie waited until Sarah was out of the restaurant and out of earshot before letting out an exhausted sigh. It had been like speed-dating for interior designers.

"I need to get the information from all three presentations together. We gave them twenty-four hours to get back to us, and keeping to that timeframe will be vital. I'm planning on spending a lot of money, but the one resource I *don't* have a lot of is time. One of them is going to respect my time, and they will get the deal. Come on, we have a cab waiting. I have something to pick up, and I need you with me."

Angie's head was spinning, but she hung in there and

followed Katie out to the car. Katie handed the cabbie an extra tip to step on it, and the cab pulled out.

"Where are we going, miss?"

"Oh, sorry. Penn Station. The Apple Store."

The cab moved quickly in and out of traffic and got them to Penn Station in record time. Katie tipped him again and thanked him for rushing. They looked through the different shelves of electronics, and Katie finally decided on a twelve-inch MacBook for Angie. Katie was fully aware that it was a nice laptop, but it wasn't as powerful or nearly as expensive as the MacBook Pro.

I'm pleased to see you're being practical about this. If this doesn't work out and she steals it, you're only out half the money.

I'm not surprised that you're taking the cynical view, but she doesn't need the Pro, that's all. Angie came into our lives for a reason. I have faith—

Ugh, not this again.

Yes, this again. Can't you see the change in her? I know she's not the whole way there yet, but she's clearly trying, and all I can do is help her. If she chooses differently, then I did my best. Besides, it's only a computer.

"Take care of this." Katie smiled and handed it to Angie. "I figured you would need something to keep up with all this."

"That is so nice! Thank you." Angie smiled as they came out of the store. "I've never—"

Angie froze on the spot.

Katie narrowed her eyes and followed Angie's frightened gaze down the block. It was her ex-boyfriend, and he was heading straight for them. He became angry when he noticed Angie outside the store. He clenched his fists and started toward her—until he spotted Katie.

Katie let her eyes flash as she stared him down. He stopped, shook his head, and flipped them both the bird. Then he turned and headed back across the street the way he came.

Angie staggered back and grabbed the railing for support, then lowered herself to the steps right there in front of the store. She began to sob, but these were not tears of fear or sadness. A river of relief flowed from her eyes. She had realized that he had no power over her anymore.

Katie sat down next to Angie on the step and placed her hand on her shoulder. "I know this is all hard, even knowing you're free—and especially after a relationship like that. But you're strong, and this will make you stronger."

Angie sniffled, wiping her tears on her sleeves. "I know. It's just...that kind of relief is almost like another blow to the body, you know? It's good, but it's shocking. I think I've had enough of shocking for this lifetime."

"Ha! You're hanging with the wrong woman, then," Katie joked.

Angie chuckled through her tears. "I kind of had a feeling that was the case."

Katie got up from the steps. "You have a decision to make. You have to decide what it is that *you* want to do, not what someone *else* wants you to do."

"I'd like to explore this opportunity you've given me."

"I'm glad to hear that." Katie smiled.

Angie looked up with bloodshot eyes. "Is there anything I should know?"

Katie shrugged. "I can't promise you it's always going to be safe, and it could get pretty scary at times. But you'll always be doing something good for the world."

Don't forget she'll be getting laid.

There's that too. Katie chuckled.

Katie held a hand out to Angie. "Come on, let's get back to the hotel. I'll drop you off, and you can take a bath and set up the new computer."

Angie nodded, laughing at herself for being so emotional in the middle of the street. She took Katie's hand and stood up, looking back toward where her ex had walked away.

He was gone, and Angie hoped it would be the last time she ever saw him.

The cab pulled up a few blocks from Sofia's house, and Calvin looked out the window at the nice suburban neighborhood. The sleepy street contradicted the bustle of the tourist spot he'd found her in. Palm trees lined the sidewalk, and every house had a perfectly-manicured lawn. He remembered the houses he'd seen coming into Cabo the first time, and how they went from run-down to affluent in a heartbeat. He had to be honest—he had been expecting a more run-down area, but he wasn't sure why. Those drug lords had tons of money.

"Okay, tell me about the layout of the house."

Sofia nodded. "This is my house, per se. The guy who bought it for me, Manuel, lives with his wife and children in a very large house a ways away from here. Mine has three bedrooms, two baths, a kitchen, and is surrounded by a tall stone wall that wraps the whole perimeter, and there's an iron gate at the front. When you walk in the front door, you'll be in the foyer. In front of you will be stairs that lead to the three bedrooms. Mine is the first on the right. Downstairs, there are three doors. The far right one goes into the living area, the middle is the dining room, and the left is the kitchen—which also has a door to the outside."

"Okay, I can see that in my mind. What about the guards?"

"On a normal basis there are two, and right now they should be Eric and Jose. They are big guys, but not larger than you, and they'll be armed. They will not be alone for long. With the news of the death of the other guards and my possible kidnapping, there will most likely be a lot more of them showing up any minute. They will all expect me to come back to the house."

"Understood. And where is your passport?"

"Upstairs in the top drawer of my dresser, under my clothes. I hid it, not knowing what Manuel would do if he found it. He doesn't want me going back to the States."

"Got it." Calvin checked to make sure his gun was loaded.

He stuck it in the back of his pants and looked at the driver. "If anything crazy happens, like shooting, you get her somewhere safe. I will make it on my own."

"Yes, sir." The driver looked terrified.

"You stay here, Sofia, no matter what. Do you understand?"

"Yes." She nodded. "Thank you."

He chuckled. "Don't thank me yet. I haven't even gotten out of the car."

After he got out, he pulled his shirt down to conceal his weapon. He checked the street, but there were no cars around and no one outside.

He dashed across the street and slid into the shadow of the wall. He peered around the corner at the large iron gate, spotting a camera pointed at it.

He looked up at the eight-foot wall and shook his head. "I knew I wouldn't get out of this without some physical exertion."

Calvin was able to jam one foot into a crack in the wall and launch himself upward to grab the edge of the wall. He groaned mentally as he pulled himself up, and stole a look over the top. There was no one on the other side. He hauled himself the rest of the way up and perched on the top for a moment before jumping down on the other side. He dropped lightly onto the balls of his feet and crouched in the yard, listening carefully. He heard footsteps crunching through the gravel path that led to the front of the building.

He hurried to the side of the house and stood with his back pressed against the wall, waiting as the man got closer. When the guard turned the corner Calvin grabbed him, putting one hand over his mouth as he pulled his gun from the back of his pants and hit the man hard over the head. He caught him before he could hit the ground, in case the noise alerted his partner.

Calvin laid the guard on the ground, then dismantled his gun and scattered the pieces before rifling through his pockets. He had no ID, and nothing else of any importance on him. Calvin dragged him out of view and crept toward the back door. He peered around the frosted glass panel and saw the other guard standing at the kitchen sink with his back to Calvin.

Calvin opened the back door and rushed the guard, giving him no time to react. Calvin slammed the butt of his gun against the guy's head, knocking him out instantly. This time he let the asshole drop. He cleared the rest of the house to be sure there were no other guards, then made his way upstairs and into the first room on the right.

He pulled open the dresser drawer and rifled through, finding Sofia's passport at the bottom. Calvin looked at the jewelry on the dresser and the clothes in the drawers and rolled his eyes, knowing he needed to bring some of her stuff with him. There was a book bag on the chair, and a quick look showed him her college books packed neatly inside. He went through each drawer, grabbing a few things and shoving them in the bag. Before he closed it, he took the jewelry box with the diamonds—obvious gifts from her asshole boyfriend—and dumped them in the front. He zipped it shut and hooked it over his shoulder.

Calvin hurried from the room, back down the stairs, and into the kitchen. It was too dangerous for him to go out the front, with the extra guards probably on their way. He stepped over the guy on the kitchen floor on his way out the door.

He made short work of the wall, hitting the ground on the other side just as a car pulled up out front. He waited by the wall until the car was through and the gate was shut again before taking off down the street toward the waiting taxi.

As he approached Sofia pushed open the door, and he passed her the bag and got inside, shutting the door behind him. He told the cabbie to take off, wanting as much distance between them and the house as possible. Sofia opened her bag and grabbed her passport, which she kissed and held it to her chest. She ran her fingers over her schoolbooks and began to cry.

Sophie turned to Calvin, tears flowing down her face. "*Gracias, señor, por enviarme este hombre para ayudar. Muchas gracias*. Thank you so much. Now I won't fail my classes, and I can get out of this place. Thank you so much."

Calvin gave her a smile, touched that something as ordinary as homework meant so much to her. It was obvious she hadn't been made for the life he'd rescued her from. She'd just gotten caught up in something beyond her power to get out of.

She closed her bag and put her head back, wiping her tears. "I met Manuel while I was here on vacation. He seemed like such a sweet guy. He showered me with gifts, doted on me, and told me how much he loved me. I eventually found out about his wife, but it didn't matter because I believed he loved me. Eventually, though, things changed, and I discovered he wasn't the man I thought he was. I became a golden girl to him, someone to put on a pedestal. If I did anything that didn't fit his image of me he would get mad, and if I argued back he would hit me."

"Well, you are out of that life now." Calvin kept a lid on

the anger bubbling inside of him. "I will do my damnedest to make sure you get to safety."

Calvin hated to see her cry, and he hated her story. He hated the fact that some man had treated her like a possession. Hers was a story like something he'd see on television, not something he'd thought actually occurred. He'd been so absorbed with hunting demons that he'd forgotten humans were evil too. Bastards like Manuel lurked in the shadows, preying on the weak and the innocent and hurting women like Sofia.

She wasn't the only one out there, but she was the only one Calvin could help at that moment—and that was exactly what he was going to do.

16

"I want you to head toward Todos Santos," Calvin told the driver.

"But that wasn't the plan," Sofia protested. She scowled at Calvin. "I thought we were going to the airport to fly out of here. We need to get to the US as fast as we possibly can. What if they're tracking us?"

"It's likely they are, which is why the airport is a bad idea," Calvin whispered to Sofia, not wanting the cab driver to hear. He didn't know who he could trust anymore, so he wanted to keep everything between the two of them for now.

Her scowl deepened. "Then we go there and wait until we know it's safe. We can't just drive thirteen hundred miles with someone we don't know, and then what? Stand at the border?"

Calvin shrugged. "Our only choices are to either rent a car and go for the border or jump on a plane. We have our passports, so we should be able to drive right over. If we try to get on a plane, we'll have to be prepared for them to find us at the airport. Right now we're moving without them knowing where we are, but soon they'll figure it out. Don't you think the airport will be one of the first places they check? You know your sugar daddy better than me, but I can assume that if he's a drug lord, he'll have eyes all over that airport looking for you. He won't even have to take the trip out to get you. He'll just have his goons bring you to him."

Sofia sighed, then looked out the window and rubbed her face, considering the truth of Calvin's words. She wanted to take the least dangerous way back to the States, but the idea of driving thirteen hundred miles to get there was terrifying in its uncertainty. Anything could happen on the way there, and Manuel wasn't just powerful in Cabo. He was known all over Mexico. However, he would *definitely* have sent people to the airport, and a small chance of getting caught was preferable to a certain one. Finally convinced that Calvin was right, she looked at him and nodded.

"I guess disappearing over the border might be the better choice. He doesn't know about you yet, or at least I don't think he does, and he won't expect me to be able to go all the way up there. He covers everything and gives me no money."

"Right, so even if they find out, we have a head start. We'll find a car rental place, get something fast and gas efficient, and make a run for the border. Once we're close, they aren't going to be able to get there in time, no matter how fast Mr. Drug Lord's private planes are."

"Yeah." Sofia nodded. She wanted to feel certain about their plan, but she knew Manuel, so she knew escaping his clutches wouldn't be easy. He hated to lose, and he would be furious to be bested by some woman, and his mistress at that.

Sofia wrapped her arms around herself and pressed her head against the window. The driver drove in silence, stopping only for gas on the way to the small town. The scenery flew past Sofia's window, making her think of home, her family, and how she had worked so hard to get into a good school in the US—for what? So she could turn around and blow it all for a man who saw her as something to be owned? She had been dumb enough to believe he loved her. She couldn't help but beat herself up for allowing herself to be tricked into his gilded cage. A shudder passed through her as she realized what a lucky escape she'd had.

Calvin noticed her shivers, and he pulled a hoodie out of her bag and handed it to her. "Get dressed. I brought some clothes. I'll turn away."

She held the sweatshirt to her face and smiled. "This is the only thing I have that isn't a bathing suit or barely clothes. I'll have to wait until we get to the next town. Maybe they'll have something for me to wear there."

Calvin nodded, looking away as she pulled the sweatshirt over her head and stuck her hands in the front pocket. He felt for her. She knew she'd made a mistake, and now she had to pay for that. It wasn't fair. Love wasn't supposed to suck that badly.

When they finally made it to the town, the cab dropped them off with all their bags at the car rental place. Calvin rented the car and Sofia climbed in, tossing her bag in the back. He started to head out of town, but spotted a Walmart and pulled into the parking lot.

"Stay here. I'm going to grab you some stuff. What size do you wear?"

She lifted an eyebrow and smirked. "Five in shorts, small in shirts."

He nodded. "Got it."

Calvin ran into Walmart, grabbed a bunch of clothes, and threw them into a cart. He walked through the toiletries section and threw a few things in from there as well, including a box of hair dye. He grabbed a pair of scissors to cut the tags and went to the checkout line. When he got back to the car, Sofia was curled in the front seat, staring out the window.

Calvin climbed into the driver's seat and passed her the bags. "I'm sorry it's not high fashion, but they're clothes."

She smiled as she looked through the bags. "This is great, honestly. It'll be nice to wear something he didn't pick out. Can we go to that gas station? I'll change in the bathroom."

"Sure."

Sofia went into the small outside bathroom and selected a pair of jeans shorts, a white tank top, and a plaid button-up shirt from the bag. She looked at the hat he'd bought and chuckled at the picture of the Mexican flag on the front. She reached deeper into the bag and pulled out the scissors, then stared at herself in the mirror. She shrugged and grabbed a chunk of her long hair, cutting it up to her chin. She then pulled down some in the front and sliced across, cutting blunt bangs. She pulled the box of dark auburn dye from the bag and went to work, giving herself a quick color change.

While she waited to rinse the dye off, she read through a magazine Calvin had thrown in the bag. It was a women's magazine, but it wasn't high fashion or how to please your man. It was about independence and taking control of your life. When the time was up, she washed the dye from her hair and flipped the hand dryer upside down to dry her hair as best she could. When she was done, she fluffed her bangs. She'd almost forgotten that in real life she actually had straight hair. She had only spent hours making it curly because that was what Manuel liked.

She tossed the hair in the trash and pulled the ball cap down over her eyes, nodding determinedly at her reflection in the mirror before she left. When she got back out to the car Calvin just blinked at her, not even recognizing her for a moment.

"Wow, I like that. You look…more yourself, I think."

"Yeah." She scoffed. "Well, it's time I became a different me. Otherwise, I might die."

"That's very true."

"Uh, you might want to get on the road, though."

"Why?" Calvin sat up, on alert as he looked around the parking lot.

She waved him off. "No, it's not that. I kind of made a mess in the bathroom. I'm not used to having such a small space, and the coloring kind of went all over the place, I won't lie. At first glance, it looks like someone was brutally murdered in there."

She held up her red-stained palms and shrugged innocently. Calvin leaned his head back and laughed loudly as he put the car in reverse. They pulled out of the gas station parking lot and turned on the GPS, setting their sights on the United States border. Calvin had already gassed up at the last place they'd gone, so he didn't have to stop for a while.

He glanced at Sofia, who, for the first time since he'd met her, actually looked like a normal person. She didn't look all glitzed and glammed, she wasn't draped in diamonds, and she didn't seem to have an issue with self-esteem. It was crazy how she was more *her*, more confident, and a lot more beautiful in just some shorts, a tank top and shirt, and a ball cap. Calvin had been right about her from the beginning. Sofia didn't belong in that world. She was just a young woman who had been pulled in over her head. She needed to get back to California and the life she had started for herself.

Katie sat at the kitchen table in her hotel room with her feet up on another chair and took a bite of her reheated donut. Pandora wasn't playing. She hadn't allowed Katie to even get *close* to ten in the morning before waking her up demanding her rotund confections. This time Katie didn't complain; she just got up and did it.

Part of the joy of waking you up is the bitchfest, but all I'm getting this morning is silence. What's with that?

I dunno. Katie shrugged. *I've just got a lot of new things going on.*

So you're as excited as a disgusting child at Christmas.

I wouldn't say excited. *I still have no idea what I'll be doing, but I guess I'm ready to move forward. It's time to explore. There's a whole new world of opportunities. Spread my wings. I may have a demon inside me, but I have something that most other people don't, and that's the funds and connections to accomplish whatever I want.*

Within reason. You're still part of the hated.

Meh, who cares what other people think? A year ago, I was facing an uncertain future. I had no idea what to expect after college, except a life with no money. The only example of adulthood I had was my mother's struggle to take care of me. More money than I knew what to do with was something I didn't even fantasize about. After you came along, my future became one of being locked in the basement, stuck fighting demons until one took me out. Now, the sky is the limit. It's intriguing, to say the least.

Pandora faked gagging. *How romantic.*

Don't worry, you'll be along for the ride. Maybe one day we'll buy a Krispy Kreme franchise, and you can have all the donuts your little heart desires.

Now, that is the kind of plan I can get behind.

Just then there was a knock on the door. Katie groaned and took her feet off the chair. She went to let Angie in with a donut in her hand. Angie looked surprised that Katie was up but didn't say a word, just followed her inside and sat down.

"You want a donut and some milk?"

"Sure." Angie smiled, reaching into the box and taking a donut.

Katie passed her a bottle of milk and finished the last bite of her own. "Once we settle on the condo and get the decorator in we can get all moved in there, not that either of us has much to move."

"Yeah." Angie chuckled.

"Then you can get set up in the office, and we can start building a business or five."

Angie laughed. "I love the way you're so motivated, even though you don't know what you're motivated *about*."

"We'll find something to put all my energy into."

How about another donut? Pandora supplied.

Katie grabbed her wallet from the table and pulled out a hundred bucks. She put it down and slid it over to Angie.

"What's this for?" she asked through a mouthful of donut. "You can't just keep giving me money."

"It isn't a gift, it's so I can contact you. If you insist I'll take it out of your salary, just as soon as I figure out how much that will be."

Angie nodded. "Okay, I understand. What is our first venture going to be?"

Katie leaned back in her chair and looked at the ceiling. That was a really, *really* good question. Whatever it was, it should be easier than her experience of building the ammunition and weapons factory with Korbin and the team. All the people who'd helped with that venture came flooding through her mind, and she realized that she was going to need some sort of staff support for whatever it would be. That made Katie mentally roll her eyes. She never was very good at the whole staff thing.

Ha! Maybe you are in farther over your head than you thought.

No, I just need to take it one step at a time. Like, what will we call my corporation? If I have one of those, I can make as many businesses under it that I want.

How about Lilith Enterprises?

No.

Fine. How about Affliction Inc or Limbo LLC?

No and no. That's just asking for trouble.

All right, how about Rogue Nation?

Again with the demon references.

Well, you are *part demon, and this is the time of the red-eye.*

How about Angelic Inc or Seraph Corp? Something with my other side in it.

Pandora made horrible gagging noises.

Katie chuckled. *How about we wait on the name until later?*

Kajesus, please do. You are making me nauseous.

Katie looked up at Angie, remembering she'd asked her a question. "Oh, uh, sorry, zoned out. I don't know what I want to do. I guess it will come to me. I'll be back in a few. I'm gonna get dressed."

Angie nodded and returned to the donuts. Katie disappeared into her room for about twenty minutes, and when she heard boots clicking against the floors, she wiped her hands and turned around in her chair.

Angie's jaw dropped at the sight of Katie entering the room wearing her leather ensemble. Her eyes widened further at the weapons strapped around her body. Her gaze went to Katie's legs. "What are *those* for?"

Katie winked at her and patted her pistols. "They're my big-ass pistols for killing big-ass demons. If *they* knock? The demons always listen."

Katie pulled on a large knee-length black coat that covered the majority of her arsenal. Somehow, even with all that gear and that big heavy coat when it was not cold outside, Katie still looked feminine and chic. She ran her hands over the white faux-fur collar and grinned.

"The fur collar always gets them. They never assume I have guns underneath a coat with a fur collar. Okay, I have to get going. You get the designers' quotes by the end of the day, get yourself a phone, and see if you can find out where all the donut shops are within a five-mile radius of the new place. You know it will be an issue if I don't find out."

"Yes, ma'am." Angie nodded.

They walked out, and Angie saluted her and turned to go to her room while Katie took the elevator down to the lobby.

Katie was on a mission. She was going to not only make the world a better place, but she was also going to make some serious cash while she did it. She walked out to the curb and got in the back of one of the taxis parked out front. The guy looked askance at her in the mirror, wondering why she was wearing such a heavy coat.

"Where to?"

"Uh, not really sure. I need you to just drive straight. I'll tell you where to stop."

The cabbie lifted an unconcerned shoulder. "All right then, lady. Your dime."

Katie paid close attention to where they were going as the cab moved through the city. He stopped at a traffic light, and the burning sensation in her chest began. It was light, so she knew they were getting close, but they weren't there yet. The cabbie drove four more blocks, and Katie rubbed her chest, feeling the pulsing.

"Take a right at this next light and stop. I'll get out there."

The cabbie looked up at the road and back at her, slowing the cab down. "Are you sure?"

"Yeah."

This is bullshit. I don't feel a damn thing. This has to be your angelic powers. I bet you that bastard Gabriel is somewhere around here being Creepy Stalker, just like before. Whenever he shows up, we end up doing some weird fucking shit.

Relax.

Relax? Fuck, no! I want to use your eyes to look around.

The cabbie made a right and pulled to the curb. Katie ignored Pandora and handed the cabbie the fare and tip, then got out of the cab and paused as the driver rolled the window down.

"Are you *sure* you want to be out here on your own? This is a bad place to be for someone as pretty as you."

"Aw, thanks for caring about me." Katie smiled and slipped him another ten. "But yeah, I've got this."

Katie walked away before he could protest further, rubbing her hand across her chest as the energy pulsed again. She entered the first building, but felt no surge. She left the building and continued her search, going from one messed-up run-down building to the next, seeking the disturbance she had felt before. She knew there was trouble nearby. It was calling to her.

The crazy thing was, she could no longer tell whether she would be facing a demon or just an evil human. Her new powers were a little confusing, but she knew that whatever was happening to her, there was a reason behind it.

17

K atie focused her senses as she passed building after building looking for the cause of the burning in her chest.

As she walked deeper into the neighborhood, the ambiance began to change. She heard languages other than English and a tang of spice lingered in the air, making her mouth water. She'd entered the part of town where the Middle Eastern community was situated. Those who acknowledged her as she passed were courteous and kind. It was actually a lot more comfortable than the gang area, but she knew something was creeping up on her.

Something in the wind that told her she was in the right place. It was an eerie feeling, and too elusive to pin down. She couldn't shake the slasher-movie vibe even though the sun was shining brightly and the people hadn't shied away from her—which just added to the creep factor.

She picked up her pace as the burning turned into a tugging sensation like a homing beacon searching out its other half. She turned right, then left, and then right again, following the intense feeling in her chest. She knew she was on the right track, but she didn't know just how much longer it would actually take to reach the source.

When Katie turned the next corner, she stopped dead in her tracks. She was facing a large mosque set back off the road. Arabic writing was colorfully painted across the front of the building, and children played happily on the playground. To the right was the minaret, square at the bottom and narrowing to a point at the top. The sounds of afternoon prayer were pumping from the attached speakers, and Katie stood with her hands in front of her waiting for it to end. When it did, many people came out of the building, all cheerful. They were shaking each other's hands and talking joyfully.

Katie didn't want to admit it at first, but the feeling in her chest was pulling her directly to the mosque. She shook her head and tried to fight the feeling, but she could almost hear Gabriel's voice inside her head telling her about the terrorist attacks using demons. Why did it have to be a religious thing, after everything New York had been through in the last decade?

"This is going to be a shit show of epic proportion." Katie sighed and set off toward the mosque as the last of the prayer crowd left for their homes.

She had been given a task, and no matter how much she didn't like it, she had to see it through. As she passed onto the property, she glanced at the children playing, laughing, and shouting to each other. She looked at the man standing outside of the doors of the mosque and smiled in his direction.

"How can I help you?" he asked, eyeing her strangely.

"I was wondering if I could speak to your Imam?" she asked politely. "It is 'Imam,' right?"

"That is what we call him, yes, but I cannot let a woman not covered modestly into this facility. It is a shame on this house and a shame on our protector, Allah. Disgraceful woman! Harlot!"

Katie tilted her head at the guy. That was when she got pissed.

The Imam put his hand on the young man's shoulder, nodding. "This is the will of Allah. If the demons are coming, so will the naysayers. We must show the world that those who go against God end up on the other side of the light."

"Yes, Imam," the young man replied a little hesitantly. "In the name of Allah."

"Exactly," he replied, an evil look glimmering in his eyes. "You will need to clear your mind and open up to let the demon enter you. Do not fight him. Remember, this is your destiny, and you will find your place in heaven."

The boy nodded, but the Imam could tell he was still very nervous. *"Adhhab mae allh. Sawf yakun maeak dayima. Tadmir alkufaar hayth yaqfuna. Sawf najid makanana fi hadha alealam."*

The boy bowed his head at those words and replied, *"Qad yakun allah maeik."*

"And with you, my son. Remember, let the change happen in the center of Times Square."

A grunt outside pulled the Imam's attention to the door behind them, and the door swung open. The man from the front was standing there with a thin stream of blood flowing from his nose.

The Imam clenched his fists tightly, enraged. "What are you doing?"

Katie put both hands on his back and pushed him hard into the room, then rapped him over the head with her knuckles as she stormed past him to the Imam. All three of them watched as his eyes rolled back in his head and he hit the ground, unconscious. The Imam backed away, throwing his arms up in outrage.

"Harlot! Infidel! How dare you walk into this holy temple with no shame? Leave at once!"

Katie looked up from the guy on the floor and smiled at the Imam. Slowly, she raised her hand toward him and extended her middle finger. The Imam spluttered and scrambled to get behind his desk. He reached for the phone, but she grabbed the cord and yanked the entire thing from the desk.

She stepped delicately toward him, slowly shaking a finger at him. "Tsk, tsk, tsk. *Bad* Imam. You are no man of God. You've tricked these poor people into believing in hate instead of love. Is *that* what Allah asks of you?"

The Imam glared daggers at her. "You know nothing!"

Katie gave him a knowing smile. "I know more than what *you* want anyone to know."

The Imam's eyes darted around the office in panic. Katie stopped just steps from his desk and pushed the chair out of the way. She watched him scramble for a moment, glad she could feel his fear.

"You have been duly Judged for dealing directly with demons. Your sentence is death."

Uh, do you have that ability? Pandora sounded concerned. *I mean, it's not like I wouldn't be against you doing it, but can this get you in trouble?*

Pandora would have pushed harder for an answer, but it became a moot point when the Imam grabbed a rifle from under the desk. She reacted before he'd even swung the rifle up.

She kicked the desk forward, slamming it into the Imam. He was knocked backward and pinned between the wall and the desk and the rifle went off, blowing holes in the ceiling. Katie squinted and waved her hand through the air, trying to clear the dust and debris that sprinkled from the ceiling.

She caught a glint of metal through the dust, and the young man screamed as he came at her, holding a knife high above his head. Katie turned around and rolled her eyes before grabbing his hand before he could strike her. She pushed him back into the table and put her hands in the air, waiting for him to regain his footing. He tossed the knife back and forth in his hand, slicing several times through the air. Katie moved and ducked, although the blade almost caught her chest.

Katie swept the guy's leg, knocking him to the ground, and the knife clattered onto the floor next to him. She stood over him as he groaned and rubbed his eyes, trying to clear his vision, then knocked him out with a kick to the jaw. She pulled her left pistol from its holster, turning around and aiming it at the Imam.

"I call this bad boy 'Tom.'"

The Imam stared wide-eyed down the barrel of her huge gun. His eyes flicked toward the rifle in his hand, but he didn't move a muscle.

Katie inclined her head toward the rifle. "Go ahead. Make my day."

The Imam shifted his eyes again, sweat starting to bead on his forehead. He glared his hatred at Katie, not realizing that her femininity had no bearing on the kind of woman she was. He didn't actually think Katie would kill him. He wasn't a demon, he wasn't possessed, and he was familiar with her and her kind.

"You're a demon hunter." He scoffed. "You do not kill humans."

Katie's lip curled as she spoke. "It really depends on your definition of 'human.' I don't think trying to kill thousands of people qualifies you to call yourself human."

The Imam smirked. "You are a woman, incapable of killing in cold blood."

"Righhht. That makes *so* much sense."

The Imam was at an impasse with Katie, and he weighed his options. Finally, still not believing she would do it, he swung the rifle up to shoot her.

Katie shot him in her next breath, splattering his skull into a hundred fragments against the wall behind him. She watched his body slide down the wall and shrugged as she put "Tom" back into his holster.

Shouts in the background let Katie know she wasn't done. She pulled out the pistol on her right hip and smiled. "All right, Harry, it's your turn now."

How the hell did you come up with the names Tom and Harry for your pistols?

Katie laughed. *Because between Tom and Harry is usually Dick, but this time it's a bitch.*

Katie crept to the doorway and peered out, pulling her head back quickly as bullets sprayed past her. She hooked the door with her foot and slammed it shut, then reached down and pressed the catch on the door handle to give herself a few moments of peace before the cavalry came charging into the Imam's office. Not even a minute later the bullets smashed straight through the door, hitting the guy on the ground and peppering the bookshelves at the back of the room.

A few moments later five men, including the guy whose nose she'd broken, charged in. Katie took three of them out as soon as they walked through the door. One headshot, one dead guy.

The other two charged at her, unloading their weapons with zeal. Katie ducked behind the desk and waited until she heard the clicks indicating empty magazines, then stood in one fluid motion, firing as she came up. Both men fell to the ground, a bullet buried in each of their brains.

Goddammit! These bullets are so fucking expensive to make. They're supposed to be for the big demons, not crazy humans. Talk about piss-poor planning. I should have known there wasn't some huge-ass demon rolling through here.

Ha! Pandora laughed. *It looks like your heaven-dar is a little out of whack. Maybe you should have figured that shit out before bursting in here.*

Well, it's done now. Shit.

Just then a bullet buried itself in the wall next to her head. A lone ranger came rolling into the room, screeching at the top of his lungs.

Katie grabbed a gun from a body and unloaded into him, only stopping when she saw light through the holes in his body. The guy hit the floor, and Katie shook her head in disgust and threw the empty gun to the side.

I think that's all of them. Fuck, I got eight non-dusty bodies here. Maybe I should have waited until the demons were inside them. It might have made it a bit easier to explain.

You probably want to explain it to the cops that way, or we are going to find ourselves up Shit Creek without a paddle.

Katie sighed and leaned back against the desk, looking around at the mess. She pulled out her phone and Schultz's number. She really didn't want to deal with it, especially since none of it could be explained, but she had no choice. There were eight bodies on the floor around her.

"This is Schultz."

"Hey, it's Katie."

"Oh, hey there. What's up?"

"Well, you're gonna want to send some men out to the mosque that we went by yesterday."

"Why?"

"There was a bit of a misunderstanding here. I came here to check things out based on a gut feeling and found that the Imam has been grooming suicide bombers, only he was going to use demons instead of bombs to attack people. I got here just as he was about to send them out to Times Square. I walked in on him talking to one of the humans he was going to use. One thing led to another, there was an argument, and it ended in a couple of fatalities."

"Wow, that's intense. So, a couple. Should I send one or two coroner trucks with the cops?"

"Um…it was more like eight fatalities."

Schultz dropped the phone. When he picked it up again, his voice was incredulous. "Holy shit, Katie! Eight is not 'a couple!'"

"Look, I stopped shooting when they stopped rushing me with automatic weapons."

"All right, all right. Hold tight. We'll be over there shortly."

Katie disconnected and sat on the edge of the desk to wait for the detectives. About ten minutes later, the sirens outside had increased enough in volume for Katie to surmise the cops had finally shown up. She stayed put, waiting until they got to the Imam's office. She pulled her coat around her again, thinking it would be best if they didn't get a glimpse of the arsenal she had strapped to her body. Not all of the cops knew who she was or what she did, and she wanted to keep it that way.

Travers and Schultz entered the mosque and made their way to the office, skirting all the puddles of blood on the floor. Katie nodded as they walked inside. Travers was still taking in the carnage beyond the office, shaking his head in disbelief.

Schultz came over to Katie and stood beside her looking around with concern. "This is pretty heavy."

"You should have seen it when it was going on," Katie replied.

Travers eyed Katie skeptically. "Why haven't any of the bodies turned to dust? I thought that was what demons did? This looks like a bunch of dead humans."

Katie was about to snap at him, but Schultz put his hand up. "I called the general as soon as I got off the phone with Katie. He told me that if Katie said there were demons, then there were fucking demons, and to write it up. So, yes, there will be a shit-ton of paperwork, but there won't be any issues with IA. You're good to go if you'd rather not stick around, Katie. We have a clean-up crew waiting outside to take care of all this."

Travers snickered as Katie picked her path carefully, trying not to get blood on her boots. He had assumed she would be squeamish about walking through all the blood and gore from the body parts spread out all over the floor.

Katie narrowed her eyes at him. "Think I'm squeamish? I could always punch you in the balls and use your body as a bridge so I don't mess up my boots."

His smile quickly faded.

Laughing, Katie strolled casually through the blood and guts as she exited the room. There was little those days that could turn her stomach, not even the entrails of a human body.

The cops were going to learn real fast that she was tougher than she looked.

Manuel paced back and forth in the house he had bought for Sofia. He stared at the picture on her dresser. It was of the two of them together on his yacht, taken just months after they'd met. He looked for her jewelry box, but it was empty, just like her drawers. He slammed his fists on the dresser, rattling the mirror on the wall. He breathed heavily, his teeth clamped together, pissed as hell that his woman had been taken from him.

"Calm yourself, Manuel. You'll get your girl back. I am the one who lost valuable men, lives that can never be returned."

The gang member who had sent his men to kidnap Sofia stood in the doorway of the bedroom. The light caught the gold rings he wore on almost every finger, complementing the pressed silk shirt tucked into his black dress pants. The men had been after each other for years. They were rivals in both their businesses and their lives, but for this, they'd called a temporary truce. They were determined to hunt down the stranger who was responsible for all the chaos.

Manuel took a deep breath and smoothed his hair back. "They caught him on camera, and they're printing us off a picture right now. They're also sending it to our men at the airport so they can keep an eye out for them."

"Do you actually think she's so dumb she would try to take a flight out? No, she is much smarter than that, my friend. She is on wheels, with this *bolsa de mierda.*"

"And what is your suggestion?"

"We take the picture, leave some men at the airport, and head north toward the border. I will make some calls to the Border Patrol, and post guards on my payroll to let them know to be on the lookout. Even if they get there before us, they will not make it to the other side."

"I want her unharmed."

"Even after her betrayal?"

Manuel rubbed his hands together. "I didn't say she would *stay* that way. The bitch will be reminded of her place, and she'll feel the wrath of my hands once again. By the time I'm done with her, she will be thankful if she can crawl out of this house and beg in the streets in her own filth."

18

Katie left the mosque, but glanced over her shoulder. She sighed, shaking her head at the bloody boot prints she'd left in her wake. There was no way she was walking the entire way back and leaving a trail of the enemy's blood behind her. She walked over to the empty ambulance sitting to the side while the coroners were inside the mosque, grabbed a clean rag and a bottle of alcohol from the back, and poured the liquid over the soles of her boots. Katie sat down on the sidewalk and scrubbed off the gore as best she could.

She took one last look around. The playground across the way was empty now, the swing slowly swaying back and forth.

When her boots were clean, she started her walk back to the Stewart Hotel. She was thankful that she wasn't tracking blood everywhere, given the number of people who had been drawn from their homes by the gunshots and sirens. They weren't looking so friendly anymore.

Most of the people she passed were more worried about what was going on at the mosque than her.

That had been a hard call. It hadn't turned out as she'd thought it would at all, and she was starting to wonder when Gabriel would show up to explain himself.

Don't you get it? Angels explain themselves less than demons do, Pandora growled. *It's the whole "God works in mysterious ways" thing.*

Yeah, well, the detectives—those two idiots—didn't make it any easier. I can't believe that after the club op, they still don't understand who I am. They didn't think for a second that I was capable of doing something like that. There was danger, and I took care of it. That's my job. It just happened that these bodies didn't disappear in a cloud of dust.

I suppose dust is easier on the senses for humans than entrails and chunks of brain matter.

Maybe for them, but it's all the same to me. But come on— they had it coming. All religion aside, I can't believe anyone would be so idiotic that they would think using demons as a weapon was a really good way of showing the public a thing or two. Have they not been watching the news? Have they not realized by now that when they plan something stupid like that, they will get their fucking asses handed to them?

It's been done like this for thousands of years. I have seen demons used for the craziest reasons. It's shocking what humanity can make itself believe when it wants to. Gore, murder, religion, politics—it always gets spun, and human beings twist their minds to believe one violent action is worth it to get their point across.

Right, and usually somewhere in their point is peace. For some reason, humans believe you can achieve peace with violence. I am human—well, sort of—and I can't wrap my head around that.

It's shock value, sister. They want you to be afraid. They rule like that in hell, too, maintaining power by fear instead of trust. What's comical to me is how your people look down so hard on the way hell operates—even the way religion operates—yet they use the same tactics up here. Rule by fear, follow because of fear, vote because of fear. It's all the same tactic, just watered down. You don't torture people in the town square anymore... Well, at least in this country you don't. But it doesn't make drone strikes, war, or murder any different. It's still an eye for an eye.

That was intense, Pandora. She found her way back to the Stewart and walked into the lobby with her coat pulled tightly around her. The day manager looked up and nodded, too busy with the line of people at the concierge desk to stop and talk to her. She was glad. She just wanted to get up to the room, change, and get some food. She was starving, and living off Krispy Kremes wasn't cutting it anymore.

Her room was quiet when she got upstairs, and she tossed her heavy coat on the couch. Katie looked longingly at the bed, wishing she could take a nap, but her hunger was in the way. She pulled off her vest and belt, and carefully set her large pistols on the bedside table. She selected a pair of black wide-legged pants and a white button-up blouse, pausing to rub her stomach.

"If it's not you hounding me for food, it's my own body," she grumbled out loud.

At least you know you'll never go hungry. There will always be someone reminding you to stuff your face. Where are we going for lunch, anyway?

We... Katie grunted as she tightened the strap on her small holster, *are going to get a delicious Italian lunch.*

Oooh, it's been a while since we had Italian, and I've heard New York is an excellent place to find authentic Italian food.

That's what I've heard too, which is why we're going to chow down.

Katie pulled on her business jacket and checked in the mirror to make sure it hid the smaller pistol she'd strapped to her hip. She still looked nice, but her outfit wouldn't hold her back if she needed to run. These days, she could never tell when she would find herself in some sort of battle. Apparently, it wasn't just when the demons called to her. Now it was a wide variety of criminals. She reached up to smooth her hair back into a ponytail.

You look like you work on Wall Street, or even worse, like one of those FBI agents right out of training. Hello, Clarice!

Katie snickered. *Well, then I make the FBI look damn good. And nobody will be pairing me with a dry white wine, I can guarantee it.*

Hell, *yeah.*

Katie checked her wallet to make sure that she had cash and her card was still in there, then put her phone in her back pocket and flicked off the lights. She grabbed the Do Not Disturb sign from her doorknob and hung it on the door outside so the maids wouldn't come and freak out when they found her weapons and bloodstained clothes. That was the one thing she struggled with when staying at hotels—she had to be careful of the most unsuspecting threats. The government might have put her up in the Stewart, but that didn't mean someone couldn't cause one hell of an issue for her while she was here.

Katie glanced toward Angie's room, but the Do Not Disturb was on the door so she took the elevator down to the first floor and did a walk-by of the computers. She didn't see Angie anywhere, but she wasn't worried. She figured the woman was holed up in her room working on her new computer. She had given her a shitload of things to accomplish. The donut list alone would take her hours, especially in a city like New York where there was something to eat every five feet.

She took the escalator to the lobby and smiled at the concierge on her way outside to grab a cab. Lunch was just waiting for her, and she could already taste the ravioli.

Calvin and Sofia drove quietly in the rental car with the windows cracked and music playing. The sun had gone down a couple of hours before, and Calvin blinked his tired eyes at the blurry lines in the road. Beyond the road, the ocean crashed against the shore, and the smell of saltwater filled the car. Calvin squinted to his left, seeing a sign for the next turnpike with the symbol for a layover area on it. He slowed the car and turned off his lights as he eased them into the small space. It was secluded, with several palm trees shielding them from the road.

Calvin yawned as he cut the engine. "Figured it would be a good time to stop and sleep for a little bit."

Sofia yawned in response and stretched out her arms as best she could. "I'm good with that."

They were far enough off the road to be safe and close enough to the shore to enjoy the sound of the waves washing up on the sand. Calvin leaned his seat back and put his arms under his head, looking at the sky through the moonroof. He closed his eyes and listened to the ocean, pretending for a moment that he was still in his hotel room enjoying his vacation.

"I'm sorry I ruined your time off," Sofia whispered, leaning the seat back and turning on her side. "I know you must work a lot, with everything going on right now."

Calvin opened his eyes. "It's all right. That was still more vacation than I've had in a long time."

"Tell me about your life," Sofia pressed.

Calvin turned over on his side and faced Sofia. "Honestly? I've been a mercenary for a very long time. I was SWAT back in the day. One day we got a call, and I went out with my boys and a priest that we always had with us. Now, don't underestimate that—this priest was a badass. Well, the entire team except me and the priest were killed, and that was when I got infected. Korbin, the old leader of the team, came right in, picked us up, and took us in. It was history after that. I became a Korbin's Killer, and that transitioned into Katie's Killers. We've been part of so many incursions, including the big one—the one that brought demons to the foreground of the media."

Sofia tilted her head in surprise. "I guess, like so many others, I didn't realize you guys were out there doing all this and saving so many lives. I can't imagine how hard it has to have been for you."

"It was rough for a while, but we became a family. We work together, play together, and make as much out of our lives as we can between the fights."

"Have you lost a lot of those people?"

"Yeah." He sighed, thinking about the family he'd lost along the way. "Not all to death. Some were exorcised and sent back to live their lives, but yeah, others were killed in the line of duty. My team is now four people. One of them isn't a fighter, one of them is intel, and then, there's Katie, who has stood by us all for quite a while now. On Incursion Day I watched men and women go into battle and make the ultimate sacrifice for the future of mankind. That's how I get past the loss. I remember that what we're doing is good. That it's for the future of this planet. I couldn't ask for a better calling in life, and I think Katie and the others along the way have felt that way too."

Sofia gave Calvin a gentle smile and turned over on her back. "You have had quite the life."

"What about you?" Calvin asked. "What's your story?"

"Oh, nothing as crazy as yours." She laughed. "My parents live in Mexico City. My father is an architect, trying to make Mexico more beautiful one building at a time, and my mother is a doctor. They work well together, always trying to make the world a better place. Kind of like you."

Calvin smiled and nestled into the seat, fascinated to hear how this girl got to that moment, running from a drug lord and trying to make her life right.

"I went to the University of San Diego to get a better education. It was easy for me to get back into Mexico with my passport, and the college wasn't too far away from family. I started out as a medical student, wanting to follow in my mother's footsteps, but once I got into the program and learned the politics of it all, I decided it wasn't for me.

My father urged me to take architecture, but it was just so boring. I didn't have a spark for it at all."

"Sometimes it's hard for us to move out of our parents' shadows to find what *we* really want to do."

"It is." She smiled. "But I finally figured it out, and it's so exciting to me. I chose genetic medical engineering. It's fascinating, especially with all the new information coming out about demons."

Sofia looked at Calvin and caught the glint of red in his eyes. She grimaced, realizing that the information she had just mentioned mostly came from the R&D on humans infected with demons. She'd heard how the infected felt about that, and it wasn't always positive.

"I'm sorry." She grimaced again. "I completely forgot that you were infected, and I went on a crazy rant about doing research on people like you."

Calvin shrugged, giving her a reassuring smile. "It's not an ideal situation, but perhaps we can make some lemonade out of lemons. We know that being infected is not a positive thing for a person. Most of us in the mercenary circle dream of a day when we won't be infected anymore, and the research offers us the opportunity to explore what really happens to us when the infection occurs. Hopefully, it will lead to a cure or a treatment that will help those who cannot help themselves. Either way, it's not a secret that this goes on."

Sofia nodded and reached up to cover her mouth as she yawned. Calvin smiled and clicked off the interior light, letting out a deep breath. They had another hard day of driving ahead of them, and he needed to make sure he was rested and ready to hit the ground running. He didn't want to give Manuel any more time to catch up to them than he could help.

"Get some sleep, Sofia. We'll have plenty of time to talk in the morning."

"Good night, Calvin."

Calvin turned over in his seat and tried to get as comfortable as he could. He was concerned about not having anyone on lookout, but they both needed their rest. He'd been starting to nod off while driving, which wasn't like him at all.

Don't worry, I don't sleep, Marty whispered as if Sofia could hear him. *I'll stay up and keep watch. You let your body rest. I gave you as much energy as I could while you were driving.*

Thanks, Marty. Calvin yawned. *I appreciate it a lot.*

Just those words made Marty feel just a little better, after being called a bitch.

———

There was no one inside the tall old vacant building on the outskirts of Brooklyn except a few vagrants and the occasional rat or stray cat. The stairs to the basement were always locked, but there was one who had the key. In the depths of the damp, dark cellar, another leader stood with his arms crossed, facing a wall lit by candles.

He turned as footsteps approached, and three men holding flashlights and looking slightly uneasy emerged from the shadows.

The leader greeted them with a wavering voice. "You came."

"Of course," one of the men answered. "*Inshallah.*"

"Good. You'll be accepting the demons, and after the events this afternoon, it all may fall on your shoulders."

"We heard about what happened at the mosque, as well as the capturing of the demons and the killing of the humans by that mercenary. We stayed away from the mosque today, and don't plan on going back. It was all a cover anyway, to help do your bidding. No one will trust us now, knowing we had strong ties to the Imam. Surely, they will not welcome us back to the mosque."

"No, they most likely won't," the leader replied, rubbing his chin and pacing back and forth. "However, that does not stop our mission. The Times Square event has of course been stopped. The police know too much about it, and extra security is already in place in that area. I have come up with another plan, though. Something that will really shake this country to the core."

The three men moved closer, curious as to what the new plan would be. They were all dedicated to the cause, some for misguided beliefs and the others for the opportunity to bring forth hell on earth.

The leader didn't care much for their motivations. He just wanted the task to be completed.

"We are going to time our effort for when the President of the United States comes to New York. He's scheduled to arrive just two days from now, and I figured that would be the perfect time. We will lie low to convince the authorities that the threat level has been eliminated, then rise up just in time to take down the leader of the most influential country in the world. We will strike fear into their hearts."

The three men listened intently, none of them fearful of

the task ahead. They had been chosen for a reason, and the leader was glad they were still there to carry it out. They had planned to be at the mosque, but by the time they'd arrived the police were there and the Imam was dead. They had discreetly scattered before anyone could notice them or point them out.

"You will be the new champions of our revolution, and when the dust settles, a new country will rise from the ashes of the infidels."

19

C alvin gripped the steering wheel loosely as they cruised down the road, heading for the Mexico/United States border. He was shocked at how well rested he felt, even with Marty waking him up before the sun had crested the horizon. He was glad of the early start. It got them on the road sooner. He let Sofia sleep for a little longer, allowing her to wake up on her own as they were driving along.

He reached down for the coffee he had gotten from the gas station, and then his phone began to ring. Calvin looked over as Sofia stirred, and she blinked at him sleepily as he picked it up to look at the screen. A deep breath escaped him when he saw the general's cell phone number on the screen. He pressed the accept call button and put the phone to his ear, having a good idea of why he was calling.

"Calvin," he boomed. "What are you up to?"

Calvin smiled. "Not much, General. What can I help you with?"

"The strangest thing just happened; some information about you just came across my desk. Apparently, there are two drug lords in Cabo San Lucas looking for you. What the hell are you doing on your vacation?"

Calvin glanced at Sofia and sighed. "I seem to have picked up one of their prized possessions."

The general put a hand to his forehead, shaking his head. Calvin wasn't going to change anything he was doing. He'd learned that trying to talk a mercenary out of doing something once they had their mind set on it was useless. Instead, he had to do what he could to help Calvin and the "prized possession" he was transporting.

"Well, be aware, son, that your face is plastered all over the border on their side. So, when you get there, you're going to have a firefight of mass proportions. Do you want us to be ready to pull you out of there?"

Calvin thought about it for a minute; a way to get them both out to safety. However, he was pissed at what had transpired. They had taken a woman hostage, beat her, and put her in harm's way, all because they had money. Calvin couldn't let that go so easily. He was determined to put the hurt on those people so they never tried to hurt Sofia or girls like her again.

"I'll make sure the woman is safe, but I'm coming through that border."

"I'll let my friends on the border know to stay out of the way." The general chuckled. "Don't kill anyone who doesn't need killing."

"I won't kill anyone who doesn't try to kill me first," Calvin replied.

Both men knew that the drug lords and their people

were out for blood, and would do everything in their power to take Calvin down. He had not only taken Sofia away from Manuel, but he had killed the other drug lord's men. That was a huge deal. Having one drug lord after you was bad enough, but Calvin was facing the wrath of two.

"Good luck, son. I'll see you on the other side."

With that, the general hung up, and Calvin considered his next move. He wasn't going to let Sofia get hurt, but it would take some help from his family to make sure that didn't happen. Calvin glanced at his phone as he drove along, scrolling down to Katie's number.

I sure as hell hope she's ready for this.

Katie sat in her living room, still full from lunch earlier. She and Pandora had gone nuts and ordered a ton of stuff, just like that night in Vegas when she could barely walk back to the SUV. It felt good to get some real food in her stomach. Pandora had made sure she didn't feel the pain from her actions, but she grabbed the bottle of Pepto from the side table and took a big swig to help. Just then her phone buzzed on the table in front of her and she leaned forward, seeing Calvin's name.

The prodigal black man returns, Pandora exclaimed excitedly.

Katie smiled and answered with a chirp in her voice, "Hello, brother from another mother. How are they hanging?"

He chuckled. "Tell Pandora they're hanging side by side, just like they should."

"Good, good," Katie replied. "I was afraid all that time in the sand with the beach bunnies had put a hurtin' on ya."

"Well, about that…"

"Uh-oh." Katie sat up, putting the Pepto down on the table. "What's going on?

"I don't really have the time to go into detail," Calvin replied.

"Give me as much as you can."

"I saved a woman from a drug lord who was trying to kidnap her, but in the process killed two of his men."

"Is she all right?"

"Yeah, she's here with me, but that isn't the whole story."

"Go on."

"She happened to be the girlfriend of a rival drug lord, who beat her and pretty much held her hostage in Cabo. Now the two drug lords have joined forces for the first time in their lives, and they're hell-bent on taking me down."

Uh-oh. Pandora actually sounded concerned.

Katie groaned. "Did you call the general?"

"The general called me. He got a memo saying the drug lords had my picture, and they and their men were going to be waiting at the border for us when we get there."

"And I'm assuming they aren't looking to grab a margarita and chat it out."

"Uh, no, more like grab a missile launcher and blow me to bits before taking Sofia back to their dark Cabo lairs and giving her the once- or twice-over."

Katie shook her head and rubbed her face. "I'm going to

go on record and say you're no longer allowed to go on any kind of vacation by yourself."

"That's probably a good idea in the future."

"All right, so we need to get the woman across the border safely, correct?"

"Yes, please, and her name is Sofia."

"I will send the corporate jet to pick her up. I'm assuming you're determined to face and destroy these guys."

"You are correct."

"Okay, I'll call you back with the location where the jet will be landing. Hopefully, it can get to you outside of a main airport."

"Sounds good. Thank you, Katie."

"Anytime, dude."

Calvin hung up the phone and smiled to himself, remembering that Katie knew him almost better than he knew himself sometimes. She hadn't chastised him, at least not too much. She simply did what needed to be done. He was glad he worked so closely with someone who understood the importance of helping innocents when they really needed it.

"Did I just hear that all correctly?" Sofia asked, giving him a stern face. "You're just going to shuttle me out of the way? You're supposed to come with me!"

"And I will, after I take care of this."

"Those men aren't demons, and they don't care how many times you flash your red eyes. They will kill you. Gun you down right there in the middle of the road. They don't care if there are US troops on the other side. Hell, they wouldn't care if the pope was on the other side. They will take care of you on Mexican soil and let the blood soak into the sand."

Calvin smiled and patted Sofia's hand, allowing his eyes to go full red. "There is one thing these guys need to understand. You never fuck with one of the Damned. *Ever.*"

Sofia pulled her hand back slightly and leaned toward the window, realizing she was out of her league. In fact, not only was she out of her league, so were the men who were waiting at the border for Calvin. She forgot what kind of damage the Damned could do, with or without demon protection.

Manuel was going to meet his match...and then his maker.

"Maybe you're right." Sofia nodded. "Going on a plane seems like a much better option for me. I don't know if I could handle the wrath of the Damned."

"Sometimes even *I* can't handle the wrath of the Damned." Calvin laughed. "So, does that mean you're onboard with this plan? I told you I would get you over the border safely, even if that means in a corporate jet high above the clouds."

Sofia eyed him for a moment and shook her head, knowing it was her only option. She was scared for Calvin, but she found that there was something in him that wouldn't let him be defeated. Calvin grinned and pressed down hard on the gas, speeding toward the border.

"Perfect. Let's get you into your chariot, then."

Katie leaned back on the couch with her phone next to her.

She had spoken to the pilot and arranged everything for Calvin. She hated that he was going to face all of it alone, but there was not much she could do. He'd decided on revenge, and Katie knew as well as the next mercenary that when that call came, they had no choice but to answer. Her phone began to buzz again.

She sighed and looked at the screen, expecting it to be Calvin or the general. Instead, it was a New York number. "Hello?"

"Katie, this is Iris, your real estate agent."

"Hi, Iris. Good to hear from you. How is everything going with the settlement on the condo?"

"Well, that's why I'm calling. The condo owners have upped the price."

"Really? So they're getting greedy."

"Exactly, which is not the first time I've seen this situation with these multimillion-dollar homes. They want to sell, but when they get some interest, they play hardball. It's annoying. What would you like me to tell them?"

"I want you to hold off a little while. Get them nervous. Let them think we're walking away, and at the last second, offer them twenty-five percent less than my original offer."

Iris went quiet for a moment, trying to figure out if she heard Katie correctly. "I'm slightly confused by your negotiating tactics. They want more money, so you're going to withdraw the offer and then put in a new one for less?"

Katie smiled, twirling her hair around a finger. "You never know what can happen in a few days. Maybe the stock market will crash. Besides, there's probably no one else trying to get it right now at that price, and I'm willing to take the chance and wait another week."

"Okay, I'll do what you ask, but if it works, I might have to hire you onto my team."

Both women laughed, knowing full well Katie would scare the hell out of anyone trying to swindle a buyer like that. Katie loved the condo since it had all the charm she was looking for and sat right on the edge of Central Park. What she *didn't* love was someone trying to cheat her. They hung up and Katie looked at Angie who was sitting in the other chair, waiting patiently to hear what had happened.

"It looks like we have a few more days to get our design quotes together. Telephone the women and give them another—ohhh…forty-eight hours or so. That way they can stop pulling their hair out."

"What if we don't get the condo? Will you choose a different one? You really loved the windows and the balconies at the Circa."

Katie winked at Angie. "Everything will be okay in the end. Trust me a little. On top of that, we will probably have an even bigger budget than before for our designers, which will be fantastic."

Katie stood up and stretched her arms over her head, already feeling better. The action earlier in the day had gotten her adrenaline pumping and sent her mind into overdrive. Not only was she helping Calvin out of whatever craziness he'd gotten himself into, she was also now on the trail of some really nasty humans and their demon accomplices.

"I'll call them right away, and I'll make a spreadsheet so you can see the whole thing easier," Angie replied, standing up.

"Perfect. I'm going to head across the street to the

precinct. I gotta run something by the detectives over there. I'll check in with you when I get back, or just knock on the door."

Katie grabbed her black suit jacket and pulled it on over her white T-shirt and jeans. She locked the door behind them and left Angie to her day.

She bounced out of the hotel and paused on the sidewalk for a moment to take in the warmth of the sun before running across the road, barely avoiding being hit by a car. The car honked and the guy shouted, but Katie just laughed.

"I've killed demons bigger than your Prius," she shouted, chuckling.

She headed inside the precinct. The guy behind the front desk offered her a sloppy salute, and he pressed the button that unlocked the door to the back. Katie laughed and gave him a return salute on her way through the doors and into the pit.

The pit was experiencing an unusual level of chaos, even by the standards Katie had seen on her previous visits. Several perps were chained to the bench as expected, but everyone else was rushing around like chickens with their heads cut off. Katie saw Travers walking into the pit from the right, his nose stuck in some papers he was holding. She reached out and grabbed his arm, startling him slightly.

He looked up and nodded at Katie. "Hey, Katie, sorry. Shit is crazy around here. I don't really have time to talk right now. The President is coming to town, and all the precincts across the city have special assignments and specific streets and areas that have to be tied down and secured."

"Right, yeah, I know. I just have one quick question. What path will he be taking?"

Travers wrinkled his forehead and flipped through his papers. "Uh, he'll be coming through Times Square. Why?"

Katie grabbed Traver's arm tightly just as Schultz walked up to them. Her eyes flashed bright red, and she could feel a flash of energy in her chest. He looked at her hand and warily back at her eyes.

"Make sure that if shit goes down, your men know not to shoot me."

She dropped his arm and spun around, heading quickly back out of the station. Travers narrowed his eyes and looked at Schultz, who looked just as confused as he was.

"Does she know something we don't?"

Calvin opened the passenger door and reached down to help Sofia out. She grabbed her book bag and slung it onto her back, then pulled her ball cap on. Calvin rubbed her shoulder, seeing the nervousness she was trying to hide.

They both looked up when they heard the hum of the corporate jet landing in the distance. They had found a tiny privately-owned airport, and Katie had paid a good sum to keep the whole thing under wraps. No one but the three of them and the pilot had known where the plane would be landing.

Sofia stepped back, nodding. "That's a nice jet. I have to admit I'm impressed."

"Yeah, it's a company thing. We only use it in emergencies like this. We have the chopper for the rest of it."

"Well, aren't you guys fancy?"

Calvin shrugged. "It's kind of essential."

When the jet came to a stop on the runway, and the guide waved his flag, Calvin grabbed Sofia by the arm and led her onto the tarmac. The plane came to a stop and lowered the stairs, and Calvin took her bag and climbed up behind her. He showed her quickly around the plane, introduced her to the pilot, and helped her get strapped tightly into her seat.

"You should have everything you need."

Sofia looked at Calvin as if seeing him properly for the first time, now that the threat of death wasn't hanging over her head. She smiled shyly and patted the seat next to hers. "I'm not a member of the Mile-High Club yet."

Calvin smiled and leaned down, whispering into her ear, "A tempting as that is, I have a personal message to deliver." He kissed her cheek and walked to the door, where he paused to look back at her. "But I'll see you on the other side of the border."

He winked and headed down the stairs, stopping at the bottom and watching the flight attendant pull up the steps and latch the door. He backed away as the engines began to hum loudly again, seeing Sofia looking down from the window above. He put up his hand and waved, not at all surprised by the turn of events. They had gotten really close on the trip, and he wasn't going to pretend that the need to get her to safety had been strictly platonic.

He grinned. "Besides, I'm already a member of the club, just not in *that* seat."

Sofia had no idea what he was saying, but she really wished he had taken her up on the offer. She knew he could handle himself since he wouldn't still be alive after all that time with mercenaries if he couldn't, but she didn't know what she would do if she were the reason he was injured or killed.

She hoped and prayed that she would see him on the other side.

20

K atie was in her room getting ready for a full day of kicking ass and taking names when there was a knock on the door. She stuck her head around the corner, figuring it was Angie. She was awake before ten again, and Pandora hadn't even had to get her up.

"Come in," she yelled.

The door creaked open, and Angie stuck her head in, looking around before opening it farther. She had her MacBook and a binder in her arms. "Hey, I just came to check in for the day."

She walked to the bedroom doorway and waited for Katie to finish getting suited up. She tilted her head to the side, running her eyes over what appeared be armor on Katie's body. Her two big guns were strapped to her legs, and she had a couple of small ones holstered at her sides.

"Is there a war coming to town that I'm not aware of?" Angie was half-joking and half-serious.

Katie smiled and shrugged. "I hate to tell you, but there's *always* a war happening around us. However, it's a bit of a special occasion. The President is coming to town today, and I think it's a good opportunity for those who want to be evil to do evil things."

Angie nodded in agreement; that was definitely a good assumption to make. There were plenty of people who probably wanted to take out their frustration on the President, as there had been with every single leader through the ages. This, however, was the perfect opportunity for the demons to cause some chaos.

Katie picked up her phone and dialed the station, tapping her foot while she waited for someone to pick up. "Yes, Detective Schultz, please. Thank you." She turned from side to side in the mirror, admiring the view. She looked badass, and she knew it. "Schultz, I need you to give me a couple of support personnel. I'll meet them downstairs in the hotel lobby. Thanks."

Katie hung up and turned to find Angie still staring at her from the doorway. Katie smiled and grabbed her coat on the way to the door.

"I don't want you to go to the President's parade. Just watch it from your room and order food. We should be done in the next two to three days, tops."

"Okay," Angie replied.

As Katie opened the door, she turned around and smiled. "Oh, and make sure the designer who's going to be our lead is ready. We will be purchasing furniture at a reduced rate."

Katie shut the door, leaving Angie slightly confused. She pulled the MacBook close to her chest and shook her head. She would never really understand what was going on in Katie's mind.

Katie headed to the elevator and took it to the lobby, where the cops were conversing with the concierge while they waited for her. She had put on her black coat, a new one that was much lighter than the other and didn't have the fur around the collar. She was wearing so much gear she didn't want to deal with the weight.

She walked up to the two cops and put out her hand. "Katie."

"Nice to meet you. I'm Jenkins, and this is my partner Roberts."

Roberts shook her hand and lifted an eyebrow. "What's up with the jacket?"

Katie looked around her for a moment and opened it up halfway, feeling a little like a flasher in an alley. They both shook their heads, their faces becoming somber when they saw her weapons and armor. All traces of humor gone, they all put on their game faces and headed out.

They rode down to Times Square and started moving from building to building. Katie stood at the window of one of the high-rises inside a vacant apartment. She stared at the street below, trying to imagine the motorcade rolling through.

"This is too low," she told them. "We would need to be higher than this to see the playing field."

"Where do you think the demons will attack from?" Roberts asked.

Katie thought about it for a minute. "I personally think they'll come infected and then carry out their attack among the crowd, but I can't be certain. If that's the case, I need to be able to get to them as fast as possible before any civilians are injured or killed. It's easy to go down, but it's a lot harder to go up, so I think getting higher in the building is going to be the best bet. If they come from a building, great. If they're on the street, I can also get to them pretty quickly."

"How will we know who's who? The streets will be packed."

"A mixture of my gut and their beady red eyes." Katie smiled. "Trust me, we won't miss the bastards, wherever they come from."

Katie tapped on the window and shook her head. She looked down at the street and up at the building across the way. She just wasn't positive she would be fast enough, even jumping through a window.

"I could use a damned pair of wings," she grumbled. "Come on, let's look out from a couple of stories above." The cops followed as Katie led them from the apartment.

When the door closed, Gabriel materialized from the shadows with a smile on his face. He nodded and clapped his hands, disappearing in a flash of light.

Katie put her feet up on the chair and bit into one of the donuts. The Hot and Ready sign had been on when they got there, and Katie couldn't believe her luck. She was actually in the mood for donuts, and not just because Pandora had willed it so.

What do you think will happen tomorrow? You think the demons will show?

Pandora groaned, nearly orgasming over how good the freshly-made donuts were. *I swear, if I could have donuts this fresh all the time, I would give up my demon card.*

Katie laughed. *Pandora, focus.*

Oh, sorry, what did you ask me?

Do you think the demons will show tomorrow?

Of course. They want to take over. This is their opportunity, and they're too stupid to realize we're on to them.

Katie sighed, looking around the small pizza shop next door to the Krispy Kreme place. There were no tables in the donut shop so they'd gone over there, buying a piece of pizza but scarfing down the donuts. On the table next to Katie was an untouched piece of extra cheese pizza, the grease staining the paper plate.

Katie looked up from her donuts as the chair next to her scraped back. Gabriel took a seat.

Would you look at this? Mr. Fucking Manners here thinks he can just roll up on our donut party, sit down without asking and take over with his weird-as-fuck eyes.

Have you forgotten about our *red eyes?*

Way better than his "I can see into the depths of your soul" eyes. That is some straight-up serial killer shit.

"Actually, Pandora, I can't quite see into the soul, just the emotions behind it," Gabriel answered, letting Pandora and Katie know he could hear what was going on inside her head. He smiled beatifically at Katie. "I took your request up to my boss."

Katie was taken aback by that. "Uh, request? I don't know if I made one, did I?"

You made a request to the man in the clouds?

No? If I did, I don't remember it. It's not like I've been on my knees praying before bed. I think you would have noticed that.

Damn right I would have.

Gabriel looked down at the pizza. "The next time you find yourself fairly high up, have faith and jump."

He grabbed the pizza from the plate in front of him, folded it in half, and took a deep whiff of the cheesy aroma. Katie looked at him, affronted, but he didn't pause. Instead, he winked and smiled in her direction. "You weren't going to eat this anyway."

He stood up, taking a bite of the slice as he pushed his chair in. He put one hand on her shoulder before disappearing around the corner.

I think I would be more pissed off if he wasn't right, Katie mumbled to herself.

Pandora shrugged internally. *You might have been tempted to be a good girl and eat all of your food. Now we have more room for donuts, and we're going to need that energy anyway. Greasy pizza would only weigh you down, so suck it up, buttercup. Let's get another dozen.*

Just then, three men came out of the train station archway and headed up the stairs. Katie stopped with a donut halfway to her mouth and watched as they walked by. All three of them were incredibly hot. The one in the front was blond with bright blue eyes, followed by a shaggy-haired brunette with deep chestnut eyes, and the guy in the back had slicked-back black hair with eyes so green they looked like colored contacts. Katie switched her gaze to their rear aspects after they passed and watched with a wistful expression until they were out of sight.

That was definitely unexpected. I should watch the stairs more often when we're here.

I'm just in shock, and completely awed that you saw them

before I did, Pandora gasped. *Either I'm off my game, or you seriously got one. The only thing that would have been better was if you'd gone after those tight asses. Though, I have to say I don't quite think you're up for a foursome just yet. They might ruin you.*

I may be noticing men, but I haven't lost all track of my personal morality. I think you can be assured there will be no threesomes or foursomes in my future. One at a time is enough for me, and probably very spaced out.

Pandora sighed. *Hey, it was worth the shot. I mean, I can't find the sky if I don't shoot for the moon.*

I'm not sure what that means, but I don't think the saying is correct.

Whatever. You know what I meant. So, how about that dozen donuts?

Katie got up from the table and threw away her trash, wiping her hands on the napkins. She walked next door and grinned as the woman grabbed a dozen box, anticipating her. Katie held up two fingers, figuring why not go for the gold? She ordered one dozen hot glazed and the other assorted, as well as several bottles of milk.

The girl behind the counter giggled. "We all had a friendly bet on whether you would get some to go. You never let me down."

"You know it." Katie smiled, throwing a tip in the jar. "See you soon!"

I thought we were doing a dozen? Pandora asked carefully, not wanting her to change her mind.

Yeah, but I figured we would eat one now back in the room and then go to sleep. That way when we wake up in the morning, we'll have a dozen for breakfast before we start our watch. It'll be one hell of a sugar rush, but I think we'll need it with the day we have ahead of us.

You're becoming a better human with every day that passes.

Calvin rolled his shoulders as he drove along, the scenery somehow a lot less interesting than when Sofia was there. A green sign on the side of the road told him he was just ten miles from the United States border. He had entered a small town, one that focused on tourists and travelers crossing the borders. There were bright signs everywhere, and enough restaurants to cater to anyone and everyone in the little town.

He pulled the car into the parking lot of a local motel. The woman at the front desk barely looked up as she took his money and handed him a key. Calvin's plan was simple. Rest up and prepare for the next day's events.

He parked the car in front of his room, grabbed his bags, and hauled his ass inside. Once there, he closed the curtains and opened the duffel bag, laying out his guns and ammo. He had enough to put a dent in whoever was at the border waiting for him, and he knew he could deal with what he had. After all, if worse came to worst, he would be able to take weapons off anyone he killed.

When he was satisfied his loadout was in good order, he zipped the bag and leaned back against the headboard. He looked around the room at the old bright-green carpet, the peeling wallpaper, and the large box tv set in front of him. It definitely wasn't the Pacifica, but the bed was clean and soft enough for a good night's sleep, and he knew he wouldn't overdo it there.

This has been an interesting trip to Mexico, Marty remarked. *I've only gone across the border once before, a long time ago when people were all about Tijuana.*

Calvin chuckled. *They still are. Only difference now is that it's mostly for illegal shit, and there's always some crazy story about a missing American being found over the border stuffed full of bags of cocaine. Not really my idea of an awesome vacation.*

That sounds disappointing. At least they have tacos, which is probably the best food I've ever had. Then again, I've always been stuck in weird bodies like this one dude who had a wheatgrass obsession. That was not a fun ride.

Well, I tell you what... You help me beat these assholes in the morning, and I'll make sure you get a whole bunch of tacos before we leave.

That sounds like a great deal to me, but they better have some kick to them.

Calvin chuckled. *I think I can handle that.*

He was taking a page out of Katie's *How to Negotiate with Your Demon* book of tricks. He had seen her do it a million times with Pandora and a box of donuts.

For his demon, all it took was the golden promise of tacos.

Brock sat on the edge of his bunk in his boxers and initialed white T-shirt, shining the last scuffs out of his boots. All around him his team were maintaining the weapons and protective gear they had rolled into battle with. Luckily for most of them, it had been so quick that barely anything got scuffed.

Unfortunately for Brock, he had rolled around through the dirt and grass with one of the bastard demons, so he pretty much had to go through each piece of his kit with a fine-toothed comb.

Everyone was tired. They all had dark circles under their eyes, their bodies were sore from combat, and their racks were calling their names. The rest of the platoon was still out finishing up some sort of assignment for the higher-ups. Suddenly, everyone jumped to attention as the captain marched through the front door.

"At ease, boys," he told them, waving them off with the folder he was carrying. "You've made the error of showing us that you're more than capable soldiers. For your crimes, you have been assigned to advanced training. Suit up and meet in the center courtyard in fifteen minutes. There will be three helicopters waiting for you. It's been a pleasure serving with you men. Good luck out there, and stay alive."

The guys waited until the captain had left the room, but as soon as the door shut they burst into loud speculation about their new assignment. They had all been pretty happy where they were, top of the barrel for the platoon, given special chow and PT treatment, and not having to do the tedious bullshit around the base. This would throw them right back into the newbie ranks.

"I *knew* we shouldn't have been such badasses in the last beat-down. Now we gotta get accustomed to everything all over again," one of the guys grumbled.

They had no choice, though. They were the best of the

best. When they'd gone out to that incursion they had proven their abilities, and they had *definitely* been noticed.

Brock personally didn't mind. The higher he climbed, the better. He'd grown to like being out in the field, and he knew that advanced soldiers got their fair share of battle time.

The guys collected their gear and put it on, each pulling out a sack and packing the rest of their belongings inside. Brock helped strip beds, throwing the sheets into laundry bags before he lined up with his group and headed out of the barracks. In the dark distance were three lit-up helicopters waiting especially for them. Several other teams were standing by to board, having been chosen as well.

Brock pulled his duffel farther up on his shoulder and smirked, ready to get out there and kick some demon ass. This wasn't a game anymore.

He had moved up into the big leagues.

21

Katie gulped some milk from the fridge and grimaced at the clock. It was six in the morning, earlier than she'd ever dragged herself out of bed before. She sighed determinedly and reached for the donuts.

There was a huge job at hand, and the demons weren't going to kill themselves just so she could sleep in. At least she had all that sugary goodness in the fridge to kickstart her day. A knock at the door drew her attention from the donuts and she opened the door, expecting to see Angie.

"You're up— Oh, sorry." She stared at one of the precinct cops from across the street. Between his pristine uniform and his earnest demeanor, it was obvious he was a rookie. She could almost *smell* the green on him.

The rookie smiled nervously and held out a couple of badges on lanyards. "Good morning, ma'am. This is your special security badge for the event. It will allow you to move along the parade route freely. Otherwise, they'll stop you every five feet. The second one is a weapons permit. It will let the Secret Service and the others know you have the right to fire your weapon if needed. That one comes in really handy after you've fired your weapon, so don't lose it."

Katie nodded astutely. "Got it."

"If there's nothing else, you're all set. Holler if you need anything, and good luck out there today."

She glanced at the badges and gave the rookie a bright smile. "I think we're good, thanks. Good luck to you guys, too."

Katie closed the door and took a closer look at her permits. They gave her official clearance to operate, which was useful but ultimately irrelevant since she was going to stop the demons with or without a permit. The politics and regulations of it all meant less than nothing to her, but she would play along if it made her job easier. She wanted the paycheck, and even more, she wanted to make sure those bastards didn't get anywhere near the President.

She slipped the lanyards over her head and went back to her room to finish getting ready. She strapped the holsters for her big-ass guns around her legs and slid Tom and Harry in carefully. The small pistols on the dresser went swiftly into her side holsters, although she hoped she wouldn't have to use both. Last but not least, she grabbed the two halves of her staff and slid them into the sheaths on her back in case Tom and Harry failed her. The staff was always her go-to in the heat of battle. She had worked hard to become one with the weapon on the hill in Vegas, and she wasn't going to forget about it because of her two new toys.

When she was done, she twisted her torso from left to

right to make sure she had a good range of motion going on around all the weaponry. She was locked and loaded, but she didn't want to be *over*loaded. What good would all those weapons do if she couldn't turn her body to grab one? When she was sure she was set, she threw on her black coat, leaving it unbuttoned.

The way it hung on her reminded her of Damian's signature trench coat, and it made her wish he was there with her. He would be all kinds of wound up over the whole angel/demon thing she had going on.

She smiled at her reflection in the mirror and gave herself a nod of approval. If anyone *did* pay attention to her, which she thought was unlikely in New York City since they were all focused on themselves, it would look like she was wearing fatigues under the coat. It was perfect, and she would blend in nicely—at least until the bastard demons decided to show up.

Then she would unveil her badassery.

Katie headed out of the hotel and pulled her coat around her to stop the breeze from blowing it open as she walked toward Times Square. Her earlier assumption had been right. Nobody paid her the slightest attention.

When she rounded the corner into Times Square, she stopped and stared at all the people who had already arrived. The place was filling up fast with excited patriots. They gathered along the barriers, waving their Stars and Stripes as they waited for a five-second glimpse of the man. This was a bad thing in Katie's eyes.

First of all, your leadership structure is bullshit, and it does not work the way all you Americans think it does, Pandora bitched. *Secondly, it does not surprise me a bit that the demons chose now to start amping up the fight. After all, the last election showed them that humans are even stupider than they had originally thought.*

Careful there, soapbox speaker. I'm actually a human.

You didn't vote for the idiot, and yes, I checked.

I didn't vote at all.

Why should you have? The pool was dank and shallow this election season. I mean, come on! This guy is a joke. All he cares about is money. He lied about global warming, he lied about working with other countries off the books, and he lied about giving two shits about the people here. And to put the fucking cherry right up there on top, he did it so badly that a two-year-old could figure it out.

Katie chuckled, not used to hearing Pandora be this passionate about something other than donuts. She didn't interrupt her, because it would do no good. When she was in that state of mind, all Katie could do was let her get it out of her system.

Then there are these religious folks saying he's the second coming of Jesus. Come on, now. Little do they know, he's just Moloch's puppet. He doesn't even know it. Sure, he'll support the fight against demons in public. It'll get him re-elected. But he doesn't give two shits about the fight as long as he comes out on top with his pockets stuffed. The second coming of Lucifer is more like it.

You really hate this guy.

Sweetie, it's nothing personal. I have hated every single President who has rolled through this country. I watched the last one with popcorn, sitting on my throne. Everyone's favorite guy, but no one noticed him illegally bombing other countries on the sly.

It's all a crooked mess. But I digress. It's not like I voted or anything.

I get it. A lot of people feel that way; more than there used to be. It's like a middle group popping up, not supporting one side or the other.

Yeah, they're called Progressives, and they're *idiots too. Politics just blurs everything up. Be free, roam like a chicken, do what you want to do when you want to do it. That's* my *mantra.*

Katie snickered. *These days fewer chickens are free-range, and more are kept in cages until they die. Just saying.*

Typical. Pandora sniffed.

I'm not here to judge their performance in office. I'm merely here to stop the terrorism that will occur if they're killed. The guy could be the biggest asshat on the planet—

He is.

It doesn't matter. I will still *be out here doing my job. No one wants to see the President killed, but I have to focus on what would happen if he were. Chaos. Pure, motherfucking chaos.*

Well, yes. I remember the last time it happened.

Exactly. It's the last thing America needs right now, and I won't let it happen on my watch.

"Here are the keys." Calvin set the keys on the counter and put his heavy bag down on the floor.

The car rental clerk behind the counter nodded and scooped up the keys. "Very good. Just give me a minute to do the inspection, and we will get you out of here."

"Thanks."

Calvin waited by the counter while the clerk went out into the parking lot with his clipboard held tightly in his hands, and a serious look on his face. Calvin sighed and looked down at the bag by his feet. He just wanted to get the whole thing over and done with so he could go kick some drug-lord ass.

When the clerk finally came back, he headed straight behind the counter without saying a word. Calvin was ready to be lectured for the hard miles he'd driven in the rental.

Instead, to Calvin's surprise, the clerk took a pile of bills from the till and handed it to him. Calvin looked at him strangely.

The clerk smiled. "We usually put the deposit back on the customer's card, but you paid cash at one of the other facilities that allows that, so here you are—your deposit returned in full."

"That's great. Um, thanks." Calvin was shocked he was getting his deposit back at all, much less in full, but he took the money.

The clerk nodded and looked down at the computer while he typed for a moment. "I noticed that no one dropped you off, sir. Did you need me to call you a cab?"

"No, thanks," Calvin replied. He picked up his bag. "I'm on foot from here."

The weapons Katie had arranged to be sent clinked reassuringly in his bag as he walked out of the car rental place. It was time to fuel up. He stood at the edge of the road and scanned the street. He spotted a small restaurant down the block and made his way over in the hot sun, feeling like his bags weighed more than his body. Inside, he sat down at the counter and had a cup of coffee and a Spanish omelet with rice.

When breakfast was done he went into the bathroom, locked the door, and set his heavy bag on the counter, then opened it and began to unload all the weapons Katie had arranged to be sent. He didn't see his armor, but he figured it was too short of notice to have it shipped with the weapons. Besides, if he *did* get hit, it would probably be by so many bullets at once that the armor wouldn't do him any good anyway. He shook the thought off and made sure each gun was fully loaded before strapping it on. He stuck two of them in the harness he'd found in the bottom of the bag.

There were no more weapons in the bag. Whoever had packed it had to choose wisely, so when his ammo ran out he would just take the enemy's. He stuffed his pockets with clips and looked into the mirror at his makeshift readiness.

I never thought I would see a day that you found facing a group of humans more intimidating than battling demons.

"Yeah, well. When it's a demon, I don't have to think of the mother whose son I just killed."

You think demons don't have mothers?

Calvin had no response for that.

Before leaving, Calvin reached in his back pocket to make sure he had his passport, which he would need to get back home after taking care of the infestation at the border. He was ready to kick some bad-guy ass, and ready to get back to his life. Sofia's dark eyes flashed through his mind, but he rolled his shoulders and pushed the image away for now.

The border wasn't far, and he was ready to face Manuel

and his men without unneeded baggage, emotional or physical.

The men lined up in the lower level of a parking garage not far from Times Square. Each of them was simply dressed in a t-shirt with the President's face on the front, a distasteful ruse to disguise them in the crowd. It wouldn't matter what they wore, once their demons took over. There were no special weapons, detonators, or bombs to conceal.

Just the human sacrifices.

The leader stood before them, his face shrouded to hide his identity. He leaned on his cane while he shared some last words before he released the demons. "The demon plague has been unleashed upon America as Allah's punishment for their sins. You have been chosen to deliver that punishment. There can be *no* greater honor than to give your lives to wipe Western corruption and depravity from this Earth so all may bask in the glory of Allah. Allah thanks you. He will stand beside you when you reach the afterlife, and you will be rewarded for your sacrifice. Your names will be spoken throughout the world! You will be heroes! Come, it is time. May Allah be with you all through the fear."

He tapped the floor with the long wooden cane to summon the portal he'd been told would come. A swirling black orb appeared beside him, but he didn't flinch; just kept his eyes on the men before him.

The temperature dropped when the first demon spirit

emerged, an incorporeal wraith that twisted the space around it into something impossible. Screams like rending metal echoed from the lightless mass as it pulled itself out of the portal and raced toward the first man in line.

The man closed his eyes tightly, clenching his fists as the demon took him over. He grabbed his stomach and bent at the waist, writhing in pain and screaming. The air vibrated around him as his body convulsed.

"Do not fight it! Release your will, soldier, and it shall be done!"

The man's shoulders went limp for a moment, then his body slammed upward, his arms flung out to the sides. Red light blazed from his eyes and his screams cut off as suddenly as they'd begun. Just as quickly as the show had started, it ended. His head fell to his chest.

Slowly, he lifted his chin to face the leader. His eyes snapped open, and the brightness of his eyes faded to a dull red ring. The transformation was almost complete.

The leader scrutinized his eyes and nodded in satisfaction. "Good, now hold onto your humanity long enough to get to Times Square and to the President. You will know when it's time."

The leader stood in place and watched as the other men were transformed one by one. They barely retained their souls, but they held on, determined to wait for the proper moment to release their demons completely. As the last man accepted his demon, the portal snapped shut and the room went pitch-dark.

They were almost ready to take over the world.

The skies were bright blue and vibrant, and a gentle breeze offered a small respite from the heat to the Secret Service agents stationed around John F. Kennedy Airport. They had shut the airport down long enough to receive Air Force One and transfer the President to the motorcade. The agents lined the runway near the waiting limos and watched the sky for any sign of the approaching plane.

Over the speaker in the tower, the pilot of the Presidential plane stated, "We are on our descent."

"We are stacked and ready for you," the agent replied.

Air Force One came into view, its landing gear slowly extending as it prepared to land. The agents remained alert as the plane touched down on the runway, ready for the first sign of trouble. The agents were nervous. They had been briefed on the threat, and in theory they understood the challenge, but it this was like nothing any of them had experienced before.

***

Katie held her two badges up to one of the agents at the front door of the building. He looked between the pictures and her several times before he nodded and stepped to the side. Katie took the stairwell to the third floor, stopping again to show her badges when she came to another agent. It was about the tenth time she'd had to do so, but it was for the best. They couldn't have crazies running around the place.

Pandora laughed. *Then how did* you *get a badge?*

Shut it.

She walked over to the window and stood with her

arms crossed over her chest. The crowds were large enough at that point that it was hard to tell who was there with her and who was just there to see the President.

Detective Lowery from the Nineteenth walked through the door and looked at Katie in surprise. "I didn't know you would be here."

Katie nodded at the detective, recognizing him from the nightclub. "Detective Lowery, good to see you."

He came to stand beside her and looked out over the crowd. "You're just going to watch this?"

She shrugged. "Maybe I'm wrong. Maybe nothing will happen."

"But you don't believe that?"

She looked him dead in the eyes. "They want to make a statement. They want to prove that they can hit the biggest guy there is. Think about how many television cameras are on him right now."

"Even so," Lowery replied. He shuffled uncomfortably for a moment. "Look... I don't mean this in any harsh way. You know I respect what you do. But what is one Damned going to be able to do against whatever army you think is coming?"

She chuckled and let her coat fall to her feet.

He took a step back and ran his eyes over all of the weaponry strapped strategically to her body. He raised his eyebrows, realizing that Katie meant serious business. "You don't play around. I'm sorry I misjudged you." He looked up and tapped on the glass in front of them. "That's not gonna stop you from getting the demons, is it?"

Fast as lightning, Katie drew Harry, chambered a

round, and holstered him in one easy twirl. She smirked at the detective.

"Nope. In my business, size really *does* matter."

Pandora burst into laughter. *Oh, holy shit, that was a good one.*

22

The President's motorcade was creeping slowly toward Times Square. In the President's overblown, overzealous fashion he had a marching band in front of the parade playing what he called "America's Greatest Hits " and a flagman carrying both the Stars and Stripes and the flag of the President of the United States.

Originally, the President had planned on riding through in a convertible to wave to his adoring fans and uphold the illusion that he was a "President of the People," but after hearing about the possible risk to his life he made sure to stay tightly snug inside his limo. He did, however, have the windows down, and planned to stand up through the sunroof when they stopped for a moment in the center of Times Square.

It was a show, one he *loved* to put on. One that fooled the American people into feeling secure. It was easy to believe that if the President was out on the streets, there mustn't be anything to worry about. It was a blind faith that was shortly to be tested.

Up ahead in Times Square, the terrorists had gotten out of the van and made their way in with the crowds. They set up in their assigned spots and waited patiently for the moment they would turn.

No one noticed anything out of the ordinary in the droves of people lining the streets.

Three stories up, Katie looked out the window at the crowd, cheerfully chatting with Pandora.

Look at the guy to the right between all the women in pink. He's got the bluest eyes I've ever seen.

Fuck his eyes. Pandora snorted. *Check out the six-pack he's rocking under that tight blue T-shirt. Wait... Dammit, is that a rainbow pin on his shirt?*

Katie laughed out loud. *It sure as hell is. That explains why he's surrounded by all those gorgeous women and not even glancing at them. You have this uncanny attraction to gay men.*

No, I have an attraction to men. *It's not my business or my fault if they are gay. I can promise you, you have looked at a man before and given him googly-eyes, and he has been gay. You just didn't know.*

Oh, I'm sure I have. I just don't express my desires out loud.

Whatever. Oh, oh, next to Detective McSlimy on the corner, the guy with the T-shirt with the President's slogan on it. He is fucking hot.

I thought you hated the President.

I didn't say I wanted to spend time talking politics with him. Shirts can be taken off, and unless he tattooed that shit on his body I am perfectly fine with it.

Don't trust it. There's a good chance he did just that. The followers of this President are a little more whacked-out than ones before, at least that I can remember. Just sayin'.

This is probably true.

Katie laughed and scanned the crowd. A bright flash amongst the movement caught her eye. Katie held her hand up to shade her eyes and squinted, following the reflection to the back of the crowd across the street. It was just a wristwatch, no weapon in sight. She almost shrugged it off, but something pulled at her awareness. Her eyes moved up the man to his face, but his eyes were shadowed by the brim of his low baseball cap, preventing her from seeing if he was infected.

Katie moved to the right to get a better view, but she couldn't see. Suddenly, there was a loud pop in the street, a kid throwing down a firecracker. The guy looked up for a split second, but it was long enough for Katie to see the red glow in his eyes. She grabbed her gun from her hip and took a step back.

You found one.

Sure did. Shit's about to get crazy. I can feel it.

Katie saw that the President was still a few blocks away, which gave her at least a little bit of time to move. Down were crowds of people, including kids sitting on their parents' shoulders.

"Damn it!" Katie snarled. She knew she couldn't blow the window. Shards of glass would fall onto all the people below and start a severe panic in the streets. Katie slammed her gun back into the holster and took off at a run. She pushed past the agent and raced to the bottom of the stairs. When she exited, she grabbed the startled agent who was guarding the door by his shirt collar.

"There's a threat. These people need to be cleared. Call it in. Tell them Katie told you."

The agent nodded and reached for his walkie.

Katie was already gone. She wound her way through the crowd to the spot where she'd seen the infected guy, but by the time she got to his position he was gone. She looked for red eyes in the faces of the crowd around her and tried to feel for the location of his demon.

There was nothing.

Katie slammed her hands against her legs in frustration, knowing that she hadn't imagined it. She flashed her badge and stepped out into the road to check the progress of the steadily approaching motorcade. It wouldn't be long until the President reached the center of Times Square, and she knew *that* was when the shit would hit the fan.

What she *didn't* know was that the demons' lookouts had spotted her. They had been warned to expect her and had prepared a distraction for Katie to ensure they got a foot forward before the mercenary did.

Screams rang out from under the famous Times Square screen. Katie jerked around, drawing Tom and Harry instinctively. A ten-foot demon tore through the crowd, scattering the people with wide swipes of his claws. He snarled and growled at the crowd, his sharp teeth dripping hot saliva. He scooped his clawed hand through the crowd, picking up several bystanders and tossing them into his mouth.

Due to the concealed pistol permits that had gotten easier to obtain since the President came into office, several lone ranger idiots in the crowd pulled their guns and fired at the beast. Their tiny little bullets struck the demon, but ricocheted off his thick skin. The only thing they managed to accomplish was pissing the damn thing off. They were lucky not to injure any bystanders.

The demon threw the half-body he was eating onto the street and splayed its claws, then bent forward and let out a ferocious roar. Those shooting at him quickly ran away through the panicked crowd.

The police nearby had Katie's bullets, but there was too much chaos around them to get off a shot. They couldn't take the chance of hitting an innocent bystander, and there were too many kids gripping tight to their parents' shoulders as families attempted to get away. There was no easy way through the panicked crowd. Navigating the press of the masses was almost an impossible feat, leaving a very tasty human buffet laid out in front of the pissed-off demon.

The demon turned toward a group of school kids.

Their teacher stood in front of them with her arms out protectively. Tears ran down her face, but she stood strong despite her fear. The beast licked his sloppy jaws and began to advance, backing them up against a building. The children screamed and made themselves small behind the teacher. The demon reached back with his sharp, scaled claws. The teacher raised her chin and screamed her fury at the demon as she waited for the impact.

There was a loud boom and the demon's head exploded, sending chunks of meat flying into the crowds.

The teacher staggered back in shock. The beast's headless body teetered back and forth for a long moment before it tipped over and fell toward them. She crouched over them to shield the children, but before it hit the ground the body burst into a cloud of dust. The teacher squinted as a red-eyed figure emerged from the ash cloud.

Katie strode toward them with Harry firmly gripped in her hand.

She nodded at the teacher and smiled at the dust-covered children. Katie holstered Harry and spun around, knowing that couldn't have been the only demon.

The demons had become too cunning for that to be the main event. They would know that the likelihood of one ten-foot demon taking out the President in a sea of people was slim, especially with how easily distracted the low-level ones could be. One minute they followed orders just fine, the next they'd tear off to make a pet shop into an all-you-can-eat buffet. The low-level ones were big, destructive, and expendable.

Katie took a careful step forward, her boots crunching in the broken glass and bloody mess on the street. Her eyes shifted left to right because she knew that at any minute another demon would show its ugly, snarling face. Sure enough, more screams came from down the block.

Katie took off, pulling Tom. She slid to a stop when she saw the demon. This one was twice the size of the last, looming over the crowd and lashing out with his claws to pick people off. A massive swipe almost knocked a cop off one of the balconies.

Katie looked up at the demon as she made her way through the crowd. *It's a big one.*

Big and dumb, just how I like them. Pandora chuckled. *This will be easy, I can feel it. Watch his right hook and stay out from under his feet.*

Got it, Katie replied. *Let's see what Tom is capable of.*

Katie advanced, Tom raised in front of her with the beast's head in view through the scope. Katie jumped up on an overturned car and took a knee. She set her sights on the demon and followed the motion of his body, waiting for the shot. As soon as the beast paused for a moment, Katie pulled the trigger. The huge bullet sped through the air and struck the demon in the side of the head. A small chunk of skin flew off—but the impact was not even enough to make the demon grimace.

"Dammit," Katie hissed, holstering her gun. "I guess we'll just have to do this the old-fashioned way."

She pulled the two pieces of her staff from her back and clicked the button to release the blades as she flung her arms down.

Pandora chuckled. *So dramatic. You know, you don't have to do that.*

I know, but it looks damn cool.

Work it, sister. Your spectators await.

People had stopped fleeing and were looking at her with wide eyes. Many had their phones in their hands to capture video of the myth-come-to-life that was Katie.

Katie grinned, twisted her hips, and threw one of the halves of her staff at the demon.

The special metal embedded itself beneath the demon's scaly skin and began to do its work. The demon clawed his neck, screeching in pain, and threw himself back, frantically searching for the cause of his agony. He finally found the staff and yanked it from his body. The thick, heavy wood looked like a toothpick in his hands. He swung his head around and stared angrily at Katie.

He doesn't seem to care that you're the Queen of the Damned.

He's too stupid to understand that.

The demon pulled his massive arm back and launched the staff back at Katie.

Katie launched herself up and reached for the staff as it whistled through the air toward her. Her fingers gripped the smooth wood, and for a moment she was victorious. However, her reaction was neither equal nor opposite, and the momentum of the demon's throw sent her crashing into the Times Square screen. Sparks rained all around her after the blade embedded itself in the screen.

She snarled and turned her body around, pushing off with her feet to dislodge her staff from the cracked glass. The staff came loose and she landed on a car below, leaving a dent in the hood. She jumped down and examined the staff, but miraculously there weren't even any scratches on it. She nodded, impressed enough to make a mental note to give Joshua a raise when she got back to Vegas.

She took off down the street, hopping over overturned cars and dashing around groups of shell-shocked people. The demon had grabbed the side of the building and started to climb.

No fucking way is he King Kong-ing this shit. Pandora, give me some super-strength.

One can of spinach coming right up.

Katie grabbed the demon by the foot and pulled him back down with a grunt. His claws dug into the building, sending chunks of brick and stone tumbling to the sidewalk below. Katie tugged again, and the demon lost his grip. She slammed him to the ground, and he bounced across the narrow New York street on his ass.

Katie chuckled as he came to a messy stop.

"Oh, bro, that is going to be a seriously acute case of road rash on your ass. You won't be able to sit for a week. Here, let me help you out and send you back for a hot sulfur bath—in *hell.*"

Katie ran after the demon. She got a few paces away and jumped, raising her poles in a high arc to skewer the demon as she came down beside him. The effect of the special metal was instantaneous. The demon squalled and growled and hissed, trying unsuccessfully to flail, but he couldn't move while she had him pinned with her blades. She pulled the blades free and steaming ichor poured from the wounds, blacker than the asphalt. Katie climbed onto the demon's chest and looked around at the crowd, who were watching in horror as the demon snapped and growled weakly at her. A cheer went up, and Katie chuckled. She bent down on one knee and looked the demon in his big, red eyes. All she could see was mindless loathing.

There was nothing human in that body; no soul, only hate and evil.

A chill went down her spine when she saw a blue-green shimmer reflected in the demon's eyes. The demon saw it and stared hard, confused.

Katie patted him on the chin and stood up, pulling Tom and Harry from her sides. She aimed them at his head and narrowed her eyes, tired of the demons fucking with what was now her city too. When she pulled the triggers, two steaming holes appeared in his forehead, and a splatter of brain matter sprayed out the back.

Katie holstered her weapons and waited for the inevitable result.

Hold your breath, dust bomb on its way!

Katie backflipped off the demon and landed on the ground just as he burst into a shimmering ball of dust. She brushed her hands and the front of her pants off, glad she hadn't landed in that mess. People were still panicked, and they ran wild through the streets, fear robbing them of logic and reason. She took in the charnel house the demons had created in Times Square. Bodies lay half-chewed in pools of blood and guts. The blood ran in rivulets, trickling down the edge of the street into the sewers below. Her fists clenched and her eyes blazed red when she saw the schoolchildren sitting on the edge of the road, tears wetting their dust-covered cheeks and fear gripping their innocent souls.

It only fueled Katie's desire to finish this.

A fresh round of screams cut the air behind Katie. She gritted her teeth and set off running. The next block over was a continuation of the chaos. People ran for their lives, stumbling over the half-eaten bodies in the street. She didn't have to look far to find the culprit: a fifty-foot demon that towered over the crowd. He shoveled handfuls of people into his gaping maw, destroying everything around him in his desire to feast.

Katie was unsure if she had seen a demon this big before, but she took a deep breath and rolled her shoulders, the stress of the situation getting stronger. She was exhausted. She wasn't going to lie—the battles so far had taken a lot out of her. Still, she couldn't tap out at this point. There was no way the cops could take on a monster of that size and survive, let alone win.

Katie sighed. *Well, this is interesting.*

That is one big stupid motherfucker, that's for damn sure.

All right, I'm tagging you in, buddy. You're up.

Yessss, Pandora hissed. *I'll make sure I look like you, though. It shouldn't be too hard. I've morphed that booty and those funbags to be just about the same as mine. It would take a trained eye to see the difference.*

Good, Katie replied. She narrowed her eyes as more screams echoed across Times Square. *Take that mother-fucker down.*

You can count on that, my pretty little angel.

23

Calvin pulled a gun out of his holster and held it ready at his side as he slowly approached the border. Manuel and his minions were there in force, men lined up and down the crossing, their weapons drawn, staring at Calvin. He flicked his eyes along the line to count the men and take note of their weapons. It seemed the drug lords were a little more pissed than he'd thought. No matter. He was ready to take the sonsabitches down and teach them a lesson.

A man started to clap, breaking the silence. He stepped out from behind one of the posts at the gate. His hair was black and slicked back, his clothes perfectly pressed, and there was no weapon in his hands. He smiled and walked forward, stopping about five steps in front of the men.

"Manuel."

"You almost eluded us, Calvin," Manuel called. "Where's the girl?"

"What girl?" Calvin smirked. "It's just me, all alone."

"Don't play games. We know you took the girl. Big

mistake. She doesn't belong to you. Here in this country, we don't look kindly upon people who take things that aren't theirs."

"Yeah, well, in *my* country we don't class people as things. Looks like we're at an impasse." Calvin stood firm, staring Manuel down, unafraid of what was to come. He knew it wouldn't have mattered if he had given Sofia to him or not. They were still going to try to kill him, and they would probably try to kill each other afterward. Drug lords didn't make alliances with other drug lords. That just wasn't how it worked, so Calvin knew it was going to be a bloody showdown no matter what transpired.

Manuel steepled his hands and pressed the tips of his fingers to his lips. "Now, we can do this the hard way or the easy way. That is completely up to you. Turn Sofia over to me, and we will give you one quick bullet to the head as retribution for killing my friend's men. You understand that can't go unanswered, of course."

Calvin raised an eyebrow. "Your 'friend,' who tried to kidnap her in the first place?"

Manuel gritted his teeth. "*That* is not your concern."

Calvin snorted. "Like I give a shit if you scumbags double-cross each other. So, what is the hard way?"

Manuel chuckled. "We riddle you with bullets and find Sofia ourselves."

"She's somewhere you'll never find her."

Manuel wheezed out a laugh. He glanced at his men, and all of them began to laugh with him. He straightened his face quickly and put out his hand, stopping all the noise. He stepped forward again with a big smile on his face. "Amusing. The only way she would be safe would be if she was dead. With all the demons running around these days, she might not be safe there either. So, what is your choice—easy or hard?"

Calvin raised his weapon and pulled the trigger twice without looking. Two of Manuel's men fell where they stood, bullet holes in their heads. All the while, Calvin kept his eyes glued to Manuel.

Manuel's lip twitched, and he put his hands up. "Have it your way, demon."

"If I die, I can promise you that everyone here will find their ends too. I come with a big team when I want to."

Manuel turned back and pushed through the men. He sneered at Calvin for a moment before giving his men permission to begin with a wave of his hand. Calvin immediately dove as the bullets blasted toward him. He rolled across the ground, firing his weapon into the group, taking down one, then two, and then one more. The gun clicked empty, and he switched it for another one in his holster.

He had to keep moving. With that many guns facing him, there was no other way he could avoid getting shot. He emptied his clip into the crowd, taking three more men down. He zigzagged across the sandy ground, tucking, rolling, and flipping. A bullet grazed his arm, but he ignored the burn and his demon went to work healing him as best he could. Calvin pulled the two small pistols from their makeshift holsters and fired them into the shooters as they reloaded. He angled the barrels up and hit the edge of the cover, sending chalky dust down over the soldiers.

As they coughed and waved their hands, he stuffed the guns back into his harness. He pulled the M16 around from his back and sprayed the front line with bullets. Man after man went down, hitting the ground with groans as their blood spilled onto the sand.

Calvin caught a glimpse of Manuel's face, which showed shock—and maybe even a little bit of fear. The other drug lord threw down the cup in his hand and shrugged his jacket off. He passed his jacket to his bodyguard and pulled his pistol out to shoot Calvin.

Calvin ducked the bullets until the drug lord's gun clicked.

He tossed it to the side and put his hands out wide. "Go ahead and shoot me, demon scum. I am Alejandro Juarez, the most powerful drug lord in all of Mexico. The bounty on your head will be great. Or you can surrender and be given an honorable quick death. The choice is yours."

Alejandro smiled, cocky. He didn't believe Calvin had the guts to kill him. Calvin stood up and dusted off his pants, staring at the guy with curiosity. He looked over his shoulder and then pointed at himself.

"Are you talking to me?" Calvin shouted. "You're giving me an option here?"

"Of course! We're all warriors here. I will give you a bullet to the brain, quick and easy."

Calvin nodded his head. "Well, that is just *so* nice of you. Seriously. I didn't think you were capable. So, in light of that option—"

Calvin lifted his gun and pulled the trigger, shooting Alejandro right in the chest. Alejandro clutched his chest, and bright red blossomed beneath his fingers. He looked down in disbelief, his mouth opening and closing wordlessly. Calvin shot him again, between the eyes this time, and the drug lord crumpled, dead before he hit the ground.

Calvin released the magazine and reached in his pocket, pulling out the spare and clicking it in place.

Manuel gaped for a moment and then screamed, "What are you waiting for? *Kill him!*"

Calvin fired at the men, pulling the trigger until no more bullets remained. He nodded to himself, knowing it was time to get a little creative. He threw the gun to the side, and the remaining men began to move forward. Calvin ran toward the line of men and slid straight between the legs of one of them.

The guy looked down at him wide-eyed, and Calvin winked before punching him as hard as he could in the balls as he slid through. Calvin rolled out of the way, and the guy dropped to his knees with a breathless squeal. Calvin jumped up and grabbed the guy, using him as a shield as the others shot at him.

He picked up the guy's gun and shot back. Two men fell and the others scattered, so Calvin threw the body to the ground and aimed at a man before he could escape into the desert. He shot him squarely in the back, the man's arms flailing wide as he hit the ground.

Calvin fired at the next, but the magazine was empty. He rolled his eyes and groaned, looking at the men on the ground and then back at the four men approaching with their weapons aimed at Calvin's chest. He chuckled, spotting the knife on the ground. He rolled across the dusty road, grabbed the knife and threw it in one of the men's direction. The knife stuck in the guy's throat, his body instantly collapsing to the ground.

He grabbed the automatic weapon lying by his feet and sprayed two of the three men standing with a hail of bullets. They flew back into the dirt, their eyes still open as they slid to a stop. Blood dribbled onto the ground.

Calvin let out a deep breath and wiped his forehead.

He turned and stared at the one remaining man, putting down his gun. The guy looked at him strangely but followed suit, rolling up his sleeves and cracking his knuckles as he approached. Calvin stood firm, his fists up in front of him, ready to fight. Calvin looked around him for a moment, realizing there was an amazing lack of people trying to cross the border at that moment. The people must have known trouble was near, which was probably why there had been so few of them in the town he'd stopped in.

It was a good thing, with the number of bullets flying around the place. Many more people would have been killed. Calvin was still slightly in awe that he had taken down as many men as he had. There were a lot of them. He rolled his shoulder as the guy got closer, feeling no pain.

You fixed it already?

Not quite, but I am blocking the pain. I'm not useless for everything.

No, my demon friend, you are not.

The two men squared off, circling one another. Calvin swiped out his fist, but the guy moved back. Calvin chuckled and nodded, cracking his neck from side to side. It had been a while since he had been in a fistfight with a human, and he had to admit it actually felt kind of good. The guy swung at Calvin, who ducked and took that moment to step forward and land an uppercut on the guy's chin. The man flew back and fell to the ground, groaning and rubbing his chin as he pulled himself to his feet.

"A tough guy, huh? Okay, okay, I got you."

Calvin lurched forward and punched him in the face with swift jabs. One, two, one, two, just like he had practiced back in Vegas with Katie.

Blood flew from the guy's mouth and ran down his chin. He stumbled backward and swiped his thumb through the blood. He slowly looked up at Calvin with a bloody-toothed grin and came running toward him, tackling him to the ground. He got on top of Calvin and swung right and left, punching Calvin in the face, the ribs, and the neck.

Calvin put his hands up and growled, bucking his body so hard that the guy flew off and hit the ground. Calvin pulled his legs toward his chest and thrust them forward, jumping to his feet. He walked swiftly over to the guy, who was now on all fours trying to get up. He kicked the guy as hard as he could in the face, spinning him onto his back. The guy was barely conscious by that point, and Calvin stood over him. He growled, the taste of blood on his lips, deciding whether to stomp the guy's face into the ground or let him live.

A loud shot crackled through the air, and a searing pain ripped through Calvin's leg, forcing him to drop to one knee. Another shot rang out, taking out his other leg. Calvin creased over, slamming his hands on the ground as the pain hit him. Marty went crazy, immediately sending his minimal powers to the two sites to block as much pain as he could as he worked to stop the bleeding.

With the pain subsiding to no more than a dull ache, Calvin put his hands on his thighs and pulled himself up to his feet with a groan. He turned around, growling angrily at Manuel, who held a gun out in front of him in shaky hands. He pointed it at Calvin's chest, and as Calvin moved toward him Manuel pulled the trigger again, but the clip was empty. He panicked, pulling the trigger again and again. Calvin swatted the gun from his hands, grabbed him by the throat, and lifted him high into the air.

"You chose to seduce that woman away from a bright future and cage her like an animal," Calvin growled into Manuel's face. "Then, when it suited you, you used your fists to beat her. You are no man, and you will remember for the rest of your life what happens to men who put their hands on a woman."

Calvin slammed Manuel to the ground and climbed on top of the drug lord to pin him so he could punch him in the face over and over. Manuel struggled to get free, but Calvin was too strong and too angry. As his fists contacted with Manuel's face, he could hear Katie in his mind, telling him to calm himself. It was hard. All of Manuel's men had tried to kill him, and he had been shot three times.

"This was supposed to be my fucking *vacation*!" Calvin screamed, punching the drug lord one last time before leaning forward on his hand and rolling over on his back.

He lay there breathing heavily, staring at the blue sky. The sound of voices behind him made him tilt his head back. On the other side of the border was a row of US military, who were waiting for Calvin to come over the border. The general stepped forward from between them and nodded at Calvin.

"You won, Calvin. Don't kill someone who doesn't need it. A little birdie told me Manuel is wanted in this country on seventeen counts of drug trafficking and three counts of murder. If he just happened to trip and fall over the line, he would never see the light of day again."

Calvin chuckled and groaned, sitting up. He looked at Manuel and smiled, smacking him in the chest. Blood trickled from the drug lord's mouth, and his face was already swollen.

"You hear that, Manny?" Calvin groaned as he got to his feet. "The US has a nice dark cell on some remote military base all set up for you. They might even serve some mystery-meat tacos once in a while."

Calvin grabbed Manuel by the front of the shirt and walked toward the border, Manuel's feet dragging in the dirt and his head lolling. Calvin stood at the border and set him down, watching as he teetered. He slowly reached out with one finger and pushed him, and Manuel fell over the border into US territory, groaning as several of the general's men ran forward and dragged him off.

Calvin looked at the border guard, who smirked and waved him through. "Tell Katie 'hi' for me when you see her next."

Calvin chuckled and slapped his hand into the border guard's shoulder, nodding and walking into the US. In the background, Sofia stood wrapped in a military jacket, her bangs blowing back off her face. She looked worried to death. Calvin moved toward her, but one of the general's men put his hand up.

"Oh, right," Calvin nodded, handing over the last gun he had in his possession, which was empty of bullets.

The guard knelt and did a quick search to make sure he wasn't carrying any more weapons over the border. When he was clear, the soldier nodded and stuck out his hand, shaking Calvin's.

"Good work out there. That was pretty much the most badass thing I've ever seen. Good work."

"Thanks." Calvin chuckled. "All in a day's work."

"Right." The soldier scoffed. "Go ahead. You're all clear."

"Thanks."

Calvin kept his eyes on Sofia as he hobbled toward her, stopping only momentarily to shake a couple of soldiers' hands. She was a sight for sore eyes, and he couldn't be happier that she'd made it over the border safely. He had to remember that he owed Katie a huge one. She had put the company assets out there, had the plane flown into Mexico, and picked up someone she didn't know, all on Calvin's word. That alone made him realize just how close the two of them were. They were family, and she trusted him.

Sofia sighed and tilted her head to the side, putting out her hand to help him over to her. She leaned in, wrapping her arms gently around him. He groaned, and she pulled back, wrinkling her nose.

"Shouldn't you get those knees looked at? I saw you get shot."

"Nah, the bullets were pushed out by my amazing demon, and he numbed them. I'm going to trust he can get the job done. It's time I put a little more faith in the guy. He's been trying hard."

She laughed. "I don't know what to say to that."

Calvin ran his finger over her cheek and smiled as she pulled out a package of baby wipes, standing on her tiptoes to wipe some of the blood from his cheeks. He put his hand over hers, and she looked at him nervously.

"I got him," Calvin whispered. "You'll never have to fear him again."

A tear pooled at the corner of Sofia's eye, and she nodded. *"Tonto loco."*

Calvin grinned. *"Tonto loco para ti."*

She giggled. "Shut up and let me fix your face."

24

The screen went black for a moment and then the Channel 8 news screen flashed up, a banner running across the bottom announcing the breaking news. The camera flashed to a mid-twenties blond news anchor shuffling papers, her face a little panicked. The music stopped, and the camera focused in on her. She stared at the screen for a moment, almost in a trance, before snapping out of it.

"Good afternoon. We interrupt your regularly-scheduled programming for breaking news. Reports have been flying in from Times Square in New York City, where the President of the United States was scheduled to make an appearance. Sources are telling us that a demon incursion has broken out, ravaging the gathered spectators. From what we know right now, the President had not yet made it to Times Square when the first of what people are describing as 'massive beasts with long sharp fangs' began to arrive. So far we have a rough estimate of thirteen people dead, but those are just preliminary numbers since the battle is still underway. Police, Secret Service, and military personnel are all on the scene, but demons are so powerful that authorities are struggling to get control of the situation. Our field reporter Ewen Gregory is on the scene and is standing by to give us a firsthand report of what's happening. Ewen, are you there?"

The screen flashed to the reporter, who cringed as another section of building tumbled into the street behind him. People were running and screaming through the dust cloud around them.

Ewen put his finger to his ear and nodded. "I'm here, Jessica. I'm currently standing one block down from Times Square. The first demon was spotted at eleven forty-three, just forty minutes ago. The beast was approximately ten feet tall, and killed many innocent bystanders as well as causing massive amounts of damage. The demon was taken down by a woman we believe to be Katie Maddison of Katie's Killers, who infamously avoids her picture being taken."

"Ewen, did you get a shot of her?"

"No," he replied. "Like every other time, she was hard to get into focus. But the story didn't end there. She then chased down a second demon, twice the size of the first. At one point he threw her into the Megatron above Times Square, and if you look in the background to my left, you can see that the screen is still emitting showers of sparks. That demon was taken down after a few good hits and turned to dust to my right."

"And what is going on now?"

"Jessica, there looks to be a third demon. I...there's..."

"Ewen, you're breaking up."

The camera showed a car door flying toward it before

the feed went to static. They quickly switched back to the newscaster, who sat there stunned for a moment.

"Uh, we've had some technical difficulties, but we will contact our other reporter, Janine, and see if we can get you back to the scene. If you are just joining us, a demon incursion has broken out in Times Square in New York, where the President of the United States was just moments from making an appearance. Since the discovery of demons at the mosque in New York just two days ago, reports have trickled in, possibly linking those to the actions today. These reports have not been confirmed, but rumors have spread that those taken down in that mosque battle were planning to use demons to attack Times Square this afternoon. With the onslaught of incursions happening throughout the country and around the world, people have hunkered down in their homes, praying that someone sends relief. News 8 spoke with a couple just the other day who lived on a small farm off the beaten path. Only one homeowner agreed to appear on camera, and this is what he had to say."

The camera switched to an interview with a farmer from rural Michigan. Meanwhile, Jessica took out her earpiece and looked at the staff. "What happened? Do we have any news? Is Ewen okay?"

"We don't know," the producer told her. "We're still trying to get back in contact with him. For now, I want you to recap the riots over the last six months, and then we should have Janine up and ready. She was hiding in a building one block over, but is making her way to the scene."

Jessica nodded and put her earpiece back in, sitting up

straight and smiling as the camera came back to her. "After Incursion Day was sealed into the history of this country and the world just eight months ago, riots began breaking out as citizens took to the streets to demand assistance for their loved ones. Since then, help centers have been set up from coast to coast, in place to rehabilitate and train those found infected, helping them suppress their demons and live a more productive life. There hasn't yet been word on whether a cure for the infections has been found, but folks are holding onto the hope that one day the demons won't play a role in their lives anymore.

"We're now getting word that one of our other field reporters, Janine Arrows, is on the scene and actually speaking with the President. Janine, are you there?"

The screen shifted to another reporter, standing beside the limo that was carrying the President. "This is Janine. Yes, I'm here. I am on the scene in New York City, standing here with the President of the United States. Sir, can you tell us what you saw, and if you know whether this has anything to do with current political movements toward refugees fleeing demon-torn areas?"

"I don't know the reason," he shouted, ducking at the sound of a crash. "I just know they came out of nowhere, and they are *big*." He held his hands apart to demonstrate, looking for all the world like a giant preschooler.

"Sir, is this your first close encounter with demons?"

"Yes it is, and all I have to say is God be with those down the block in the street."

The Secret Service agent grabbed the President and guided him back into the limousine as a building crumbled behind them, the crash echoing in the background. Janine turned back to the camera and moved to the right, letting it pan behind her. On the side of the building was a gigantic demon hanging onto the side of the brick wall. Behind him was a female with long black hair, black spandex clothing, and massive guns hanging from her hips.

"It seems to me, Jessica, that this situation calls for the big guns."

Pandora rolled her shoulders, reaching back and taking the ponytail out of her hair. She made sure to keep as many of Katie's attributes as possible, but anyone who knew Katie would know she wasn't her by her features. Having her hair down would hide that issue, especially from afar, which was where the reporters seemed to be staying for the moment. Her body, though, was almost identical to Katie's and that didn't take much effort since Pandora had purposely been structuring her body to resemble Pandora's own.

All right, Katie told Pandora inside her head, *this demon is huge, and it's vital we move it away from the President. No matter how you feel about the guy, you can't let him die.*

Got it. Now shush, I need to concentrate.

Pandora jumped up on the side of an overturned bus to get a better look at the demon. He growled loudly as he tore through cars and buildings like they were candy wrappers and devoured the humans inside. His messy bites left a trail of half-chewed limbs in his wake.

He's so wasteful, not even eating the humans when he pulls them apart. Someone's mommy never taught him to take all you want, but eat all you take.

The demon jumped on top of a parked bus, the top caving in as he leaped off and landed on another car, which swerved down the road as the driver tried to get away. The demon stepped down from the blue sedan and plucked the door off, shaking the car until the human fell into its hand. It looked at the screaming guy for a moment and closed its clawed hand around him, squishing him into paste. He swung his arm wide and wiped the remnants of the guy across the side of the nearest building.

The demon looked down the block at the President's motorcade. There were over three dozen agents armed with automatic rifles loaded with demon-killing bullets. Pandora knew, though, that with that bastard's size it was going to take a special hand to take him down. The demon lunged toward the President, and Pandora took off faster than the human eye could see. She stopped at the next block and looked around. She picked up an empty Ford 150, swung it around her head, and let go, standing still to watch as it soared through the air and hit the demon in the back of the head.

The demon roared, stopping when he saw Pandora—or Lilith, to be more accurate. The demon grumbled, obviously rethinking his movements. He ran toward a skyscraper and leaped onto the side, smashing windows and throwing people out of the building to tumble to their deaths. Pandora growled and started running again, leaping off the fiery crashed bus to land on the other side of the skyscraper.

They sat there for a moment, staring around the edge at

each other. The demon leaned his head back and roared loudly, pounding his scaly fists into the side of the building.

Pandora rolled her eyes and sighed. "Don't be such a fucking baby. You made this mess, and now you're going to pay the price for it."

The demon snarled and started climbing the building. Pandora drew Tom, pointing him at the demon's ass and pulling the trigger. The bullet hit him hard in the right butt cheek and the demon reached down, squealing like a pig.

Pandora threw her head back and cackled. "That's what you get, motherfucker. Where are you going? You're fucking up the beautiful buildings."

The demon whimpered, digging his claws deep into his ass cheek to get the bullet and throwing it to the ground below. He snarled at Pandora and showed his teeth; he wasn't backing down. The demon looked at Pandora and then back down at the President, trying to figure out his next move.

"Whatcha plannin', big guy? I ain't got all day. I mean, the view is cool from up here, but I'm not a fan of just hanging around like this. Make a choice, or you'll be wishing you could pluck this bullet out of your demon balls."

The demon let out a roar, blowing spit into Pandora's face. She wiped off the slobber and looked up as he continued to climb the skyscraper. She sighed and put Tom back into his holster.

"I guess that's how we're playing this game, then."

She grunted, lifted her legs up onto the exposed beam and pushed upward, soaring up through the air. She grabbed the side again, digging her demon claws in and pushed up, leaping like a frog up the side of the building. With every thrust, she got farther ahead of the demon. On her last push, she dove over the edge of the roof, rolling across the sticky asphalt. She stood up, grimacing at the gunk stuck to her hands.

She strolled over to the side of the building and looked down, just as the demon was looking up. She tilted her head and looked at her nails, yawning loudly.

"You just take your time, okay? I'll be up here waiting for your fat ass to join me."

The demon snarled and continued to climb as Pandora backed up, leaning against the door to the inside. She sighed, looking down at her nails and then at the sky, watching the helicopters attempt to get close. She tapped her foot on the ground and kicked a rock, watching it bounce across the roof and get stuck in the goo.

So, do you think we'll get this condo?

Katie chuckled. *After this, I definitely do. The owners would be pretty dumb to deny the heroes of New York City. That is, if that damn demon ever makes it up here.*

I know, right? Just then, the demon's large paw came over the edge of the roof, and the top of his head began to appear. *Oh, there's my cue.*

Pandora slowly walked forward, pulled the staff's poles from her back, joined the halves, and flicked the blades out. The demon pulled itself onto the roof and let out a Hulk-worthy roar.

Pandora and wiped the new spittle from her face with a hand, shaking her head. "You have *got* to stop that. It's fucking rude. Is that how you show respect to your queen?"

The demon growled, balling his fists. He took off at a run, leaping through the air and pounding his fist down toward Pandora. She lifted an eyebrow and took four large steps to the right, and the demon's fist broke through the roof. He spun, whipping his arm through the air, but Pandora ducked. She rolled to the right as he attempted to smash her again, almost falling through the hole in the roof.

"That was close." She chuckled as she regained her footing. The demon growled at her, but she kept advancing while whirling the bladed staff. The demon backed away until its heels were on the edge of the roof and it had nowhere else to go, and Pandora snickered and darted forward to slice his jugular. The demon grabbed his throat with wide eyes and a gargle, his black blood flowing out over his claws. Pandora watched the demon with pleasure, waiting until he was almost unconscious. As the demon teetered on the edge, she pushed the tip of her staff, blades now retracted, into his chest.

The demon flailed and overbalanced. His arms windmilled out to the side, and he fell off the roof.

The people below screamed in fear, trying to run as far as they could go. The President got out of the limo and looked up with wide eyes as the demon plummeted toward the ground. He would smash and kill them all, but there was little to no time for anyone to get out of the way. As the demon passed the seventh floor the people stuck below crouched, awaiting their impending doom.

The President shrugged the Secret Service off and straightened his jacket, watching the beast plummeting toward him. Just as the demon passed the fourth floor and all was thought lost, it burst into dust, which drifted down to cover those below. The screaming stopped, and mass coughing broke out. The President blinked his eyes, dust covering his eyelashes and silvered hair. He blew the ash off his lips and shook his head, brushing the rest off his perfectly-pressed suit.

Everyone looked around in amazement, shocked that they weren't dead. The demon had turned to dust at just the right moment. They stood and looked up through the cloud and the sparks coming from the broken sections of the building above them. A breeze blew through the nearby streets, and the dust began to clear. Standing high above them and peeking over the edge of the roof was Katie, her body reclaimed.

Everyone erupted into cheers, and Katie let out a deep breath, just glad Pandora's little stunt hadn't gone terribly wrong. After all that, the last thing they needed was for the President to be killed by a falling demon. She might have lost some of her contracts. Katie pulled back from the edge of the building and walked to the other side of the roof. She sat down and pressed her back against the ledge, leaning her head back and smiling.

That, my dear, was some mighty fine demon slaying. Katie sighed.

I would have to agree with you. I think I have two favorite parts to the day. When you blew that first demon's head off his shoulders and part of his brains hit a man in a top hat on the sidelines, and of course, my own dramatic ending.

Katie laughed, shaking her head. *I didn't see the brains, but God, I wish I had. That would have topped my day, for reals.*

I offer the top award to you, but I think you just did it to scare the living shit out of the President.

Maybe. She giggled. *Do you think he shit his pants? Possibly just a little?*

For your sake, I hope he did. It'd be like a prize for all your hard work.

Damn straight!

2 5

K atie paced back and forth on the roof, her phone to her ear. She looked down at the ground, letting her hair fall to the sides of her face as a news helicopter swooped overhead. When it was gone, she pulled her hair back and looked out over the city, Central Park in the distance. The real estate agent had called her before she could even get her ass down off the roof, not that she had tried that hard.

"First, I want to say that what you did today was poetic," Iris squealed. "You are the city's hero. The world's, really. You saved the President."

"Well, it's part of my job, so I had little choice." Katie chuckled. "But thank you."

"And on that note, the owners of the condo have seen the video of the demons, and they want to sell the condo to you at the original price."

Katie snickered. "Oh? Well, I gave them my other price. They can have that."

Katie pulled her phone from her ear and ended the call,

hearing Iris from a distance trying to convince her otherwise. Katie laughed, knowing they would take the deal. It was too good of a public connection for them not to. Katie wasn't a rich and famous snob, but most of the people who owned condos like the one she was buying were. They would *kill* for the opportunity to be able to tell people that they had sold their condo to Katie from Katie's Killers. It would make them famous in their group of friends.

Katie's phone buzzed again, and she looked down, figuring it would be Iris.

"That was fast," she mumbled to herself.

Instead of Iris' name on the screen, though, it was Calvin. Katie let out a deep breath and raised the phone to her ear, thankful to finally hear from him. She hadn't gotten the chance to find out what happened at the border.

"Hey there, gunslinger."

Calvin laughed. "Hey there. What are you up to?"

"Oh, you know, just enjoying the view of the city. You?"

"Yeah, just finishing my leisurely stroll over the border."

Both of them laughed, Calvin having already seen the footage from New York, and Katie knowing better than to believe he hadn't taken down a dozen or more drug dealers.

"So, what's up? You coming home? I got a new pad for us to chill in when we're in New York."

"I leave you for a week, and you go buying condos in the city?" Calvin chuckled. "Actually, I decided I'm going to spend the rest of my vacation in San Diego. I can eat tacos, get to know the locals a little better, relax."

"Mmmhmm," Katie murmured with a raised eyebrow. "Are you getting to know *the* locals or *a* local?"

Calvin laughed, knowing Katie was too smart to fall for that. "A local, if you must know."

"Well, enjoy yourself, because I'm putting you to work when you get back."

"Deal." Calvin laughed and hung up.

Schultz and some other detectives from precincts all over the city had made their way up onto the roof, half to see Katie and half to get away from the crowds below. Two officers came up behind them carrying pizza boxes and six-packs of beer. Katie clapped her hands excitedly, ready to chow down after that whole affair. Before she could join them, her phone buzzed again, and she groaned as she pulled it out of her pocket.

"You thought you wouldn't be popular after that stunt?" Schultz called out, laughing with everyone else.

Katie smiled and looked down at the general's name on the screen. She put her hand up to the detectives and put a finger over her lips. She mouthed the word "general" to him and stepped off toward the giant hole in the roof.

"General Brushwood, how are you?"

"A lot better now that the President is safely onboard Air Force One and headed back to Washington. That was one hell of a stunt you pulled, and I have to say I'm really relieved it worked out as it did. I was afraid we would be scraping the President off the sidewalk."

Katie laughed. "Nah, just dusting him off a bit."

"I won't lie, that part was kind of funny. I do have a question for you, though."

"Shoot."

"Why in the hell are you still on the top of the building?"

"Because the building is surrounded by hungry reporters. I really don't want to deal with them. Plus, these guys brought me pizza—and, if they love me, donuts. They really don't want to have to deal with me going down there either. It would be like throwing me to the wolves. So, we decided the view was too good not to just hang out up here."

"Now, I don't mind you hiding from the reporters since we don't need any clear shots of you hitting the news, but I do have to ask that you go inside. Your plan has a bit of a flaw."

"Oh? What's that?"

"The news helicopters keep showing pictures of you guys from above."

Katie looked up at the choppers floating in the air around them. She hadn't even thought about it. She was hoping they would have the airspace cleared out soon, since it was technically illegal to fly their choppers that close to the buildings in that area.

"Yeah, sorry about that. I'll move everyone inside."

"Good deal. And good work, Katie, and Pandora of course. You guys really saved the day. I knew sending you to New York was a good idea. I just wasn't sure how the opportunity would present itself."

"I kind of like it out here, too."

"Uh-oh, don't go all *Sex and the City* on me."

Katie laughed loudly. "Goodbye, General."

"Goodbye."

Katie put the phone back into her pocket and turned around, putting her hands in the air. "All right, boys. Let's move it inside. The general said there are too many pictures from the choppers. I think there's enough room in the stairwell for us to post-op—if the building doesn't fall down around us."

"That would be a really shitty end to this day." Schultz scoffed as he walked toward the stairwell.

When they entered the enclosed area, the news reporters began to move out, pissed that they'd missed their opportunity to get a good shot of Katie. They assumed the guys on the ground would be waiting when they came out the other side, but those below didn't have the same confidence. They had waited for Katie before, thinking there was no way she could get out of the place, but had never run into her.

Katie and the officers sat joking around, enjoying their pizzas and donuts. Katie leaned against the wall, munching on a Krispy Kreme as the cops hilariously replayed the events of the day. They especially loved the part where the demon had to pick a bullet out of his ass. It had been the perfect moment to capture a meme-worthy photo.

"Hell, there are already memes flooding Facebook."

Katie laughed. "Hey, if you don't try to have fun in your job you'll end up hating it, right?"

Later on, after the sun had gone down, the detectives and officers headed down to the bottom of the broken building and came out the front doors. The reporters jumped to their feet, cameras flashing and questions being shouted. After a moment, though, they settled down, realizing the officers were alone. Katie was nowhere to be seen. Instead, they carried seven empty pizza boxes and five empty Krispy Kreme containers.

"Detective," one of the reporters yelled. "Where is Katie? We've been waiting to talk to her."

The detective shrugged and smirked slightly. The other reporters shouted questions to the officers, but they acted like they had no idea where Katie had gone. The reporters dropped their mics and watched the detectives walk down the sidewalks. One reporter stepped forward and put his hands in the air.

"Come on, you gotta give us something. We've been out here all day. We need to know where Katie went. Is she safe? Is she okay? Why won't she talk to us?"

Schultz turned around, rubbing the pizza sauce out of his goatee. He smiled and let out a breath, finding the whole situation more than amusing. He put his hands up to quiet the reporters and cleared his throat.

"The mission, though brutal, was a success."

The reporters groaned, having heard the same scripted speech repeatedly that day. The detective laughed and shook his head.

"Katie is safe, but we don't know where she is. Perhaps she grew wings and flew off."

The reporters rolled their eyes and started packing up their bags. Schultz looked at the roof with a smile and headed to his car. He didn't know how she planned to get down, but she'd asked for privacy, and she deserved it.

Katie stood on the edge of the building, her hair blowing wildly around her. She could see the oranges and reds of the setting sun in the distance. Below, it was dark, the buildings blocking the last of the sunset, but up here she felt like she could see the whole world. She stepped closer to the side and peered over the edge, mumbling to herself.

What are you thinking? Pandora asked.

"You just have to have faith," she whispered.

Oh, faith? I have to be honest with you here, Katie. That's never been one of my strong suits. I'm more of a realistic kind of girl. If I see it, I believe it.

Katie stared out, lifting her arms in the air and shutting her eyes, feeling the wind whipping around her. Pandora started to stir, very nervous that Katie was acting so weird and standing so close to the edge of the building. Katie whispered the phrase again, this time tilting her head toward the sky.

You are kind of close to the edge there, dude. Seriously, you're going to fall off, and I can't fix smushed.

Suddenly, the phone in Katie's pocket began to buzz, bringing her attention back to the present. She stepped off the ledge and pulled her phone from her pocket, ignoring Pandora's sigh of relief. It was her real estate agent again.

"Hello?"

"Katie, it's Iris, and I have some brilliant news. The owners have accepted your offer, and they're pushing it through first thing tomorrow. Congratulations! I have to admit, you kind of made me nervous. I didn't know what you were thinking with that counterbid, but as sure as I stand here, it worked! They couldn't pass up the opportunity to tell people they knew Katie from Katie's Killers in some way. I told them you're very shy so there will be no meet and greet, which they were disappointed by, but they were still excited to sell to you."

"That is really great news." Katie smirked. "I had a feeling they would come around. Circa is where I wanted to be, but I wasn't going to let them bully me into a higher price than I originally offered. I don't care how nice the place is. I was ready to go to Hoboken and get a really nice place there for half the price."

"Oh, God," Iris exclaimed. "The thought of living in Jersey gives me chills. I'm extra-glad we were able to make this all work out, knowing that."

"I'm glad too." Katie laughed. "And I'm glad it helps you as well. I know you get a killer commission off it."

"Yes. Yes, I do," she agreed happily.

"Well, thank you for all your help, and I will look out for your call when it's time to sign the papers and transfer the funds."

"Sounds great. I'll be in touch."

Katie hung up and smiled, excited that she had gotten her way and now had a brand-new home in New York City. Calvin was going to freak when he found out how much money she'd spent, but it was well worth it. After a demon-slaying like today, the cost of the condo would be a drop in the bucket. She called Angie, knowing she was waiting.

"Holy shit," Angie cursed when she answered the phone. "Thank God you're okay. Where the hell are you?"

Katie chuckled. "Aw, you care!"

"Of course I do."

"I'm on a roof, but that's not why I called. We got the call, and the condo is mine!"

"Yay! That's awesome!"

"I need you to get everything set up now because we

should be closing on the house in the next day or so. Set up the proposals from the designers and we'll go over all of them tomorrow."

"I'm already right on top of it, boss. The three proposals and quotes are all lined up on my kitchen table, waiting on you. One of them is pop-up."

Katie laughed. "Above and beyond."

"Yeah, if you like dragons."

"Uh, what?"

"You'll have to see it to understand."

"Right." Katie giggled. "All right, I am going to head out of here. I'll be home in a bit, and we can go to some greasy spoon if you're hungry. I ate a pizza and a box of donuts, but I'm always up for a second dinner."

"I don't understand how you don't weigh three hundred pounds."

"I'm on the demon diet, and it's fabulous. It even sculpts and tones."

Angie chuckled. "Goodbye, and for God's sake, be careful coming home."

"I always am." Katie smiled and hung up.

She put the phone to her lips and looked at the sparkling lights across the city. She smiled to herself and put her phone in her pocket, making sure all her weapons were secured in place. She rolled her neck and stretched her arms over her head.

You getting ready to work out or something? Pandora asked.

No, but I think I understand now what Gabriel was telling me.

Huh?

Without another word Katie took off across the roof,

heading for the ledge. Pandora started screaming and panicked, sure Katie had finally lost her damn mind,

What the fuck? *Slow down! Stop!* Don't you do it!

Katie leaped off the side of the building, swan-diving out and down. She grinned, feeling the wind against her face, nothing but Pandora's screams echoing through her ears. She was completely, one-hundred-and-ten-percent calm. When she was halfway down the building, giant wings sprang from her back and spread out wide, stopping her plummet and lifting her on the air. Katie put her hands out and opened her eyes, laughing excitedly.

Oh, this is just fucking beautiful. What the fuck are those things? Duck wings?

Oh, Pandora, let it go a little and enjoy the ride.

Possibly after I stop my heart from beating out of my chest and clean up the shit in my pants. Maybe then *I will enjoy the fact that you have fucking angel wings and you're soaring through the streets of New York fucking City.*

Katie laughed as she swooped down and back up again. The people in the street stared up in wonder. They swore they saw someone, a person with wide, feathered angel wings, but the city was so dark, they couldn't be sure. Katie laughed wildly, swooping between the buildings before soaring high up in the air over the tallest and gliding for a moment. She let out a deep breath, staring down at the beautiful lights of the city below and the Statue of Liberty in the distance.

As they swooped over the 9/11 memorial, Katie hovered for a moment, thankful that what had happened earlier that day had been nothing even close to *that* tragedy. She soared over the Brooklyn bridge and watched the cars for a short time. She moved through the suburban areas, smiling at the people in the windows, having dinner, talking and laughing with their families.

So, Falcon. Pandora chuckled. *What are we going to do now? We saved the city and the President and decided to start a new business. I know you have something else up your sleeve.*

I think now I'm looking for the right man.

Pandora snorted. *Well, honey, you're demon-infected, a Damned mercenary with angel genes and huge feathered wings on your back. Granted, you still have perfect hips and tits, but I don't know if you will ever find the* right *guy.*

Katie laughed as she soared through the city, shaking her head. *I didn't say a man for forever. I just need a man for right now.*

Pandora snickered, relaxing a bit and enjoying the view through Katie's eyes. She couldn't help thinking that maybe—just maybe—the whole flying thing wouldn't be that bad. No more cabs, no more choppers, just clear, clean skies. Pandora'd had a feeling all along that there was something angelic about Katie, but it took her a while to admit it to herself. The Queen of the Damned, stuck in an angel body, what kind of weird shit had she ended up involved in? The thought made her laugh, and she hollered as Katie swooped about ten more blocks and landed on the empty sidewalk.

Katie folded her wings and reached for the front door, smiling as she swung it open and disappeared inside.

WOOT!

First, thank you for reading our stories, and of course in particular this one!

We are smack-dab in the middle of major changes in the war and society with Katie and the rest of the Damned. Brock is updating his life as he moves forward, and what the hell is up with Mr. Casanova (commonly called *Calvin*)?

That man escapes from Pandora for long enough and he gets involved with a damsel in distress and stays with her.

If that doesn't scream "the rules have changed," nothing will. For those who have not read the *Protected by the Damned* series, before Incursion Day, those who are Damned were not allowed to interact with normal society —especially in the area of romance.

We know that Katie is special now, and due to that, we see how she has been able to be the vessel that is strong enough to contain Pandora.

Personally, I believe there is more in store for the two

of them as together they start to learn more about Katie's abilities, and her desire to feel like she is a bit more in charge of her life. While Pandora has shown aspects of her personality that lean towards Katie's, we see Katie start to lean towards Pandora.

I believe most older readers will remember the adage, "You become who you hang around with" and it is proving true for our troublesome duo.

In the next book (which will be here in about two to three weeks—look for a pre-order opportunity soon) Katie and Calvin have some unfinished business to clean up, the condo is moving along, and there is a new threat exploding underneath a church.

Moloch and Baal are back, and they decide to attack somewhere unexpected.

Personal Thanks!

I'd like to take a quick moment to thank EVERYONE who is a part of making these stories. From collaborators, to cover artist(s), to JIT and editors, Stephen and Jami and Amazon's infrastructure as well.

We (indie publishers) can't do what we do at the speed we accomplish our production without a LOT of people being involved.

Including you, *the fans!*

I try to get to Facebook on the Kurtherian Gambit page, the KG Group and the Protected by the Damned group as often as I can. I read the posts going back and forth amongst the fans and smile, knowing that this is beyond me now.

Our stories have taken a life of their own.

Thank you for giving a guy like me the blessing of your time, your support, and your encouragement as we build new worlds of characters who give a damn about each other.

So that we as readers can occasionally dip into a place where friends are there for each other, as I think we all enjoy.

At least, I can say that I do.

EAR CRUSH

Do you like to read, but sometimes life intrudes? Hit up *Ear Crush* and listen to LMBPN Stories read *TO* you...

For free!

I know many of you are Audible listeners, but some of you aren't and that is ok.

Stephen Campbell is your host for a podcast (downloadable audio) called *Ear Crush* that has our Award nominated and award winning talent reading short stories NOT AVAILBLE on audio anywhere else!

For example, our first short story, already available, is *Tabitha's Vacation*, narrated by Emily Beresford. This short story was produced for an anthology called *Beyond the Stars – At Galaxy's Edge* and recently recorded for *Ear Crush* as the first short.

Many more are in production.

I encourage you to check out Steve's effort to bring great stories in audio to you for no charge. Just click the link, and see if Apple iTunes or Stitcher (which has a web option) will work for you.

APPLE (iTunes)
https://itunes.apple.com/us/podcast/ear-crush/id1399011477

Stitcher (web or other podcast solutions)
https://www.stitcher.com/podcast/camven-media/ear-crush

LMBPN Website (You can find other podcast locations on our website)
www.lmbpn.com/earcrush/

Thank you for entrusting US with your time.

Ad Aeternitatem,

Michael

Hey! Happy Summer to you!

Hope this note finds you enjoying snow cones and sliding down a slip and slide. That made no sense, but it sounded good in my head.

I'm a zombie right now and not in a good way. (I feel like I'm losing brain cells reading this letter I'm writing. Accept my apologies in advance.) We're moving! Or rather, we're going nomad again. So, packing up and cleaning out this week has been less than pleasant.

Sneaking away to my office to write has been the joy of my life. It's a great excuse, and some days, I'd just rather spend time with my characters than the old fam! You too?

I get asked what "going nomad" is when I mention it. Jacob (the hubster) and I jumped into publishing in 2015 when I decided to start writing books, and over the course of many hours, tears, and Google searches, we were able to retire him from being a coach.

When we did that, we sat back and thought, what could we do? I'd built up a great fan base in romance (Ali Parker), and we thought maybe going on the road for a year would be cool. We'd do fan dinners, go to events, and I'd write on bumpy roads and in shady hotels. You get the picture.

So we did. January through August of 2017, we did the southwest to the northwest. We fell in love with Utah and Denver, as well as Seattle and Portland. It was hell trying to write books at the speed I usually do, but we made it.

After settling down in Texas for a year to get my middle child (the one my mom says I deserve, you know the one) through high school, we're finally done and picking back up. The Great Lakes are home for the summer, then Toronto and the Northeast. I'm ready to get back on the road.

Funny when you get the travel bug, you just can't shake it. AND I always find time to go see Mike in Vegas and get him to take me to the restaurants he's slipped into our books and some of his. Delicious!

Strangely enough, I need a donut. All that being said, I hope you get some down time this summer, and when you do, I hope you read a great book or binge a series. There are so many awesome tales out there to disappear into. I know I'll be doing just that!

Prayerfully, this book made you laugh, think, and cringe a time or two. We appreciate you spending your money picking it up. It means more to us than you know.

Slave to Many Stories,

Laurie Starkey